Back-Slash

Back-Slash

Bill Kitson

To Sara,

With love at Christmas,
from Uncle Bill

ALIAS

Bill Kitson

December 2011

ROBERT HALE · LONDON

© Bill Kitson 2011
First published in Great Britain 2011

ISBN 978 0 7090 9316 9

Robert Hale Limited
Clerkenwell House
Clerkenwell Green
London EC1R 0HT

www.halebooks.com

2 4 6 8 10 9 7 5 3

Printed in Great Britain by the MPG Books Group,
Bodmin and King's Lynn

This book is dedicated to the memory of Nell (1992 – 2006)

Her gentle, sweet nature made her everyone's friend,
and gave me the perfect model for the forester's dog

acknowledgements

I'd like to thank everyone who has contributed towards the book you are holding. 'Freddie Green', who taught me the sure-fire way to extract information from a prisoner. Don't look for Freddie in your phone book. That isn't his real name – for obvious reasons.

To the very real Julian Corps whose charity donation gave him the chance to become a character in this book.

My wife Val, whose editing, proof-reading and continuity skills contribute more and more to the series.

My readers, Pat Almond and Cath Brockhill, who gave their opinion on the original draft.

Derek Colligan, whose splendid covers have done much to attract potential readers to the Mike Nash series.

And above all, to everyone at Robert Hale for their continued support – and patience!

chapter one

Anna was late. Her clattering footsteps on the concrete steps of the multi-storey car park reflected her haste. Although she was behind schedule she had taken precious minutes to check her appearance in the mirror before leaving the office. She wanted nothing to give Alan cause for suspicion. She felt a twinge of guilt at the thought of Alan. Deceiving him was the worst part of the whole business.

The car park was deserted, badly lit. Most of the light bulbs had succumbed to the attention of vandals. Anna wrinkled her nose in distaste, the stairwell smelt of stale urine and vomit. Her car was on level seven, parked against one of the concrete supports in the most remote corner. She unlocked the door and was about to step in when she heard a rustling sound. She glanced round. Surprise turned to shock, shock to horror and she opened her mouth to scream.

2000

The trial lasted three days; extremely short for a murder case. The evidence was circumstantial but convincing. The plea of not guilty had little to support it. Faced with the allegations of the prosecution and with little to refute them, the judge's direction to the jury was disposed heavily in favour of the Crown. As one reporter whispered to another, 'Why bother with a jury, the verdict's already been handed down.'

The jurors needed less than an hour to consider their

findings. They filed back into the court, conspicuously avoiding the defendant's gaze. Their foreman rose in response to the usher's call.

'Have you reached a verdict?'

'Yes, my lord.'

'And is that verdict unanimous?'

'Yes, my lord.'

'On the charge of the murder of Anna Marshall, how do you find the defendant Alan Charles Marshall?'

'Guilty.'

'Alan Charles Marshall, you have been found guilty of the murder of your wife Anna Marshall, a verdict with which I entirely agree. This was a brutal crime carried out in cold blood. You knew your wife's love for you was dead. You knew she was on the point of leaving you. You could not tolerate that rejection so you slit her throat in the cruellest and most gory manner; using such violence you almost decapitated her. Then you calmly drove more than sixty miles to dispose of the body into the North Sea. Hoping no doubt that it would remain there so that the evidence of your foul deed would remain undetected. However, the sea gave up the corpse, your wife's body was identified and the police investigation uncovered the motive behind your evil action. In view of the nature of the crime, the complete lack of remorse you have shown, and your refusal to acknowledge your undoubted guilt in the face of unchallenged evidence, I therefore sentence you to life imprisonment with the recommendation that in this instance that should mean a term of no less than twenty-five years.'

2006

'It is the opinion of the Court of Appeal that this conviction is not safe. Our findings are based on inconsistencies in the evidence presented by the prosecution at the original trial and we are less than satisfied that the direction to the jury was other than prejudicial to the defendant. This court deems that the defendant's guilt was not established beyond reasonable doubt, and therefore determines that the conviction of Alan Charles Marshall for the murder of Anna Marshall be set aside. The defendant is free to return to the community.'

As the handful of attendees filed out, Marshall stepped from the dock. He was greeted by his counsel with a curt nod. As the barrister stuffed the case notes into a folder, Marshall asked, 'How much is this going to cost?'

'No concern of yours. The bill's been paid. You're a free man, what more do you want?'

'I want to know who paid.'

'I'm not at liberty to say. Accept your freedom and be grateful. If you want something to worry about, prepare yourself for the press when you walk through that door.'

The small dwelling was more than remote, it was isolated. Although the scenery was beautiful there was little else to recommend it. The single-storey cottage had nothing in the way of luxury apart from an ancient, but serviceable, Aga. It was no place for the social-minded. For a hermit it was ideal. The prospective tenant nodded approvingly. 'It'll do.'

'You understand the terms? If you leave your job you've to leave the cottage.'

'I understand.'

'You're quite sure? It gets lonely out here and pretty bleak in winter.'

'Suits me.'

'Then it's yours, and the job with it.'

2008

There were only ten shopping days before Christmas. DI Mike Nash grimaced at the thought; office parties, drunken brawls, domestic violence and opportunist thieves. That's what Christmas meant to him. When he walked into Helmsdale police station he was surprised to see the reception desk manned by

Sergeant Binns, who'd been working at HQ in Netherdale. 'What are you doing here, Jack?'

'I've been sent back. Flu!'

'Who's gone down with it now?'

'Almost everybody. Apart from you, me and your visitor.'

'My visitor? Who?'

'The chief constable, no less. She doesn't visit many of her officers' – Binns gave a sly glance – 'but we all know she has a soft spot for you.'

'You've been listening to Clara too much; you're getting to sound like her.'

Nash hurried upstairs to his office. 'Morning, ma'am.'

Gloria O'Donnell, the highly respected chief constable, known irreverently as 'God' because of her initials, more than for her rank, looked up from his desk. 'Morning, Mike. I came to ask for help because of the flu outbreak, but it seems you've got your own problems.' Nash raised his eyebrows questioningly. 'I've taken two phone calls since I got here. Both Mironova and Pearce have gone down with the virus. Netherdale station is like the Marie Celeste. You're the only CID officer in the area who's fit for duty. There seems little chance of any of them returning to work this side of New Year.'

'That's going to be fun, with the mayhem the festive season brings.'

'Tell me about it. The only solution I can come up with is to let civilian clerical staff run the desk at Netherdale. You'll have to make do with a community support officer here. That'll free Binns up to work with you in CID. I've just got hold of DC Andrews. She's been on attachment to Yorkshire Central. I told them I needed her back. She's on her way. They squealed a bit, but I pulled rank. She lives in Netherdale, so that helps. Oh, and I've had a word with HMIC. In view of the circumstances, they're prepared to lend me Superintendent Edwards again, short term. You've worked together before, so that shouldn't be a problem.'

'That would help. Don't suppose a recruitment drive's on the cards yet?'

O'Donnell sighed. 'Let's not talk about that. The cutbacks are getting worse. I can't have a new deputy, vacancies aren't being filled; even civilian staff levels are being culled. Put it this way, if you drop a paperclip, pick it up.'

'That bad?'

'With the whole country having to tighten its belt, then so must we. With rising unemployment there's bound to be a hike in the crime rate, but that carries no weight. We've to knuckle down and get on with it. It's not much I'm afraid, but it's the best I can do for the time being.'

'That means Helmsdale has four officers, Edwards, me, Binns and DC Andrews, plus a rookie for the desk? I should be able to cope.'

O'Donnell paused before telling him the worst. 'No, Mike, that's to cover Netherdale as well.'

The buzzing took on an angrier note as the chain made contact with timber. The process had been going on for three days. The pile of stacked lengths of wood at the edge of the clearing, and the pale tops of exposed tree stumps testified to the level of activity.

The chainsaw operator paused. Despite the cold December wind he was sweating from both the thickness of his quilted shirt and the effort. Wiping his brow he transferred liberal quantities of sawdust from his shirtsleeve to his forehead. He switched off the saw and rested it against one of the stumps. Thinning trees was a job he enjoyed most, in hindsight. He didn't even have the distraction of a companion to enliven his rest breaks. He reached for his knapsack. A pale winter sun hung low in the sky. He reckoned it was about 2 p.m. Time for lunch.

Taking his flask, he brewed a mug of tea and examined the clearing as he ate his sandwiches. With luck he'd have the job finished by the weekend. He thought briefly of Nell; wondered whether she gave him a thought out here on his own. He smiled wryly; he of all people should be used to being alone.

Using a long-bladed knife from the sheath on his belt, he sliced effortlessly through an apple; then tossed the core into the long grass. He stood up, flexed his arms and back, repacked his knapsack and fired up the chainsaw again.

Some accidents are down to carelessness; some are pure misfortune. In this instance it was both. As the chainsaw bit into the trunk of a silver birch the head of a nail snagged one of the teeth. The chain snapped, but the drive continued feeding links round the blade. It unwound with the speed of a striking rattlesnake. His hands felt the change first. He slackened his grip on the trigger. A split second later he saw the chain arcing towards him. He ducked to his right.

The last few links caught against the side of the guard, slowing the chain and slewing it slightly. The reduction in speed and the change in its path undoubtedly saved his life.

Shock deprived him of movement. He stared down at his quilted shirt, ripped apart in a long gash across his arm and chest. Blood began to spurt from the wounds. He was alone, miles from help. He took a deep breath, let the saw drop and cut the motor off with the toe of his boot.

Using his right hand, he unbuckled his belt, wrenched it from his jeans and looped it tightly round his upper arm, manoeuvring the improvised tourniquet above the wound. He took another deep breath. Shock was making him dizzy. He'd over a mile to walk. Even then he'd be little better off. Without a phone, the cottage was as remote as this wood. There was no alternative. He'd have to drive or bleed to death.

chapter two

Lisa Andrews wasn't happy. She'd arrived in Helmsdale late morning; had only been there five minutes when she was sent on a job. Sergeant Binns had greeted her briefly then tossed a patrol car key to her. 'Andrews, I've a nice drive for you.'

'Where to?'

'Far side of Kirk Bolton. Chance to make a name for yourself: the only detective in the county investigating a rustling case.'

She shouldn't have got her hopes up. Her thirty-mile round trip had been for nothing. The old farmer stared at her in dismay. 'Eeh, I'm sorry, lass. I forgot I'd arranged for them to be tupped. Spoke to a mate of mine at mart yesterday.' The old man scratched his head ruefully. 'Thing was, we were in Cobblers Arms, having a pint. It weren't my last, though.' He cackled with laughter at the pun.

His laughter died as he saw her expression. 'I forgot he'd said he'd send his wagon for 'em yesterday afternoon, so when I saw they weren't in t' field this morning I thought they'd been nicked. 'T weren't until after I rang your lot I remembered. Sorry, an' all that.'

Frustrated at the waste of time, Andrews reversed too quickly into the lane and ended up in a ditch. The patrol car was not as damaged as her pride. It took nearly an hour for the farmer to fetch his tractor from the field and get her back on the road. As she left the farmhouse the old man watched her go, aware of her frustration.

The scenery went unnoticed. She failed to register the change from wild moorland to the gentler pastures and forestry of the lower slopes of the dale. The dense woods concealed a side road that spewed on to the lane at an acute angle. Her attention was brought back abruptly as a Land Rover cut across her bows and careered in front of her. The rear door of the vehicle was so close it filled her windscreen.

She slammed her foot on the brake. The Fiesta snaked wildly as she fought for control. The Land Rover was pulling away. She gritted her teeth. 'Right!' Her foot hit the accelerator as her hand flicked on the siren and lights.

He heard the sound but failed to identify it. Consciousness was beginning to slip away. He tried to fight the lethargy, muttering through gritted teeth. 'Must get to Barry's, must get to Barry's.' It became like a mantra. Barry would be out shooting. He prayed Barry's wife would be home.

The noise filtered through a fierce wave of nausea. His vision blurred as he saw the red and blue lights in his mirror. 'Oh shit.' He stopped. The road was moving, up and down, then side to side. He stared at it, nausea rising, senses failing.

Andrews flung her door open and leapt from the car. This was no false alarm. The man's erratic driving marked him down as a drunk. She reached the Land Rover and looked in. The driver was around forty, she guessed, his dark hair was going grey early, his face was deathly pale. He was lolling back in the driving seat with his eyes closed. The classic drunk's pose.

She tapped angrily on the window. The driver opened his eyes and looked at her. How keen his focus was she couldn't be sure. She flashed her warrant card and gestured for him to open the door. 'Get out of the car please.'

As he fumbled with the handle she saw his face screw up with pain. She took an involuntary step back. Something wasn't right. He looked drunk. He drove as if drunk, but there was something strange about him. As he put one foot on the road he half fell, half knelt; then vomited violently. A second later he straightened up. She stared in horror at the blood-stained mess that had been his left arm and chest. 'Oh God, what happened?'

'Chainsaw,' he muttered through gritted teeth. 'Must get help.'

Stating the bleeding obvious she thought, without noticing the pun. 'You can't drive. You're in no fit state. Can you make it to my car?'

He nodded.

'I'll get you in the passenger seat; try not to bleed on the upholstery. I'll move your vehicle off the road then drive you to Netherdale Hospital.'

The nausea eased momentarily. 'There's a ditch on the left–'

'I know,' she snapped.

When the Land Rover was secured she hurried back. 'Can you manage your seat belt?' He tried but the effort caused him too much distress. 'OK, let me do it.' She leaned over and gently eased the belt across his chest; trying to avoid as much of the bloodstained gash as possible. She put the car into gear and hit the siren and lights. After a few abortive attempts she managed to get a strong enough signal to talk to the control room. 'I'm taking a badly injured man to Netherdale General. He's had an accident with a chainsaw. He's got wounds to the upper arm and chest, severe loss of blood and is in shock. Pass that to A and E.' Glancing sideways she added, 'Tell them he's been vomiting and now he's lost consciousness.'

The staff nurse looked harassed. 'Can you tell me the patient's name and address?'

'I'm sorry,' Andrews replied. 'I don't know them. I stopped his car because he was driving erratically. Before I'd chance to question him, he collapsed.'

'Do you know anything about him?'

'Not yet, but I soon will. I have his registration number. Unless he stole it, I'll find out his details.' She pulled her mobile phone from her pocket, only to receive a glare from the staff nurse.

The nurse pointed to the phone on the end of the reception counter. 'Use that one.'

Andrews read out the Land Rover's details to Jack Binns.

'OK, I'll check it out then ring you back. Give me that phone number.'

'Hang on a mo.' Andrews hailed a passing nurse. 'Does this phone accept incoming calls?'

The nurse nodded. It was ten minutes later when Binns phoned back. 'The Land Rover's registered to Winfield Estate, which doesn't get us a lot further. I've rung the estate office but got no reply. I'll keep trying.'

'The hospital needs to know his details. Also his car's stuck out on a country lane and I've got the keys.'

'I'll get back to you as soon as I have anything.'

The A and E department had changed shift before the information came through. Andrews put the phone down and smiled apologetically at a nurse waiting to speak to her.

'Are you with the patient who had the chainsaw accident?'

'Yes, how is he?'

'He's recovered consciousness, but he's very weak. He lost a lot of blood and had to have a transfusion, so he'll be kept in for a few days. He's been moved on to a ward.'

'Can I speak to him?'

'As long as you keep it short. Have you found out who he is?'

'I've just got the details.'

His eyes were closed as she approached the bed. She thought the nurse had been over optimistic in assessing his condition. His wounds had been bandaged, the dressings revealing the full extent of the injuries. He looked pale and ill. Far worse than when she'd found him. 'Mr Myers,' she said softly. His eyelids flickered but didn't open. 'Mr Myers.' She repeated his name, this time a little louder. The second time he opened his eyes. He stared at her without recognition. 'Mr Myers, can you remember what happened?'

At first she thought he was too heavily sedated to take in her question, but after a few moments he gave a minute shake of his head.

'You had an accident with a chainsaw.' She spoke slowly and clearly as if to a small child. 'I had to bring you in.'

He frowned slightly, whether from pain or what she was telling him, she couldn't be sure. Then she heard him whisper, 'Sorry.'

'We need to get your Land Rover off the road. Is there anyone at your home to drive it?'

Another fractional head-shake.

'You live alone?'

There was no answer for a moment. Then after moistening his lips he whispered, 'Barry,' he paused for a second to allow a sudden bout of pain to pass before adding, 'Barry Dickinson.' His voice was so weak she'd to strain to hear him.

'OK, I got that,' she told him. 'Can you tell me where he lives?'

'Cottage, Winfield Estate.' It was by no means a long sentence but he was gasping by the end of it.

She heard a voice behind her. 'OK, I think that's enough' – a doctor was standing by the end of the bed – 'unless you want to undo all your good work. Sorry and all that' – he gestured towards the door – 'but he needs rest and quiet.' He gently but firmly ushered her away and out of the ward.

The following morning she was back at the hospital before 8.15. She was anxious to interview her mystery patient, but first she had to get past the ward sister. 'I'm glad you've turned up,' the sister informed her as she paused at the reception counter. 'You've saved me a phone call. I need to check the information you gave us.'

'Why?' Andrews asked.

'According to the details you gave his name is Andrew Myers, his address is Woodbine Cottage and his date of birth is the first of February 1971.'

'That sounds right,' Andrews agreed. 'We got it from his employers, Winfield Estate.'

'Well I think someone's been feeding you bad information. According to our computer Mr Andrew Myers with that address and that date of birth doesn't exist.'

'I don't understand.' Andrews stared at her blankly.

'Our computer can trace anyone who's been allocated an NHS number, providing we know their name and date of birth. No NHS number has been issued to an Andrew Myers born on that date.'

Lisa frowned. 'Is he awake?'

'Yes, and I asked him for his details.'

'What did he tell you?'

The sister pursed her lips before replying, 'Andrew Myers!'

'I'll have a word.' Lisa headed for his bed.

'You've caused a lot of bother.'

He frowned. He should remember her, but his recollection of recent events was more than hazy. 'How did I get here?' His voice sounded pathetically weak.

'I brought you in. I'd to stop you because your driving was all over the place.' She smiled. 'I thought you were drunk, until I saw your injuries. You shouldn't have driven in that condition.'

He remained silent.

'How long are you in for? Have they told you yet?'

'Another two days perhaps.'

'I have some questions.' She looked at him as she spoke and was shocked at the change her innocuous remark brought about. His face became a mask of wary tension. She pretended not to notice. 'How did the accident happen? Can you remember?'

'I think the chain hit something, a nail or maybe a hard knot. Anyway it snapped and flew back at me.'

'Where did it happen?'

'In Layton Woods.'

'Is that where you work?'

He shook his head. 'I work for Winfield Estate. It borders Layton Woods. I was clearing a section of woodland that crosses the boundary between the two estates.'

'Can you confirm a few personal details for my file? Your full name, address, date of birth and occupation.' She waited, biro poised, as he hesitated.

'Andrew Myers, Woodbine Cottage, Kirk Bolton. I'm a forester employed by Winfield Estate and my date of birth is the first of February 1971.'

'Married or single?'

Again she noticed the momentary hesitation before he replied. 'Single.'

'OK, I've only one more question. Can you explain why you don't appear on any official records? The hospital computer fails to recognize an Andrew Myers with that date of birth as having ever been allocated an NHS, or National Insurance number.'

She was uncertain what to expect. Fear, possibly anger. What she saw in Myers' expression was a mixture of bitterness, resignation and sadness. His reply was a long time coming. 'A man may call himself whatever he wants. If I wake up tomorrow and decide to call myself Geoffrey Thompson for the day, nobody can stop me. If I want to change it the next day, I can do that too. There's no law against it.'

'Listen,' she said; her voice low but firm. 'You've caused a lot of trouble. Not just for me, but for your friend Mr Dickinson, and for the hospital. I didn't get home until gone midnight and my shift should have finished at 6 p.m. And no, we don't get paid overtime. Apart from that, if I hadn't stopped you when I did, you'd probably be dead.'

His mouth twisted bitterly. 'You wouldn't have to do crowd control at the funeral.'

'Oh for God's sake, spare me the self pity.'

He tried to shrug then winced. 'Look,' he said firmly. 'It isn't that I don't appreciate your help, but I just want to be left alone. Is that too much to ask?'

'Mr Myers. All I'm trying to do is wind up this matter. I need to know why you insist on calling yourself by a false name.'

He sighed wearily. 'Don't you lot ever give up? Don't you ever let a man alone once you've had your teeth into him? It's as if you piss on him and leave a scent for others to follow. Why can't you simply take it on trust that I've done nothing that would remotely interest you? Can't you leave me alone to get on with my life? All I want is to remain anonymous.'

There was a long silence before she said, 'Trust? OK, I'll do a deal with you. Tell me why you want to remain anonymous. If I'm satisfied you're on the level I promise it'll go no further. How's that?'

He nodded agreement. 'But not here though, and not yet. When I get out of this place. I'll tell you then.'

'It's a deal.'

21

chapter three

'Morning, Lisa, finding your way round?'

'Yes, sir.' Lisa grinned and jumped to attention.

'Don't take the piss. I understand you were thrown in at the deep end yesterday. Manage OK?'

'I had no problem solving the theft that turned out not to be a crime. Had a few problems with the accident victim though.' Lisa related her experiences. She'd just finished her tale when Nash's phone rang. He picked it up. 'Ruth? How are you? And more importantly, where are you?'

He looked up and made a drinking motion with his hand. Lisa nodded and left his office. Binns was in the CID room staring at a computer screen that stayed stubbornly blank. 'Bloody computer's on the blink.' He scowled at the monitor. 'Third time this week it's been out of action. I reckon it's caught the flu bug.'

'Do you want a coffee? I'm making Mike one, for when he comes off the phone.'

'Talking to one of his lady friends, is he? Or is it work?'

'Someone called Ruth, so probably not work.'

Binns laughed. 'Think again. That would be Superintendent Edwards. She was attached to us after Tom Pratt's heart attack, before she joined the Inspectorate of Constabulary. The chief's got her back on a temporary secondment.' Binns paused. 'She's a top-class copper.'

'How did the chief get her to agree to come back?'

'Power of persuasion. When she sets her mind to it, not many would have the balls to refuse her.'

The cottage felt cold, uninviting. As soon as he opened the front door he could smell the closed-up atmosphere. The door opened directly into the lounge. The room was spartan in appearance. Along one wall was a small dresser, on another, a large bookcase whose shelves were crammed with a wide selection of books. There was no television, but there was a modern music centre and a vast collection of CDs in a rack alongside. For the rest there was only a single armchair, coffee table and a standard lamp. A solitary man's room.

Although the drive home by taxi had tested him, Myers ignored the armchair. His priority was the Aga. Without it the cottage would remain unheated. He'd seen a weather forecast on the TV in the hospital. It was threatening a hard frost. It would be pointless surviving the chainsaw massacre only to succumb to hypothermia. Cleaning out and relighting the stove normally took ten minutes. On this occasion it was over half an hour. He was sweating slightly and felt in urgent need of a cup of tea, but knew he'd have to wait.

He remembered a distasteful task left over from the accident and walked slowly through to the bedroom. The sheet on the single bed had been ripped to provide a makeshift dressing. Myers picked up the remnants and carried them through to the kitchen for incineration.

He heard the engine long before Barry Dickinson reached the cottage. He opened the front door as the gamekeeper's vehicle pulled to a halt.

'Now then, Andy, how're you doing?'

'Not too bad. Did today go OK?'

'Ay, well enough.' The gamekeeper opened the Land Rover's tailgate. Myers stepped out of the doorway and the next second a black shape hurtled past him.

'She doesn't seem tired,' Myers commented.

'Not her. I hope her tea's ready.'

'No problem. Would you like a coffee?'

'I would that. Here let me do it.' He handed Myers a foil-topped plate. 'Your supper,' he said by way of explanation. 'Shirley said to warm it through.' Myers thanked him as Barry brewed them a drink.

The Labrador had demolished her meal, wandered over to her bean bag and lain down, head on paws. 'Nell did you proud today,' Barry said. 'Sir Maurice was capped with her, and I'd someone wanting to buy her. Sean Parker also had a couple during their shooting week. He told me one bloke refused to believe Nell wasn't his to sell, got quite shitty about it.'

Myers looked down at the Labrador. She twitched one eyebrow and gave a perfunctory wag of her tail. 'She doesn't seem to have come to much harm, despite her amateur handlers.'

The keeper winced. 'Who made you an expert? Anyway, I've a couple of messages from Sir Maurice. Firstly, he wants to know how you are, and he wants to know if you're interested in breeding from Nell. There's a bloke near Helmsdale has a right good dog, a Field Trial Champion. Sir Maurice reckons there'd be some grand pups in a litter from that mating. He's already talking about buying one of the bitches' – Barry grinned – 'for me to train.'

Myers stared at the keeper coldly. 'Is that supposed to be an inducement? I'd have to give it a lot of thought. These things can go wrong and she's all I've got.'

Barry's eyes softened momentarily. Although he'd often wondered why Myers chose such a hermit-like existence, he'd never intruded with questions.

'Ay, well we might be able to change that. Get you fixed up if you fancy it,' he said mischievously. 'You'll have to wait till after Christmas though. Sir Maurice told me to invite you to the shoot supper on the twenty-ninth. He warned me there's only one answer to the invitation and it isn't "no".'

Myers shook his head. 'I don't do the social bit.'

'I told Sir Maurice that. I said you'd rather curl up with a good book than a bad woman.'

'What was his reaction?'

'He wasn't impressed. He threatened to get Falstaff to come and collect you.'

Sir Maurice's butler-cum-chauffeur was built like an all-in wrestler with a ferociously piratical beard. The likeness to a Shakespearean character made the nickname inevitable. Local rumour was that Sir Maurice had been involved with the security services long ago and that Falstaff was his lifetime bodyguard. Neither master nor man commented on the rumour, which did nothing to quell it.

'I've nobody to take; nobody to ask,' Myers objected. 'Everybody else will be there with wives or girlfriends. I'll be a real gooseberry.'

'I've an idea. Why not ask that nice lady detective who rescued you? She's a fit-looking bird.'

Myers smiled ruefully. 'The trouble with fit-looking birds is they're usually either married or in a relationship with some hairy-arsed bloke twice my size. Anyway she's far too young for me and, as I said, I don't do the social thing.'

Barry couldn't restrain his curiosity. 'Why, Andy? I mean, you're not exactly hideous. You know how to behave, you don't have BO and you don't fart or pick your nose in public.'

'I prefer it that way.' Myers' face darkened. 'All right, I'll go to the shoot supper. Let's just leave it there, shall we?'

'OK, Andy, I wasn't prying. We can sort the arrangements out on Boxing Day. You'll be right by then? It's the biggest day of the season, bigger than ever this year.'

'I should be. I don't want to miss it.'

'Grand, because I'll likely be rushed off my feet and you're the best picker-up around, especially when you're working her.' Barry pointed to Nell.

'Why will you be extra busy?'

Barry pulled a face. 'Sir Maurice has added extra guns for Boxing Day, because in the first shoot in the New Year he's invited half the Cabinet and a fair number from the House of Lords, as well as the local bigwigs. That's going to mean a big Special Branch contingent and the like, all fidgety because of the guns about. A right headache, I can tell you.'

Stuart Moran was tired. As senior partner of the Leeds office of a national firm of solicitors, he had plenty of work to tire him, but this was a different weariness. He couldn't afford to ease up; not with two avaricious ex-wives to support. He needed a break.

Christmas was approaching but Stuart wasn't going to follow his normal routine. Instead of stuffing his diary with social engagements, he declined every invitation. This came as some surprise to his personal assistant. Exactly how personal her assistance reached was known only to a select few, but Lesley had been Moran's mistress long before the end of her marriage and Stuart's second.

'I've had an idea about Christmas,' Moran told her. 'Let's do something different. I've got this brochure.' He passed it over the desk. 'See what you think.'

'"The Golden Bear at Netherdale",' Lesley read aloud. '"Why not make it a romantic festive season, a time for lovers?"' The brochure described a programme of dinners, dances, outings and walks. Lesley was no fan of the open air; social events were more up her street.

Moran braced himself for stiff resistance and was surprised when Lesley agreed with seeming enthusiasm. She didn't relish the idea of Christmas buried in the countryside, but she had ambitions to become Mrs Moran mark III. As she left to make the booking his direct line rang. 'Moran,' he identified himself. 'Oh, it's you. What do you want?'

'Have you thought over my latest instructions?' his caller asked.

'No,' Moran stated with a touch of bravado. 'I've told you before, Harry, I don't want any more to do with it. I want out; for good.'

'I think that would be a mistake.'

'I mean it, Harry,' Moran insisted. 'As far as I'm concerned it's all over.'

'You can't walk away. You're in too deep.'

'I can walk away whenever I want. Don't forget, I hold the evidence.'

'I don't like the sound of that. It sounds almost like a threat. That would be a serious mistake, Stuart. If I was you I'd think again.'

'No, Harry, my mind's made up.'

'There's no way I can persuade you?'

'No there isn't!'

'Very well. We shall see.'

The line went dead, but for a long while afterwards Moran stayed clutching the receiver, the dialling tone unheeded in his ear. Eventually, he took a sheet of notepaper and began to write. Slowly, with several pauses during which he stared at the wall, his eyes unfocused, Moran filled the A4 sheet. He reached into the drawer, extracted another sheet and continued. When he'd finished, he read the document through a couple of times before signing it. He placed it in an envelope before reaching for the phone book.

Nash was daydreaming, idly toying with his wineglass as he waited. The casserole he'd prepared was simmering gently. The doorbell rang and he wandered down the hall, opened the door and smiled at the visitor. 'Hi, Ruth, come on in.'

'Mike, this is really good of you. I couldn't get a hotel room for love nor money. Everywhere is booked solid for the next three weeks.'

Nash took her case and pointed down the hall. 'I'll show you your room. Would you like a shower or anything before you eat?'

'Just a pee and a wash; I'm ravenous. I've been driving over six hours. I left Bristol and hit one of the worst traffic snarl-ups in history.'

Nash showed Ruth the spare room. 'That's great.' She peeled off her coat. 'Now, I'll go to the bathroom, while you pour me a large glass of whatever you're drinking. After that, show me the food and stand well back.'

Nash laughed. 'That hungry, are you?'

The meal over, they relaxed in the dining alcove. 'That was terrific,' Ruth told him. 'I couldn't have got a meal like that in a hotel.'

'My pleasure; and the least I could do considering you're helping us out.'

'When Gloria asked, I couldn't refuse. How busy are you?'

'Not specially, not at the moment. But I reckon it's the calm before the Christmas storm.'

Ruth yawned. 'I'm going to turn in soon. All that driving, I need an early night.'

'Mr Brown?'

'Who's asking?'

'Mr Jones.'

'I know several Mr Joneses.'

'I'm sure you do. Let's just say I'm one of the Yorkshire Joneses.'

'Oh, that Mr Jones. We haven't spoken for some time.'

'I haven't had the need for your special talents until now.'

'Then I take it you have a commission for me?'

'Yes, and it's quite urgent. I assume you're still engaged in that line of work?'

'Most certainly,'

'As we haven't done business recently you'd better tell me your current fees.'

Brown named a figure and added, 'Plus expenses.'

There was a pause. 'I see. You're right, it has been a while. Inflation I suppose. Can I assume your terms are still the same?'

'You can.'

'And my order should still be delivered in the same way?'

'Absolutely correct.'

'Very well, I'll attend to it immediately. One other thing; when you've completed this commission there may be others. I assume that presents no problem?'

'Certainly not. However, I need your security name to satisfy myself everything is as it should be.'

'Of course. The secure name is Harry.'

chapter four

The newsagent's was on the corner of a long terrace of houses.
The proprietor had owned the shop longer than most of his
neighbours had lived in the area, or in some cases, the country.
Shortly after he had bought the shop, he was approached by a
man who asked if he would receive letters for him, a service
for which the stranger was prepared to offer the sum of fifty
pounds per item. He'd thought about it, but not for long. Fifty
pounds to hold a letter was easy money. The service had been
running ever since. The stranger had said the letters would be
addressed to Mr Jackson Browne.

A week before Christmas, Mr Browne arrived to pick up a
letter. As he watched the stranger leave his shop, the proprietor wondered, not for the first time, what the process meant
and whether it was legal. He glanced down at the money in his
hand, put it into the till and forgot all about Jackson Browne.

Lesley Robertson sat in the bay window of her flat. Christmas
lights from the surrounding buildings reflected in the raindrops
on her window pane. She saw Moran's BMW coming down the
street and reached for her handbag and coat. By the time she
returned she'd be well on the way to being Mrs Stuart Moran.
She wheeled her suitcase to the lift, then to the car, where Moran
helped her stow it in the boot. Neither of them noticed the small,
nondescript saloon that pulled away from the kerb shortly after
they set off.

They arrived at The Golden Bear late on the afternoon of
Christmas Eve. Netherdale's wide cobbled market place was
alive with last-minute shoppers. The Christmas lights were
augmented by those from the market stalls where the traders

were doing good business. Outside The Golden Bear six giant Christmas trees were festooned with a myriad of tiny white lights. Lesley began to revise her opinion. Maybe the festive season would be more fun than she'd thought.

They walked into reception and checked in. As they waited for the lift neither of them noticed the man who approached the desk. Had they seen him they wouldn't have been interested.

'Good afternoon,' he greeted the receptionist. He gazed at the headdress the management had insisted she wear. 'Nice antlers!' The joviality was lost on her. 'I want to enquire about a room during February, from the fourteenth to the twenty-first to be exact. A double en suite if you have one.'

'Just one moment, I'll check for you.' Before she could input his request he'd scanned her screen, which was showing details of the previous registration. He had them memorized before the receptionist turned and informed him, with mock sympathy, that there was nothing available for the dates he required. That'll pay you back for the antlers, she thought.

The unlucky visitor went to the bar. If he was disconsolate about the missed booking, it didn't show. He sat amid a crowd of festive drinkers, making notes in a small Filofax. The notes were about Stuart Moran's registration. They also described, down to the smallest detail, the uniform of waiters and porters employed by The Golden Bear. Nowhere in the notes was there mention of a visit in February.

The week leading up to Christmas had proved boring for both Myers and Nell. He was still unable to work because of his injuries; neither could he give his dog the exercise she needed.

His most adventurous outings were both to Netherdale Hospital. The first was to have his dressings changed, the second for the removal of the stitches. The staff nurse on the ward professed herself satisfied with the way the wound was healing. The visit to the hospital reminded him of his promise to the detective. A promise he'd not yet kept. He felt guilty at breaking his word, but eased his conscience by telling himself she'd have forgotten about him by now.

On Boxing Day morning he and Nell were collected early by Barry, en route for Winfield Manor. They found Sir Maurice and several members of his household, including the impressive Falstaff, directing the small army of keepers, under-keepers, beaters, loaders, end stops and pickers-up. In an unoccupied stable, tea, coffee and bacon sandwiches awaited them. Competition to work on Sir Maurice's shoot was fierce, the principal reasons being the food, and Sir Maurice's attitude to those he employed.

'Treat them as servants and they'll act like servants,' he'd told one of his neighbours. 'Make them part of a team and they'll give you more work than you pay for. What's more they won't resent you.'

Barry parked his Land Rover and opened the tailgate. Nell jumped athletically down and dashed off to renew old acquaintances, both human and canine. Sir Maurice noticed the dog before he spotted Myers. 'Andy, how goes it?' the baronet asked.

'Fine, Sir Maurice,' Myers responded.

'Your injury healing OK? Nasty things, chainsaws.'

Myers nodded. 'I've had the stitches out and the hospital gave me a clean bill of health.'

'Excellent.' Sir Maurice beamed. 'As long as you're not going to sue me. Barry tells me he's managed to persuade you to come to the shoot supper. I'm pleased about that; you'd be very much missed if you weren't there.'

'I'm really looking forward to it,' Myers told him, whilst trying to ignore the faces Barry was pulling behind the baronet's back.

'We can't have you turning into some sort of latter day St Anthony, can we?'

'I think Godric might be nearer the mark, Sir Maurice.'

The baronet looked at him in mild surprise for a second, then blinked. His shoulders quivered with laughter as he replied, 'In that case I'd better keep Lady Winfield and my daughters out of your way.' He was still chuckling as he turned to greet a couple of new arrivals.

'What was that St Anthony and Godric stuff about?' Barry asked.

'St Anthony was one of the earliest Christian hermits,' Myers explained. 'He was very pious and extremely chaste. By contrast, Godric was a self-confessed lecher, despoiler of virgins, adulterer, rapist and thief. Even after he became a hermit he continued his wickedness, but only in his dreams and memories.'

'Sounds like the wife's brother,' Barry remarked sourly. 'Now, about this supper. Shirley's volunteered to drive so we can have a few pints. If we pick you up at your cottage about 7 p.m. how will that suit?'

'That'll be fine.'

The keeper's attention was claimed by one of his deputies, who needed to consult about sending the end stops to the first drive. As he was discussing it, Barry wondered what it was from Myer's past that he remembered in the style of Godric.

'Mr Brown?'

'Who's calling?'

'Mr Jones, secure name Harry.'

'Yes, Mr Jones.'

'Can you give me a progress report? The first part of the payment has been transferred.'

'I've researched the item you enquired about, and your order will be dispatched by Monday – at the latest. The delivery address is a town called Netherdale.'

'That is excellent news. Once I have confirmation I'll be able to place my next order, will that be acceptable?'

'Quite acceptable.'

The shoot supper proved less disastrous than Myers feared. The meal was a buffet as Sir Maurice had requested. 'I prefer it this way,' he explained to Myers. 'Gives everybody a chance to circulate and chat, if anyone can talk above this racket.' He winced as a fresh wave of sound from the DJ's speakers assailed them.

'Led Zeppelin not to your taste?' Myers asked in a muted roar.

'Not bloody likely,' the baronet screamed back. 'Give me The Beatles or The Beach Boys any day.'

With typical generosity Sir Maurice paid for most of the drinks. Myers didn't abuse the hospitality. He wasn't used to drinking, and although he'd only had a couple of pints, he knew one more would have him on the edge of indiscretion. As his gaze turned towards the door of the function room he noticed a couple standing by the lift. He stared at the man's face which was in profile. He couldn't be sure, yet the resemblance was uncanny. His senses swam. It couldn't be the same man. He felt physically sick. As the man entered the lift he turned full face towards Myers.

Myers' eyes dilated as a cold murderous rage overcame him. He began to walk through the foyer, his eyes fixed on the closing lift door. Someone attempted to speak to him. They were saying something, he wasn't sure what. He pushed them aside as if they weren't there. At that moment nobody existed for Myers except the man he'd just seen. The man he hadn't seen for nearly nine years.

He reached the lift and watched the indicator. It passed the first-floor mark, and continued smoothly towards the second. It passed that, and Myers knew the couple's room was on the top floor of the building. He turned and sprinted towards the stairs. He took the shallow treads two at a time in his haste to reach the third floor; in his haste to get to the man he was going to kill.

It had been the worst possible Christmas for Lisa Andrews. She found herself working the oddest hours and returning home at the strangest of times. She couldn't really object. She knew that Nash and Superintendent Edwards were working even longer shifts. With no easing of the staff problems, the position was getting worse, rather than better.

She certainly wasn't expected home at midday two days after Christmas. If she had been, her boyfriend Donald would surely not have invited her neighbour Jackie into Lisa's bed. The row that followed was witnessed by the other occupants of the flats. Donald was flung out on to the pavement, wearing little but an expression of pain from the kick in the genitals that Lisa had delivered. Jackie bolted into her own flat and locked the door before Lisa's wrath turned on her. Lisa had flung Donald's car keys and clothing out of the window to him whilst he squirmed with embarrassment. No, Christmas had certainly not been good. Her only respite came from having to work the long, busy shifts, distracting her from the desire to strangle her ex-lover and her ex-friend.

Donald phoned her several times. Begging for forgiveness, reconciliation, a meeting, a chance to explain. Eventually, wearied by his persistence, she agreed to meet him for a drink in the bar of The Golden Bear on the evening of December twenty-ninth.

The meeting wasn't a success, only the public place preventing Lisa from starting a slanging match. Tersely she told him, 'Donald, why don't you piss off back to Leeds? I don't want any more to do with you. You can come to the flat tomorrow morning at 9 a.m. Your belongings will be outside on the pavement. Be there; or they go in the nearest skip.'

After he walked disconsolately away, Andrews finished her drink and stood up to leave. As she moved towards the door of the public bar she glanced across the foyer and recognized the man heading for the lift. It was another man who'd broken a promise and lied to her. 'I want a word with you, Mr Myers,' she muttered. When he turned and raced towards the stairs, Lisa set off in pursuit.

Myers reached the third floor. The climb had done nothing to cool his rage or weaken his resolve. He pushed open the glass door at the head of the stairwell alongside the lift. The brightly lit corridor stretched away to the right and left. He stood for a moment, undecided. The corridor was empty. Short of knocking on every door, his only option was to listen for the sound of movement and hope he'd picked the right room.

He heard footsteps, but was still undecided which direction they came from when the door behind him was flung open. The handle caught him painfully in the small of the back. A hand descended on his shoulder and turned him round none too gently.

His rage seemed to dissipate as he saw Lisa Andrews. 'You broke your promise,' she told him flatly. 'I thought better of you than that.'

He gaped at her in astonishment. 'Were you following me?' He clutched the wall for support, his fingers closing round the brass handrail. He looked pale and upset.

'Hah! What makes you think you're so important? What are you doing up here anyway?' she demanded.

He shook his head like a boxer who'd taken a heavy punch. 'If I told you, you'd arrest me.' He sighed heavily. 'Look, I had a good reason for not telling you about myself. I'm still not sure I should. But I reckon I owe you, not once but twice. You just might have saved me from doing something rash, so I'll tell you what I promised. But not here.'

She looked at him, unsure how far to trust him. Eventually she said, 'You said that before. But no mistakes this time; I'll come out to your cottage tomorrow morning around eleven.'

Myers was waiting, standing in the open doorway as she pulled her car to a halt. She locked the door and looked up in time to catch his fading smile. 'I don't suppose I needed to do that, did I?'

He shook his head. 'No. The pheasants round here are an honest bunch.'

'Don't rub it in. Force of habit.'

'Do you realize you have me at a disadvantage? You know who I am and where I live. I don't even know your name.'

'At least it's my own name,' she retorted.

'Ouch,' he exclaimed. 'Come inside.'

She looked around the sitting room; it was like a hermit's refuge. 'What, no TV?'

'No desire for one,' he told her succinctly. 'The problem is TV leaves nothing to the imagination. When I read a book I can make the characters look however I want. I can turn a hill into a mountain, a pond into a lake or a stream into a river. You can't do that with TV.'

'You may have a point.'

In the kitchen Myers brewed coffee. Lisa sat on a chair

sipping it whilst Myers perched on the table cradling his own mug. She was about to bring up the subject of their meeting when something cold and wet touched her hand. She gasped and looked down into a pair of beautiful almond-shaped brown eyes. 'Oh, hello,' she said. 'Who are you?'

'That's Nell.'

'Hello, Nell.' She stroked the Labrador's head. 'I'm Lisa Andrews.'

'Well, Lisa Andrews,' Myers began, 'I promised I'd explain myself. I'll tell you everything, except my real name. Will you excuse me that?'

'It depends on the reason for withholding it.'

'It's because I was tried, convicted and sentenced to life imprisonment for murder.' Myers paused and looked at her face for traces of shock, before continuing. 'The victim was my wife.' When he spoke again his voice was distant, remote. 'There was a young ambitious civil engineer who lived and worked in Leeds. Whilst he was at university he met and later married a pretty girl, equally ambitious. He'd graduated and been head-hunted by one of the top firms in the area. He was headed for the very top. Everyone said so. His wife was working in a solicitors' office in Leeds: a real golden couple. Nothing could go wrong.' He smiled mirthlessly.

'This was you?'

Myers nodded. 'Our marriage was allegedly failing. I didn't even realize it. Then one day my world fell apart. It wasn't an avalanche, just a slow collapse. It started as a trickle. My wife didn't come home one night. I wasn't as surprised as you might expect, she'd been acting out of character. I was angry, jealous, bitter, but not surprised. Instead of ringing round, making a fuss, I opened a bottle of whisky and drank the contents. That was a big mistake. Not my last, by any means.'

'What happened?'

'I woke up the following morning with a king-sized hangover. My wife still hadn't come home. So I made my second mistake: I went to work. Probably because I didn't want to admit the marriage was over. When she didn't come home that night

I decided to face her, get it over with. I went to her office next morning. That was when I was told she'd not been at work the previous day. It was only then that I reported her missing.

'Three days later her car was found abandoned in a car park in Scarborough. It was unlocked and the back seat was covered in bloodstains. Blood later identified as hers. The following spring a body, or what remained of it, was washed up along the coast near Robin Hood's Bay. DNA testing was the only way they could identify the corpse. The body had been in the water too long. If people knew what creatures in the North Sea feed on, they'd never touch fish and chips again.'

Lisa shuddered. 'Please, too much information.'

'The pathologist's report showed her throat had been cut with such violence that a vertebra at the back of her neck was notched. She'd almost been decapitated. The pathologist gave his opinion that the wound was either inflicted with a razor-sharp knife, or in great passion. I was charged with murder.

'The trial only lasted three days, during which the prosecution drew the jurors' attention to the damning evidence. They were told about blazing rows reported by a neighbour. Then her boss told them he and the dead woman were lovers. They heard the solicitor say that my wife believed I knew about the affair. They were told of the suspicious lapse in time before I reported her missing, making it sound as if I used that time to cover my tracks. They listened; then convicted me of murder. They only took forty minutes to reach the verdict. Not to be outdone the judge got in on the act. The sentence was life, with a little additional clause recommending a minimum term of twenty-five years.'

Myers was watching Lisa as he related the story. If she was repelled or frightened she didn't show it.

'What happened next?'

'Durham gaol maximum security wing. Category: extremely violent and dangerous. That means they locked me up for twenty-three hours a day. Unless you've experienced prison life you'd think someone was making it up. Even now the mention of the place is enough. I can almost taste the foul stink of it. I wasn't a model prisoner. My parents had disowned me. I have a brother living in New Zealand. He wrote twice telling me I was a disgrace, and that he was arranging for my parents to go and live with him.

'It was years before I had a visitor; then, out of the blue, a solicitor came to see me. He'd been instructed to commence appeal proceedings. The only stipulation was I was not to be told who funded the appeal. When I got in front of the Appeal Court judges the barrister retained on my behalf started taunting me. In the end he riled me into saying I adored my wife, had no idea she was having an affair, wouldn't have harmed a hair on her head. He asked why I hadn't reported her missing, making out I was guilty. I told him I drank a full bottle of whisky and got absolutely pissed.' Myers stopped and laughed.

'What's funny?'

'Those judges live in a different world. One of them stopped proceedings and asked me, "Would that be a litre or seventy-five centilitres?" Then my counsel went into his closing statement. He said there was no proof I'd killed my wife. No DNA, no witnesses, nothing to show I'd ever been to Scarborough. The judges agreed, said there was sufficient doubt; that the original conviction was unsafe.'

'So you were acquitted?'

'Not really. I mean I was never acknowledged as innocent.'

'What do you think happened to your wife?'

'I've absolutely no idea. God knows I'd enough time to think about it. I'm nowhere nearer the truth than I was when it happened. Someone knows though. Somebody apart from the killer, I mean.'

'What makes you say that?'

'When the solicitor came to visit me, it wasn't at my request. Somebody went to a great deal of trouble and enormous expense to bring about my appeal and pay for it.'

'Have you ever been tempted to try to find out the truth?'

'Occasionally, but whatever I do won't bring her back.'

'Do you still love her?'

'I thought I'd fallen out of love with her when I heard she'd been having an affair. Now I'm not so sure. Above all, I regret that she died so horribly. She was a lively, happy person, who should have been given a better chance.'

'Her death put you through hell,' Lisa pointed out.

'Yes, but that wasn't her doing. Anyway it's all over now. A sorry tale, I'm afraid.'

'Well, Mr Myers, or whoever you are, you've done what you promised. I can see why you live the hermit existence out here. Does all that bitterness not have an end, though? Why did you seem so angry last night? What were you doing on that third floor of the hotel?'

'First, tell me something. Did you believe me, when I said I didn't kill my wife?'

'Without examining the evidence it's not easy to say, but you certainly don't seem the type.'

'What I'm about to say might shake your belief. I said you'd saved me from doing something rash. When I was at that party, I spotted the man who'd been my wife's lover. The one who told all those lies about me in court, the man who got me convicted. If you hadn't come chasing after me there's every chance I might have killed him last night.'

chapter five

On New Year's Eve the dining room at The Golden Bear, transformed into a ballroom for the night, certainly looked festive. Large Christmas trees were spaced at intervals down one wall of the room, each ablaze with a mass of lights. There were also twinkling light displays around the temporary stage, where a jazz band was entertaining the diners. The tables were decorated gaily with centre displays, Christmas napkins and crackers on each setting, whilst those reserved for the ladies had a small gift parcel in addition. The whole effect was enough to lift the spirits of even the most reluctant reveller, and the partygoers were far from reluctant. The evening was a great success.

On New Year's Day the staff faced a daunting task. First, they had to clear the debris from the previous night's function; then set up the dining room for breakfast. They did this knowing that the few residents who would partake of food had opted to eat it in their rooms. That set them their next task, preparing and delivering the trays.

The knock on the door of room 37 came earlier than expected. Stuart Moran had vacated the shower in favour of Lesley and was about to start dressing. He opened the door to find a liveried waiter standing outside. 'Breakfast, sir.'

'Thank you. Put it over there please.' Moran turned to take a pair of slacks from the wardrobe. The waiter placed the tray on the table, took a large knife from it, stepped up behind Moran and slit his throat.

As he watched the solicitor slump to the floor, he was distracted by a sudden noise. He looked up to see Lesley standing in the shower room doorway surveying the bloodbath in front of her. She opened her mouth to scream but the sound was never uttered, for by then her windpipe had been severed.

New Year's Eve saw Nash and Andrews stretched to the limit, whilst at Netherdale. Ruth Edwards and Binns struggled to cope with the usual round of drink and drug-fuelled offences. It was 4 a.m. when they eventually got some respite. Nash sent Andrews home. They'd agreed beforehand that he and Ruth would take the brunt of the night's work.

Lisa reached her flat and opened the communal front door. She climbed the stairs slowly, too tired to relish the prospect of a few hours off duty. She could hear a stray reveller rolling home, and thought briefly of Myers, alone in his remote hermitage. She'd pitied him his lonely existence, his isolation from society. Had he been telling the truth, or was he a clever, cunning murderer who'd got away with it? Lisa didn't think so. The way the Labrador looked at him was the only basis for her opinion. It wasn't very scientific but Lisa had read somewhere that animals usually have a much better instinct in such matters, and it was obvious that Nell adored her master. Obvious too that the Labrador was the only thing Myers cared for. Lisa had found it easy to pity his loneliness but after a night such as she'd just experienced she began to think he was more to be envied. She couldn't think of anything worse than a shift such as she had just worked. She trudged off to bed, to get what little rest she could.

'Morning, Mike.'

'What is it, Jack?'

'Sorry, Mike. Control rang five minutes ago. Didn't know you were in the office. There's been a murder. Well, two murders to be exact.'

'What!'

'It's a New Year's Day special offer. A bog-off, buy one get one free. If Sainsbury's can do it why can't we?'

'Just what we need. Got any details?'

'A few. The victims are a couple from Leeds. They were

41

found in their suite at The Golden Bear about twenty minutes ago. Throats slit from ear to ear, apparently. The waiter taking their breakfast discovered them. The room's a bloodbath by all accounts.'

'Better phone Andrews. Then get hold of Mexican Pete and the forensic lot. Superintendent Edwards and I will meet you there.'

Nash and Edwards hurried through hotel reception and headed for the lift. When they reached the murder scene, men in white forensic overalls were everywhere. Andrews and Binns were standing outside the suite. 'What have you got?' Ruth asked.

Binns glanced at his notebook. 'The victims are Stuart Moran and Lesley Robertson, both from Leeds.'

'Is that all you know about them?'

'At this point, yes. The room looks to have been ransacked. SOCO say there's no cash, jewellery or credit cards around. Mexican Pete won't be here. He's still in some unpronounceable place in Spain. His flight back's not until Sunday. Netherdale General are sending a doctor to certify death, but with it being New Year's Day, it might not be until later. They seemed to think the living have priority.'

'Curious notion, that,' Nash retorted. 'Well, it can't be helped. Let's get suited up and we'll join you inside.'

The room was as big a mess as they'd imagined. Both victims had bled copiously. The gaping wounds at their necks were still wet. 'How do you think the killer got in?' Nash directed the question at Andrews.

'There are two breakfast trays. My guess is the killer posed as a waiter and brought them breakfast. When the real waiter found the bodies he dropped the breakfast he'd brought on the floor.'

'Good; now, I want you to liaise with SOCO. Let me know if they discover anything significant. Have a word with reception and the porters as well. Find out what luggage the couple brought with them. I want to know what's missing from this room. Speak to the other members of the staff, and any guests you can find. I need a picture of the couple, what they were doing here, what they said or did, and particularly who they talked to. Find out if they had any visitors, or asked for directions to any particular place.'

Nash turned to Binns. 'Call Yorkshire Central Task Force. Ask if they know the victims.'

'I'll do that if you want, Jack,' Ruth volunteered. 'You'll be needed here for a while, I reckon.'

Sean Parker, on the Layton Estate, wasn't as good a gamekeeper as Barry Dickinson. If he had been, the row would never have happened. If he'd been more confident he'd have organized the guns in time, insisted they get into position.

It was the Layton estate's shoot on New Year's Day. The first drive was due to commence at 8.30. Myers had agreed to help. He rose early and sent Nell outside whilst he made a cup of coffee. He listened to the radio, using the time signal to set his watch.

The first drive would begin from the strip of forest adjacent to Woodbine Cottage. The plan was for Myers to walk through the wood with Nell, pushing any pheasants to the far end where the guns would be waiting. If they took flight early they would alert others, and there would be a steady flow of birds over the guns. The result would be an impressive show for the start to the visitors' day.

Myers got into position and checked his watch. At exactly 8.30 he set off, thrashing to the left and right with his stick, and making strange noises he hoped would prove startling to pheasants. 'Hey, hey, hey, whoosh, whoosh,' he cried as he slashed at the thick briar and tapped at tree trunks. Nell knew her part in this game and dashed to and fro seeking out and scenting any pheasants still cowering in the undergrowth.

They moved slowly through the collar of woodland, pushing the birds steadily before them. A couple of cock pheasants took off followed a few seconds later by four more. Each time the pursuers halted, unwilling to flush too many at once. After the first two rises, Myers was puzzled by the lack of response from the far end of the wood. Had the birds gained too much height, or had they slipped out sideways, flying out of range of the waiting guns?

He knew he could do nothing about that, but as rise followed rise without response from the guns he grew more perplexed. By the time he reached the end of the strip he was convinced something had gone wrong. As he came out of the wood he saw what the problem was. The visiting guns, that should have been in position fifteen minutes earlier, were just arriving in a string of 4 x 4 vehicles. Parker was already there, as was his boss, Piers Layton. Parker's face darkened with annoyance as he saw Myers appear. 'What the hell are you doing here?' he bawled angrily. 'You shouldn't have set off yet.'

'I set off at 8.30 as agreed.'

Layton, an irascible man in his middle years, glowered. 'I don't care how it happened but this drive is ruined. The guns will demand a share of their money back. Between the two of you this has probably cost me the thick end of ten thousand pounds.'

'It's ruined because Myers is incapable of listening to instructions,' Parker shouted in a tone that was not as convincing as he hoped. 'I told him 8.45, not 8.30.'

Myers knew this to be a lie. Also knew that Parker was terrified of losing his job. Contradicting him would only make matters worse. 'I'm sorry the guns will be disappointed, and I'm sorry if it costs you money, Mr Layton,' he said quietly. 'As I'm incapable of listening to instructions the best thing I can do is leave.'

He whistled Nell to heel and strode off in the direction of Woodbine Cottage, leaving the two men staring after him. Something in Layton's expression boded ill for the hapless Parker.

Myers was now restless. His injuries were healing well but he knew anything too strenuous would jeopardize the recovery. The rest of the day was spent doing very little. He tidied the cottage. That took five minutes. He prepared his evening meal, which accounted for half an hour. After that he decided to exercise the dog. Even the couple of hours' walking failed to quell the discontent he'd begun to experience. He sat down with a mug of coffee and tried to analyze his dissatisfaction. For two years he'd lived alone; the solitary life had become second nature. The spell in prison had prepared him well.

He should be grateful; at least he was free. He had the cottage, a job he enjoyed where he was his own master, and he had Nell. So why was he restless? Telling his story to Lisa Andrews had invoked painful memories. His quandary was what to do about the past. He'd attempted to let it lie, but it didn't seem to want to stay buried. Should he abandon the attempt, rejoin what he'd heard called 'the rat race'? He looked down as he felt a paw on his knee. The Labrador stared at him, her eyes mournful and her distress apparent. Something was troubling her deeply. Myers glanced at the kitchen clock and laughed. 'OK, I'll get your tea.'

'Good morning, Mr Brown. Jones here, Harry Jones.'

'Good morning, Mr Jones.'

'I've been listening to local radio. I see an unlabelled package was dispatched. I assume it was mine, as required, together with a bonus, I understand. I take it there were no snags connected with the delivery?'

'None whatsoever. Although there has been an unexpected development. One I feel sure will interest you deeply. Not in connection with the dispatched article itself, more to do with the information I gathered at the time.'

'Really? What might that be?'

'When I was looking through the papers and documents I'd collected, I came across a very significant name. One we both know from a long time ago.'

'Would this name by any chance be connected with a much earlier dispatch?'

'That's right. If I remember correctly, it was a name you were most anxious about at the time.'

'The fact that this name should come to light is interesting, though hardly surprising.'

'I think you should take it seriously.'

'I'd be concerned if I thought the two parties had got together and

exchanged information. That would be highly dangerous. The problem is we have no way of knowing whether they did or not. Maybe it would be better not to take any chances.'

'There's something else that might be relevant to your concern.'

'What might that be?'

'You remember the location chosen by the party concerned with this commission?'

'Yes, it seemed an odd choice.'

'Perhaps it would seem less odd, if I tell you that according to the paperwork, the other party lives in a small village no more than eight miles from there.'

'Now I'm more than concerned. This demands urgent attention. How swiftly can you rectify matters? We're talking extreme damage limitation here.'

'I would need to do some research before I can deal with it. Given the location, it will be a couple of days at the very soonest before I could deliver.'

'Then do so, as early as possible. Lay the ancient history to rest. If you can make it appear to be voluntary retirement, so much the better. Will you trust me in the matter of payment?'

'No, Mr Jones, I never trust anyone in the matter of payment. However, should the money not be forthcoming, I would be more than a little unhappy. I'm sure you wouldn't wish me to be unhappy, Mr Jones. Unhappy enough to arrange a meeting with you?'

chapter six

When businesses resumed work after the holidays, Ruth's enquiry about Stuart Moran yielded a result. 'Moran's a solicitor,' she told Nash and Lisa. 'He's a partner with Hobbs and Hirst, a nationwide practice. I've spoken to one of the other partners. It took a while for the news to sink in. Once he got over the shock he told me Lesley Robertson also worked there. In fact, she was Moran's secretary. He'd no clue as to a possible motive for the murders. It gets to look more and more like a chance robbery, which will make it harder to solve. I've to go through to Netherdale. I'll bring the chief up to date whilst I'm there. Save you a job. And I'll release the details to the press.'

Nash raised his head. 'I thought we'd a press liaison officer?'

Ruth made a sneezing gesture as she left the room.

Nash smiled as he reached to answer his phone.

'Nash, Ramirez here. Did you think I'd miss you so much, you arranged for me to have a corpse or two ready for my return?'

Nash grinned at the pathologist's sarcasm. 'I don't want you to lose your touch for lack of practice,' he agreed gravely.

Ramirez snorted. 'Little chance of that with you around. Anyway, I can't spend all day gossiping. For all I know you could have arranged the slaughter of a football team. Or a rugby team,' he added caustically. 'I want to get on with the post-mortems; can you send someone through?'

'Certainly, Professor, I'll send DC Andrews across. She should be there in about half an hour.'

Later that afternoon when Lisa returned, she relayed a message from the pathologist. 'He said to tell you there's something you should know. At first glance he assumed they'd been killed by that well known cliché, the left-handed killer. The wounds are deeper on one side than the other, that's how you can tell. But he's not convinced that's the case. He said don't rule anyone out because they're not left-handed. As for the rest, you'll have to wait for his report.'

Close to Leeds city centre there are a number of squares of Victorian terrace houses, once the domain of the managerial classes involved principally in textiles and engineering, two of the driving forces in the city's rise to prominence. These dwellings had long been converted to office suites, and it was here that some of the smaller professional firms based their operations. Carnforth & Lancaster, Solicitors and Commissioners for Oaths, was one such organization. Nowhere in Leeds were old-fashioned values more rigidly observed. As one of the newer generation of lawyers remarked, 'You expect the clerks to be sitting at roll-top desks scratching away with quill pens. You want to ask to speak to Bob Cratchit.'

Albert Carnforth, senior partner in the practice, started work prompt at 9 a.m. every morning. His first twenty minutes in the office would be spent reading the *Yorkshire Post*, the *only* newspaper as far as Carnforth was concerned. One of the pages he scrutinized carefully was the obituaries section. Contrary to rumour circulating amongst some of the more flippant members of staff, Carnforth wasn't checking to see whether he was listed there. Tuesday morning was no exception, until the intercom buzzed. 'Miss Burns?'

'Yes, Mr Carnforth?'

'Would you come into my office and bring your keys?'

Hilary Burns didn't hurry. Hurry wasn't something they did at C & L. When she entered the office, Carnforth was waiting by the document safe, keys in hand. On his desk lay the morning paper, the headline declaring 'Prominent Leeds Solicitor Slain'. Together they put their keys into the twin locks of the massive door and turned them. Carnforth opened the door and removed a slim envelope.

The envelope had been signed and sealed. Carnforth took it across to his desk. 'I was entrusted with this quite recently and given instructions not to open it except in certain circumstances. It would appear that time has arrived sooner than anticipated.' He slit the envelope with his paper knife and removed a sheet of A4 paper, which he read before up-turning the envelope. A single key fell on to his blotter. 'It appears we have to remove the contents from a safety deposit box at the bank and dispatch them to a chosen recipient. This is the key. I'll attend to the matter this afternoon. Thank you, Miss Burns.'

He watched as Miss Burns walked back to her own office. He admired the long graceful shape of her legs, the rhythmical sway of her hips, as he'd been admiring them for the last twenty-five years. Fortunately, for both his peace of mind and hers, she was completely unaware of his admiration.

Later, Carnforth examined the contents of the safety deposit box. These comprised a large addressed envelope together with a smaller one addressed to him. He read the instructions in his envelope, then summoned Miss Burns.

He handed her the larger envelope. 'Kindly see that this is taken to the post office. It must go by registered mail.'

Myers and Nell were picking up again. This time they were back on home ground, at Winfield Estate. The morning progressed well, with Nell distinguishing herself, much to the chagrin of one or two other pickers-up.

Sir Maurice arranged the drives so the morning session finished close to the house. The break was a social event as much as a meal. With everyone from the most distinguished VIPs to the youngest beater on an equal footing. The food was held back until every member of the gamekeeper's staff arrived.

During the wait Myers listened with a modicum of interest to the various conversations going on around him. These were mostly about politics, a subject that bored him. The group he was closest to comprised Sir Maurice, a treasury minister, the Lord Lieutenant and the chief constable of the neighbouring county. They were discussing a forthcoming by-election. 'Our man's a virtual shoo-in,' the treasury minister told them. 'The party's very keen for him to get into the House as soon as possible. The Prime Minister's already indicated he'll only stand once more, and we need a replacement of the right calibre. He fits the bill to a T.'

'Do you think he's got what it takes to go all the way?' the Lord Lieutenant asked. 'The House can be a crucible for those not used to the rough and tumble of politics. I assume you know a bit about his background?'

'He's got a track record second to none in industry. He's made himself a fortune, not a small one either. He started with nothing. Built his own company from scratch, had years of struggle before he got where he is now. It's the sort of rags-to-riches story voters and media alike love. Self-made men are the type they trust.'

'I must admit you hardly seem to pass a building site that hasn't either got his company name or his biggest rival's sign on it,' the chief constable agreed.

The minister lowered his voice. 'Strictly between ourselves, I understand he's about to launch a hostile takeover bid for his competitor; but that's highly confidential of course.'

The rest of the group nodded understandingly. Myers concealed a smile. The fact that they hadn't mentioned any names seemed good security to them. However, they'd littered the conversation with clues. Perhaps it was as well he had little interest in such matters.

As their conversation petered out Myers caught the tail end of another discussion, gorier in nature than politics. Two of the beaters were close by and were talking about a murder, or as Myers gleaned from what little he could hear, a double murder.

He strained to hear, but as he did so Sir Maurice claimed him and insisted he joined their group who wanted to praise his dog. Whilst listening to their compliments Myers was only able to pick up snippets of the beaters' talk. 'Golden Bear, breakfast', and 'solicitor from Leeds, I think', were the only words he could be sure of. They were enough.

Sir Maurice laid a solicitous hand on his arm. 'Are you all right, dear fellow? You've gone quite pale.'

Myers recovered his wits. 'Yes, Sir Maurice, I'm fine. I think I need a breath of fresh air. I'll pop outside for a few minutes.'

He walked out through the long french windows on to the broad stone terrace and stared at the rolling parkland that swept down to the lake; without seeing any of it. Had he heard correctly? If he had, and the beaters had got the story right, it had to be Moran who'd been murdered.

Only a week ago Myers had been found on the third floor of The Golden Bear. That was bad enough in itself. The fact that the witness was a police officer made it worse. In view of his past, few people would believe he hadn't murdered Moran.

The one thing he had going for him was that nobody knew his true identity. Nobody apart from DC Andrews knew his past. How long that would remain secret he couldn't be sure, but for the moment he had to act normally.

The lunch dragged, the afternoon dragged, but eventually they completed the final drive before the light began to fade. The guns thanked the gamekeeper and his staff. Sir Maurice paid them, and added the customary brace of pheasant for those who wanted them.

Myers reached the cottage without knowing anything about the drive home. As he let the dog out of the car she bounded towards the house, then stopped. She began to cast about, scenting. Myers frowned. She normally headed straight inside. Straight for the food bowl. 'What's matter, Nell?'

The dog barked, then began sniffing at the ground. As they neared the cottage door she barked again. Myers looked round. Everything seemed normal. He opened the door and stepped inside. The sitting room looked undisturbed; except for one thing. Myers stared at the armchair; it had been moved. Not much; and not far enough to be apparent to the casual glance. But he'd spent so many hours in that room, he knew to an inch where everything should be. He looked at the carpet. Sure enough the indentations where the chair legs had been were visible. Someone had been in the cottage.

He got no further with his speculation. Out of the corner of his eye he saw a blur of movement. He turned and ducked. The knife that was intended for his throat sliced the air close to his ear.

51

Myers tried to grapple with the intruder; tried to reach the knife hand which was arcing towards him. Suddenly, the assailant's wrist was grabbed, vice-like; a powerful set of teeth sank deep into his flesh. The attacker wrestled furiously in a vain attempt to loosen the dog's grip. He swung his fist, and hit the animal on the head. The dog let go and dropped to the ground, stunned. The intruder turned back, sliced again at Myers and made contact. Myers reeled back and fell across the chair, blood oozing from his chest. His assailant saw the dog lumbering to her feet, snarling and baring her teeth. The knife was thrown at the dog, narrowly missing her, as he bolted through the door, slamming it behind him. He ran round to the back of the building, where he'd hidden his car. He reached over into the back seat, grabbed a plastic carrier bag, which he tossed into the thick brambles and put his foot hard down on the accelerator. As he raced past the front of the cottage his eyes were on the narrow, bumpy track. He failed to see Myers stumbling through the cottage door, staring after him.

Myers stared down at the blood seeping through his shirt. He gently eased the shirt clear and examined his chest. The knife had partly re-opened the gash caused by the chainsaw. The flesh had barely knitted. Now the damage looked even worse. He walked slowly through to the bedroom, trying not to stretch the wound-site. He gingerly peeled the shirt free, using a handtowel to mop the blood from the cut. Another sheet would have to be ripped up to provide a dressing, if only as a temporary measure. One thing was certain. There would be no emergency dashes to hospital this time. Hospital staff would have to report such injuries. Besides which, if what Myers had heard that lunchtime was accurate, it wouldn't be long before he was being sought by the police. For Stuart Moran to have been murdered in such close proximity would never be seen as a coincidence.

He needed time, time to think. He also needed to be away from the cottage. Once it had been his refuge against the world. Now it was anything but safe. Above all he needed space to try and work out what was happening. Why had he been attacked? And why had these figures from his past come back to haunt him?

His first priority was his dog. He had to ensure she was safe before he could think of anything else. After all, she'd saved his life. He knew Barry and Shirley Dickinson would look after Nell. How far their willingness to help would stretch was something he'd find out in the near future. He bound his wound as best he could and donned a clean shirt. On an impulse, he reached into the wardrobe and from behind the stacked shirts pulled out a slim document case and stuffed it inside a carrier. He collected the dog, closed the door and set off in his Land Rover down the lane; each bump and pot-hole sending fresh waves of pain through his body.

Barry and Shirley Dickinson listened to Myers' tale with growing incredulity. When he blurted out the news of the attack Barry immediately said, 'I'll phone the police.'

'Hang on. Don't do that. Please, hear me out. There's worse to come.'

They were in the lounge of the keeper's house. Myers was in an armchair, or rather perching on the edge of the seat, with Nell sitting leaning against his knee.

Barry and Shirley sat on the sofa. By the end they too were on the edge of their seats, staring at the man they thought they knew. The man they realized didn't even exist.

'Christ, Andy, what a bloody mess.' Barry said.

'Alan,' Shirley suggested.

He turned to look at his wife. 'What?'

'His name's Alan,' Shirley said.

'Look,' Myers/Marshall said. 'If this is too much for you, just say so and I'll push off.'

The couple looked at one another. 'You'll do no such thing.' Shirley spoke for both of them. 'Just give us time to get used to it.'

'I keep thinking you could have been lying dead in a pool of blood on your kitchen floor,' Barry said. 'Why the hell were you attacked?'

'Let's go back to when Anna was killed. If you take my word that I didn't do it, then who did? Suppose that same person killed Moran and discovered where I was living. It would be dead easy to frame me for Moran's murder. I'd be the obvious choice. Who had more reason to hate Moran? To be sure I

53

couldn't defend myself, they dispose of me. What I can't for the life of me work out is how they knew where I live?'

'So who are *they*?' Barry asked.

'That's the problem. I've no more idea than I did when it happened. At least I didn't, until now.'

'What do you mean?' Shirley asked.

Marshall took a piece of paper from his pocket. 'When the car drove off I made a note of its number plate. Not too difficult for me as it turned out: ACM, my initials. All I have to do is find out who the car's registered to.'

'How can you find out who owns the car?' Shirley asked. 'I thought that sort of information was only available to the police?'

Marshall told them. They listened with even greater incredulity than before. 'You're mad,' Barry said. 'You'll finish up in the slammer.'

'I agree,' Shirley said. 'Are you sure there's no other way?'

'None that I can think of. I know it's risky, but what have I got to lose? Before long every police officer in the land will be dreaming of the promotion he'll get by capturing me. I might as well go for broke. The only way I can stay out of prison is to find out who actually committed these murders.'

'How will you do that if you're on the run with no one to help you?' Shirley asked.

Marshall shook his head wearily. 'I don't know. But I have to try.'

'What do you want us to do, Alan?' Marshall was mildly surprised that it was Shirley who asked the question, her husband Barry was less so. Shirley was soft-hearted and the sadness behind Marshall's story would have engaged her sympathy. Even before this latest bombshell he knew Shirley felt sorry for Marshall in his lonely existence.

'I don't like to ask,' Marshall replied. 'I don't want to get you into trouble. If the police find out you've helped me they might class you as accessories.'

'That would only be true if you'd committed these murders,' Barry pointed out.

Marshall laughed, but it was a laugh devoid of humour. 'I didn't kill Anna either, but I still had to serve nearly six years. My appeal only succeeded for lack of evidence, which hardly classes as a pardon. So I wouldn't hold too much store by the fairness of British justice.'

'Nonsense,' Shirley's tone was bracing. 'We can do what we like. No copper's going to push us around. If they try to come the heavy, all we have to say is we don't believe you killed anyone. Let them go ahead and try to prove the accessory bit.'

'I need someone I can keep in touch with locally. I've no idea where this is going to lead. I've got one tiny piece of evidence: this number.' He held up the slip of paper. 'That's more than I had when Anna was killed. If I don't go for it I'll finish up back in Durham; or worse.'

'How do you mean "or worse"?' Shirley asked.

'If it hadn't been for Nell I'd already be dead. How much easier is it to pin the blame for Moran and his girlfriend's murders on a man who can't answer back? A dead man. Not only that,' Marshall said grimly, 'the killer can still use me as a scapegoat. He can do it far easier if I'm unable to deny the charges. To make his scheme work he needs to kill me. I'm in more danger now. Keeping clear of the police is one thing. The killer is a far more potent threat. That's why I have to disappear. It's my only chance of staying alive.'

'You're not going anywhere, the state you're in. Not until I've seen to that wound,' Shirley told him. 'We've left it too long already.'

He thought over what had happened. He reckoned he had two chances of survival. Slim chance, or no chance at all. The slim chance was finding the killer before the killer found him. The no chance was the killer finding him first. To take the slim chance meant desperate measures. Marshall was about to take the first of these. He was going to tell his story to the police.

'Have you seen the headline in this morning's paper, about Moran? What the hell's going on?'

'I'm afraid I've had to use Brown's services again.'

'Oh dear God no. Why? After all this time. I thought we were clear of all that. Why didn't you tell me earlier?'

'It was unavoidable, believe me. I thought you had enough on your plate at the moment and I didn't want to burden you with this.'

'Unavoidable? In what way, unavoidable?'

'He was becoming difficult. He refused to cooperate with the next part of our plans for one thing. Besides which I found out he was planning to ditch us.'

'How do you mean, ditch us?'

'Not to the authorities. Even he wouldn't be that much of a fool. I learned he was planning to go see someone, somebody who would be more than interested in what he had to tell them.'

'Good Lord, you don't mean Mar—?'

'Careful, no names. Let's just say someone we've upset.'

'I see. I thought we'd got clear of the need for Brown.'

'Far from it. The need is greater now than ever. It's become obvious from certain other people's reactions that our plans are in jeopardy. So I fear Brown will have more work to do.'

'Is there no other way?'

'Absolutely not. It isn't a decision I took lightly, believe me.'

'You must be sure nothing can be traced back to us.'

'Don't tell me you're getting cold feet too?'

'Of course not. It's just that we've so much to lose, and we're close to achieving all we set out for. I dread to think of things going wrong.'

'Your trouble is you worry too much.'

'Yours is that you don't worry at all. One of us has to.'

'In that case, I'll leave you in charge of worrying. One more point. As things are at the moment, I think we ought to consider our own security more carefully.'

'Sorry? I'm not with you.'

'We're approaching a critical stage in the operation and we can't afford anything to go wrong. Even the slightest whisper of what we're hoping to achieve would ruin the whole thing. I propose we abandon any procedural discussions over the telephone until matters are resolved. Unless it's of the utmost urgency, only use the phone purely to arrange meetings.'

chapter seven

Lisa Andrews was weary. She couldn't complain. Nash and Superintendent Edwards were working even longer hours than she was. On her drive from Helmsdale, and as she parked her car and walked across the car park towards her flat Lisa, was too tired, too preoccupied, to notice what was happening around her. In other circumstances she would have spotted the vehicle that had followed her at a discreet distance.

She stopped outside the front door and fumbled through her bunch of keys, searching for the right one in the meagre illumination provided by the street light. 'Good evening, Lisa.' The voice was soft but it made her jump nonetheless.

She spun round, instantly alarmed. 'What are you doing here? What do you want?' Her voice contained a rising note, of panic and anger combined.

'Relax. I just want to talk to you. I thought we could at least behave like civilized human beings.'

'Civilized, that's a laugh. Civilized people don't pester others and make a nuisance of themselves. Besides, they don't shag their lover's best friend.'

'Lisa, I'm not going to stand here arguing the toss with you. You owe me. Half the stuff in that flat is mine by right. If I don't get my share I'll make your life a misery.'

'I don't know how you work that out. You've paid for none of it, so don't come that game. I've told you before, you can piss off back to Leeds; you're getting nothing from me.'

Donald Smailes drew his arm back. A good slap might change her mind. Before he could strike, he felt his wrist gripped, then wrenched, then twisted behind his back. Then he felt himself being lifted by the arm alone. There was another slight twist and Smailes felt an excruciating pain leap from his wrist to his shoulder. He heard a popping sound from close to his collar bone. Screaming in agony, he squirmed to escape the grip, but the pain got instantly worse.

'You heard what Lisa said. She told you to piss off. If you don't, I'll break your arm as well as dislocating your shoulder. Now, do you understand?'

Donald had a brief glimpse of the man holding him. Then he was thrust away towards the gate. He squealed at the fresh bout of pain. 'Oh for goodness' sake, don't be a wimp. It's only a dislocation.'

They watched the injured man stumble down the street with the sound of his moans fading into the distance. Lisa took a step back as she turned to face Alan Marshall. 'Thank you, but how did you happen along at the right time? How did you find out where I live?'

'Easy. I followed you home.'

'Why did you do that?' The recent encounter had unnerved her. The apprehension in her voice showed.

He smiled. 'Not for that,' he said a trifle obscurely. 'The fact is, I'm in a bit of trouble and I need a favour.'

Lisa eyed him suspiciously. 'What is it?'

'I need to find out the name and address of the registered keeper of a car.'

'You've got to be joking,' Lisa spluttered; then added, 'why do you need to know?'

'I can't tell you. All I can say is it's vital. A matter of life and death. Mine to be exact.'

Lisa swung open the door and gestured him inside. 'Upstairs, first floor, front,' she commanded. He'd heard that tone before. He didn't argue.

She opened the flat door, flicked the lights on and pointed to an armchair. 'Sit down.' He sat down feeling helpless in the face of her determination. 'Right! I've had a busy day, a very bad day. To cap it all I had to endure meeting that dickhead. You rescued me and I'm grateful. So go ahead with your story; talk.'

Marshall tried once more. 'If I give you a full explanation, you might arrest me for murder! To be exact, two murders.'

'So, tell me. I'll leave the handcuffs off while you explain. Everything!'

It was no contest. Lisa held all the aces. What was more they both knew it. Marshall took a deep breath. 'OK, first I'm going to tell you my real name. That's only jumping the gun anyway. Within the next few days everyone will know it. My real name is Marshall, Alan Charles Marshall. The solicitor who was murdered in The Golden Bear was the principal witness at my trial, my wife's lover. Reading between the lines, the way he and his lady friend were killed seems identical to the way Anna was murdered. I believe that was done to throw suspicion on me.

'The first I heard of those murders was at lunchtime today. I was on Sir Maurice Winfield's shoot. It was only a passing reference but it put the wind up me, made me wonder what was going on.' Marshall paused, Lisa saw his face was sombre, troubled. 'That was bad enough, but then I went home....' He explained about his return to the cottage.

Lisa studied him. 'If you really are innocent you ought to give yourself up.' She thought for a moment. 'You reckon the man who attacked you committed these murders?' Marshall nodded. 'Then I need some proof. Show me the wound.' He hesitated. 'Look,' Lisa insisted, 'if you want my help you've got to give me some evidence. Something to make me trust you. Otherwise I'll phone my boss right now. The only reason I'm not already on the phone is because I owe you for sorting that pillock Donald out.'

He stood up and slid his jacket off, then his shirt, not without difficulty. Blood was beginning to seep through the dressing Shirley Dickinson had applied. Lisa nodded. 'OK, I believe you. But, Alan – can I call you that?' Marshall nodded. 'You really ought to go see DI Nash. Mike's a decent bloke; he'll not rush to judge you. He won't assume you're guilty just because of what happened years ago. I admit things don't look good for you, but I'm sure it's the best thing to do.'

Marshall looked alarmed. 'No, not yet. I daren't. Not after what happened last time. You don't know the half of it, Lisa. When I was questioned about Anna's murder, it was as if the police were on a mission to make sure I was convicted. Admittedly the evidence didn't look good, but they didn't take account of anything I said. And there were others too, people who lied in court. Neighbours who said we were rowing constantly. That just didn't happen. That's why I can't trust the police. What I need is time to get well clear of here, try to work this out.'

'You mean time to get away; to avoid being arrested.'

'No, things are much worse than that. The police are the least of my worries.'

He explained his theory. Lisa listened in appalled silence. Eventually she said, 'It sounds like something from a gangster movie.'

'Unfortunately, it's all too real.'

'What do you intend to do? You can't spend the rest of your life running and hiding from a killer and possibly the police?'

'I've spent long enough hiding from a past that was none of my doing. I've lost years of my life. I'm not prepared to lose any more. Whatever happens, I'm not going back to hiding from it. OK, I might have to, short term. This is why I need the details of that car owner.'

'I assume you're about to ask me to use the police computer to find this out for you. There's no way.' After a moment's silence Lisa asked, 'Do you have any idea who might be behind this?'

'Not the foggiest. I almost convinced myself Anna's death was a chance killing. A robbery that got out of hand perhaps, but deep down I never believed it. I reckon whoever murdered Anna had a logical motive. I believe the killer is someone I know, or knew. That makes it even scarier, if that's possible.' He smiled, but the smile didn't reach his eyes. He looked up. 'So now you know everything. Will you help me?'

Lisa paused, staring straight at Marshall as she gathered her thoughts. She paced the floor, then sighed. 'At this moment you're a free man, not suspected of anything. Give me the number and I'll see what I can do. But, I'm going to tell my boss what we've talked about. I won't do it until tomorrow, I promise. I also want you to keep in touch; by phone or text or whatever.'

Marshall agreed. He knew he'd no choice. 'Phoning might not be easy. If I can't phone, I'll get someone else to. Probably the people who will be looking after my dog. I'll not give you their names; it would compromise them and you. I'll tell them how to identify themselves so you'll know they're the genuine article.'

'OK, now tell me something.'

'I've told you everything I know.'

'Tell me what you did to Donald?'

He was surprised at the question. 'A friend of mine taught me the trick. I've never used it before, never had cause. He said if you lift someone with their arm straight, then twist, the shoulder will dislocate. I had my doubts, but it appears to work.'

'It sounds as if you've some interesting friends.'

After copying down Lisa's phone numbers, Marshall left. When he'd gone, Lisa was plagued with doubt. She'd acted on instinct, on a whim she might regret. She'd made her decision so she'd stick to it, and to hell with the consequences. Marshall seemed a decent man. Decent men don't slit people's throats, no matter how strongly they're provoked. Beside which, he'd sorted that worm Donald Smailes out. She decided to let things ride. Shelving her anxieties might not be so easy. Nor was she looking forward to her meeting with Nash tomorrow. She knew she'd be lucky to escape without being suspended from duty. All she could do was explain and hope Nash understood her reasons.

Marshall drove back to the Dickinsons' house with one eye on the rear view mirror, his ears attuned for the sound of a siren. It was with great relief that he pulled the Land Rover into the safety of their back yard. 'I'll need to get rid of that in the morning,' he told Barry. 'I'll do it first thing.'

He settled for the night in the Dickinsons' spare room. Nell curled up on a blanket on the floor beside him. As he fell asleep he wondered if this would be the last decent night's sleep he'd get for a while.

The following morning the household was up early. Marshall took the Land Rover and parked it deep inside the forest at the end of a little-used ride, where he was reasonably sure it wouldn't be found. After he returned, having given Nell a good walk, Shirley presented him with a plate of bacon and eggs.

'When you've finished that I'll re-do your dressings.' She watched him start to eat before asking, 'Why ditch the Land Rover? Won't you need a car?'

'I'll have to rely on public transport. The Land Rover's too well known. Once the police make the connection, both they and the killer will be on the look-out for it. They'll be convinced I've got it. I want them to keep looking. They'll be looking in the wrong place, which suits me.'

He finished his breakfast and submitted to the discomfort of having his dressing changed before hurrying out to join Barry. His greatest regret was the look of accusation in the Labrador's sad eyes at his desertion of her. As Barry drove him to Netherdale, Marshall checked that he'd given Lisa's number to him. 'Don't worry, Alan. Shirley's got it safe. Have you got our home number and my mobile too?'

'Yes.' Marshall patted the document case. 'I'll call as soon as I've found a bolt-hole. It'll take me a day or two to make sure I'm safe.'

Shirley had a moment's panic as a shadow passed across the kitchen window, then realized it was the postman. Seconds later the doorbell rang. 'Morning, Shirley, parcel for Barry. It's to sign for I'm afraid. Everybody's got something needs signing for this morning,' he grumbled. 'I've even got a registered letter for Woodbine Cottage. That's the one at the end of that long track isn't it? It must be over a year since I was out there. Not even junk mail, would you believe. Now all of a sudden the bloke's got a registered letter. I didn't even know his name until this morning.'

'I'm afraid you're going to be doubly unlucky,' Shirley told him with a smile. 'I can save you a lot of wasted time and effort if you want. I'll sign for this parcel of Barry's first. He's away early this morning. You'll have no joy at Woodbine Cottage either. He's gone off with Barry. If you want, I'll sign for his letter as well; give it to him when they get back. It'll save you another trip.'

'Thanks, Shirley, you're a pal.'

Shirley examined the registered letter. After a quick glance she darted through to the kitchen, glancing at the clock en route. If she was lucky she might just be in time to catch Barry before he dropped Alan at Netherdale railway station. She dialled her husband's mobile but heard the distinctive call alert ringing out in the hall.

When Barry returned, Shirley was waiting at the kitchen door. 'Did he get off safely?'

'As far as I know. There were no screaming sirens before I left anyway. I didn't hang about though. What's that you've got in your hand?'

Shirley showed him the envelope. 'What do you make of that?' Barry asked.

'I think it proves we did the right thing. I admit I had my doubts about Alan's story, but this suggests he was telling the truth.'

Lisa was anxious. Nash and Ruth Edwards were discussing staffing rotas, trying to relieve the pressure on them. She wanted to speak to Mike, but while she waited she took a call from the fingerprint officer, who asked for Nash.

'Sorry about the delay, forensic officers are as rare as flies in January at the moment; this damn flu bug. But I've got a print that might interest you,' he said. 'We gave priority to the victim's suite itself, the rest had to wait. Have you any idea how many staff that place has? They all had to be eliminated. Anyway, this one's not from in there, it's from the corridor close by.'

'There must be a lot of prints there. What's so special about this one?'

'This one's got form.'

'Who is it, a hotel thief with a propensity for throat-slitting?'

'Not exactly; although you got the throat-slitting bit right. I've arranged for the file to be sent straight over to you from Yorkshire Central. Least I could do with the delay we've caused.'

A couple of minutes later Nash explained to the others. 'I think we've got a breakthrough. SOCO found a print in the corridor. It belongs to an Alan Charles Marshall, convicted in 2000 for murder. Victim was his wife, Anna. Her throat was slit. SOCO gave me some details from their records. Anna Marshall had been having an affair with Moran. She worked for him. He was the star prosecution witness. The contention was that Marshall found out about the affair and was known to have a temper. The prosecution said he slit her throat in a fit of jealousy, drove to Scarborough and dumped her body in the sea.'

'What happened to him?' Ruth asked.

'He got life. Then he appealed successfully; got released back in 2006.'

'So all we have to do is locate Marshall and we'll have the case sewn up.'

Nash smiled at Edwards. 'Sounds easy, doesn't it? Have you any idea where to begin looking? It's a shame we don't keep tabs on released prisoners.'

'I thought we did?' Lisa asked as she began nervously chewing on her lip.

'We do when they've been convicted. When they've had the conviction quashed we're not allowed to. It's against their human rights or something,' Ruth explained.

Lisa hardly heard what the other two were saying; she could feel the panic rising. She knew he hadn't gone into the suite that night. But had he returned? Had he tried to convince her of his innocence so he could get away? 'I know this sounds a bit naïve, but do Marshall's fingerprints prove he killed Moran. Surely he'd be extra careful given their past history.'

'Not in itself it doesn't,' Ruth replied. 'But it's as strong a piece of circumstantial evidence as I've ever seen. I'm off to Netherdale with this lot.' She waved the sheaf of timesheets. 'Ring me if there's any development.'

Lisa was torn with doubt. She decided to wait until the file arrived before she told Nash all she knew.

Binns brought it to the office, where he and Nash stared at the attached photo in dismay. Taken years earlier, it demonstrated how times and fashions had changed. Aged twenty-nine, Marshall's face glowed with health and a sort of cherubic innocence. Any trace of these would have long vanished. Time and the ageing process would have taken care of much, the spell in prison the rest. As a tool for apprehending Marshall it was tantamount to useless. Nash put it on one side and they began studying the rest of the file's contents. As they were reading the phone rang. Binns moved across the CID room to answer it. When he'd picked up the receiver Lisa leant forward. 'Mike, I need a word. It's important.'

Nash noticed her troubled expression. 'Give me a couple of minutes. Let's see what Jack's dealing with first.'

Binns replaced the handset. 'That was a chap called Parker, gamekeeper from Layton Estate. He went to see a friend of his yesterday evening; owed him an apology of some sort. There was no sign of the bloke, his dog wasn't there either. The guy's name is Myers, lives in a remote cottage. Anyway, the keeper went back this morning. Still no one there, and when he tried the door it was unlocked. He went inside and found a lot of bloodstained sheeting, towels and so forth.' Binns paused then added, 'He also found a bloodstained knife on the floor.'

'Will you have a run out there, Jack? Lisa and I'll concentrate on this. Let me know if there's any mileage in it, or if this keeper's panicking over a shaving nick.'

They watched Binns depart. As soon as the door closed behind him Lisa said, 'He isn't.'

'Isn't what?'

'That keeper. He isn't panicking over nothing.'

'How do you know?'

'The man who's been living in the cottage, his name isn't Myers. It's Marshall. Alan Marshall.' Lisa began to explain. It took a while and when she finished Nash sat looking at her in silence. 'I'm sorry, Mike. I was about to tell you everything before that call came in. I suppose I'm going to be suspended or sacked or something,' she said miserably.

'Not necessarily. You might have been' – Nash pointed to the file on the desk – 'if I hadn't read that first.'

Lisa looked up in surprise.

'I wouldn't convict anyone of shoplifting on that evidence,'

Nash told her. 'I'm not surprised the Court of Appeal tossed it out. I'd have done the same. It's possible that Marshall got a raw deal. Which begs the question, why were there so many people anxious to have him convicted? OK, he could be a wife murderer, and he might have taken a sadistic revenge on his wife's lover and the woman he was with; but I find that hard to believe. From what you tell me, Marshall's been living in that cottage quite peaceably since his release. Now, I'm expected to believe he's suddenly gone on the rampage. It doesn't make sense. Of course I could be wrong' – a grin passed across his face, fleetingly – 'it has happened before. So what I want to know, Lisa, is what do you think of Marshall? You've met him, talked to him, and what's more you've done so in highly stressful circumstances. What's your assessment of his character?'

'He seems a normal, calm, even-tempered individual,' Lisa stated. 'All right, he had a bit of a chip on his shoulder about his conviction, and about Moran, but I'm not sure he really meant to kill him; despite what he said at The Golden Bear.'

'In that case we'd better follow Jack out to this cottage, see what went on there. Don't mention anything about this to anybody else, right? Before we go, get the details of that car from the computer.'

'Harry Jones here, Mr Brown. What's happening?'

'Everything's been dealt with, Mr Jones. The item for urgent delivery has been dispatched. I can't say when you will hear that it's been delivered as the address is remote. However, it has been done.'

'That's exceedingly good news. Rather than waste time I think we should move on. I have another order to put your way. The dispatch isn't as urgent but the sooner the order's been executed the more content I shall feel. I'm sure I can trust to your expertise. I'll send you the order form in the next few days.'

'I'll see to that, no problem. I take it payment for the urgent delivery has been sent?'

'Naturally.'

'Then I look forward to receiving your further order.'

chapter eight

The officers stood in the lounge of the cottage. 'We need a SOCO team out here. Organize it will you, Jack? Lisa and I will have a look round the rest of the place, then see if we can find anything outside.'

They walked into the bedroom. 'This looks as if someone's been wounded.' Nash pointed to the torn, bloodstained sheet and equally soiled towel. 'Unless they were left over from the chainsaw accident.'

Lisa shook her head. 'Marshall told me he'd burnt those; made a joke of it. Said when he put them in the Aga they created so much smoke anyone passing the cottage would think he'd been elected Pope.'

They were wandering round the back of the cottage when Binns joined them. 'I can't get a signal on this side of the woods. Do you want me to drive over to Bishop's Cross? It's a lot nearer the mast.'

'You'd better do. Ask them to send a sniffer-dog. That's if the handlers haven't got flu or the dogs contracted distemper or rabies. It'll take us weeks to search all this. A dog will do it in hours.'

They watched Binns depart and Lisa asked, 'You don't think Marshall's returned here, do you? I got the impression he was leaving the area.'

'Maybe that's what he wanted you to think. The other thing is, it takes two to have a fight. For all we know, Marshall could have killed someone and hidden the body.' Nash gestured to the surrounding woodland. 'We might as well make a start whilst we're waiting.'

Binns returned with the news that SOCO and the dog

handler wouldn't be available for another two hours. As he was speaking, Lisa shouted to Nash, 'Mike, you'd better come and have a look at this.'

Nash looked down at the plastic bag she had found. Stuffed inside were several items of clothing. They donned latex gloves and carried it into the cottage. In the bag they could see the familiar livery worn by staff at The Golden Bear. Nash slid the trousers out and held them up. 'Lisa, how tall do you reckon Marshall is?'

Andrews replied instantly. 'Just over six feet, at a guess.'

'What about his chest measurement? Approximately, I mean.'

'I'd say he was about your size, a forty-two or a forty-four, why do you. . . ?' She stared at the blood-splattered jacket Nash had taken out of the carrier. 'Oh, I see.'

'If those bloodstains prove to be from Stuart Moran and Lesley Robertson, Alan Marshall couldn't have been the killer. Not wearing those clothes anyway.' Lisa looked at the suit and realized what Nash meant. There was no way Marshall could have squeezed his six feet two inch frame into trousers made for someone six-inches shorter, nor get his forty-four inch chest into a thirty-six inch jacket.

Nash explained his theory to Binns. 'There's something else. Marshall's been living like a hermit. At a guess, I'd say when he goes shopping, it would only be to Helmsdale or Netherdale, right?'

Binns nodded. 'Seems logical.'

'Look at the logo of the supermarket on the carrier. Their nearest branches are York and Harrogate. I can't see Marshall travelling that far for his cornflakes and sliced loaves, can you?'

The sergeant grinned. 'You might make a detective one of these days, Mike. What do we do next?'

'I want you to remain here and liaise with SOCO. Make sure they give the contents of that bag priority. Lisa can come back with me. I'll sort out a press release, and then I'm going to see if I can get an interview with Marshall's employer, Sir Maurice Winfield. If anyone round here knows what's going on, he will.'

'I thought he was retired?'

Nash gave Binns an old-fashioned look. 'Don't believe all the rumours you hear, especially those that might have been started deliberately.'

As Marshall turned to walk into the railway station he felt totally alone. Quite unlike anything he'd experienced even during his long sojourn in Woodbine Cottage. This was an altogether different emotion compounded by fear. Fear of the ruthless unknown enemy, and the apprehension of an approaching battle, in which Marshall was without ally. He was up against an opponent who appeared to know everything about him, whereas Marshall knew nothing about his enemy. He had only one tiny scrap of information, and even that would be useless without Lisa's cooperation. She'd agreed to help, but was that merely to rid herself of a man she saw as a dangerous killer? Had she gone straight to the phone, once he'd left her flat? Even now the police could be on the lookout for him. By entering the railway station, was he about to walk into the arresting arms of waiting detectives?

Marshall glanced back towards the Dickinsons' Land Rover, an unconscious plea for reassurance. But Barry was manoeuvring into the early morning traffic that was about as close to a rush hour as Netherdale High Street achieved. Marshall walked towards the station's ticket office, his thoughts as grey and cheerless as the January skies.

Netherdale railway station had been simplified to the point of stark necessity. It comprised only the waiting room, located in the middle of the single platform that segregated travellers wishing to go north from those heading south. Within it were the ticket office, a set of toilets and a food-and-drinks machine, the only requirements deemed necessary for the few passengers to use Netherdale.

'Single to Leeds,' he asked the official behind the screen. As the man brought the details up on his computer Marshall glanced apprehensively round the small room. A slightly spotty youth, his eyes narrowed with concentration, was seated in one corner, his fingers moving rapidly over the keys on his mobile phone. Further along an immense woman in her late thirties was attempting to pacify a toddler in a pushchair whilst dealing with the highly vociferous demands and complaints of a couple of older children. At the far end of the bench, as opposite in attitude as in location from the youth, was a middle-aged man who was struggling with the *Daily Telegraph* crossword. At his feet was a briefcase and alongside him on the bench another case whose dimensions betrayed its contents: a laptop computer. The rest of the waiting-room was empty.

'The 8.55's your first train, then there's another at 9.25,' the railway official told him. 'You'll need to change at York.'

Marshall paid for the ticket and walked out on to the platform. He wandered across to the southbound side and sat on one of the slatted benches. Their uncomfortable design was surely intended to avoid passengers missing their train, for there was no chance of anyone dozing off on those unyielding surfaces.

The earlier train was crowded, but Marshall wanted to get clear of Netherdale as fast as he could. Losing himself in the mass of humanity in and around Leeds represented his best chance. He was unable to find a seat but after twenty minutes or so the train stopped at Throxendale. A large, noisy family got up to leave the train. Marshall slid into the seat vacated by one of them.

The first thing he needed was money: cash, to be specific. Paying for goods and services with a credit or debit card was as good a way of advertising his whereabouts to the police as waving and shouting, 'Yoo-hoo, here I am, come and get me.' To get cash involved a visit to his building society, where his account had been active since he was at university. There he'd be able to withdraw sufficient for his needs. Cash would be anonymous, untraceable and had several other advantages. Traders liked it, because cash never bounced, and it didn't cost the trader a commission. If cash brought the trader peace of mind it bought the same for Marshall.

Leaving the cottage so hastily had been a panic measure. Marshall acknowledged the fact, but he'd no experience of being a fugitive. He'd need to think out every move with greater care from now on. He'd collected his few valuable possessions such as driving licence, bank and building society passbooks and one or two private documents but had completely overlooked the matter of clothing. If his period in hiding was to be lengthy, he'd need not one, but several changes. He'd have to buy these and something to contain them to avoid drawing attention to himself, to appear normal.

Marshall smiled ruefully. What was normal about his life? Was it normal to be on the run? Was it normal to be on the run from both the police and a ruthless killer who'd slit your throat as soon as look at you? Was it normal to have spent so long hiding from your past, from the consequences of a crime you hadn't even committed? No, whatever else could be said about his life it certainly wasn't 'normal'.

Marshall remembered everything about his arrest with hideous clarity. The journey from Leeds to Scarborough in the back of the police car, sandwiched between the two officers leading the enquiry. The mortuary: its chill, damp air, musty with the smell of death and formaldehyde. The drab green paint on the doors, the faded magnolia emulsion on the walls. Then the examination room, the cold clinical look of stainless steel everywhere. Everywhere, except in the middle of the room where a central spindle supported the table, ominously covered with a heavy green sheet. He knew what lay beneath that sheet. He knew he'd been brought there only in part to identify the body: an impossible task. The real reason was to allow the detectives to pressure him into confessing to Anna's murder.

Marshall felt the tears pricking at the corner of his eyes as he remembered the obscenity that was revealed when the sheet was pulled back. The ocean and its creatures had ravaged her beyond all recognition, ripping to shreds his memory of the beautiful girl he'd courted and married.

At his trial he had been made to listen whilst the prosecution seeking his conviction exposed Anna's infidelity in lurid, lascivious detail for the world to see and hear, and drool over. No matter that every word was a fresh torment to him. No matter what his feelings were. He was only the defendant. His feelings didn't count. He might have protested but knew his protests would carry as little weight as his plea of not guilty.

His conviction had been inevitable. He'd seen it coming from early on. As shock followed shock, lie followed lie, he began watching events unfold with a detached, almost neutral viewpoint. As if the events in court were happening to someone else.

He didn't dwell on his years in Durham. There were some things that should remain buried. It was a life sentence he'd been given. It had seemed like several lifetimes before the successful appeal. Outside the court following his release, Marshall remembered the senior detective telling him, 'Don't think of coming near Leeds, Marshall. One way or another I'll have you. I'll find some way of putting you back where you belong.' Marshall had glanced to the right and left. The corridor was deserted. He'd learned a few tricks during the past few years. He was fit. As lean and tough as a spartan regime and less than appetising diet could make a man. The detective was overweight, had spent too long in too many bars, drinking too many pints and smoking too many cigarettes; a coronary waiting to happen.

Marshall had brought up his knee sharply and seen the detective's face whiten with pain. He'd held him upright against the wall, stuffed his tie into his mouth and grabbed his bruised testicles. 'Keep out of *my* way or I'll present these to you as a souvenir,' he told the man. He'd squeezed and heard the man gagging against the silk fabric, saw his eyes bulging with pain. 'I'd stay out of dark alleys too,' he advised the detective, before moving away to face the press.

Despite the success of the appeal Marshall felt cheated and betrayed. That was why he'd retreated from the world. Not from guilt or shame but to stay clear of the risk of being hurt again.

Roundhay Park was deserted. Not surprising at that time of year. Apart from an occasional dog walker there were few pedestrians braving the cold, windswept expanses of that area of the park known as Soldiers' Fields. The two men who approached one another were muffled up against the weather. They met and began to walk alongside one another.

'What's the latest? I need to know what's going on.'

'I've had to get Brown to do an urgent job for us. I'm pleased to say he did it quickly and efficiently, and in difficult circumstances too.'

'What was it about this time?'

'A potential problem came up.'

'I've heard nothing, so why all the panic?'

'It hasn't come to light yet. It wasn't so much a panic, more of a precaution. I wasn't sure if our legal friend had renewed an old acquaintance or not. Something we didn't want to happen. I thought it wise to ensure nothing came of such a meeting, even if it did take place.'

'You're certain it was necessary?'

'I'd say vital. If that meeting had taken place it would have had disastrous consequences for us. Having the chance to sever the last link with the past was too good an opportunity to miss.'

'I'm not sure I follow.'

'Put it this way. Who were the last two people we'd want to meet up and reminisce about old times? I'm not sure it happened, but I wasn't prepared to take the chance. Even if it did, there's now no reason to believe the result of their conversation will become known.'

'I take it you must be referring to Moran on the one hand. Who might the other party to the conversation have been?'

'Ah, now that's where it gets very interesting. You remember I said I was having grave doubts about Moran's frame of mind and where that might lead him? I was right in one sense, wrong in another. He did seem to have been afflicted with a sudden attack of guilty conscience, but instead of rushing to tell all to the officers of the law he headed quite the other way. To talk to the husband of the dear departed.'

'How did you find out about it?'

'Brown found Marshall's address amongst Moran's possessions. The location was so close to where he was staying I can't believe it was a coincidence.'

'You're sure nothing remains to link us to these events?'

'I think it highly unlikely. I pressed Brown into urgent action. He examined the scene and found no incriminating evidence. I'm sure we acted fast enough to avoid repercussions. If that's the case Brown's erased the last link with what happened nearly ten years ago. There's *no one left to tie us in to those events. Marshall would have been a great threat. You didn't know him. He was highly intelligent and very determined. I believe he was capable of discovering us and ruining us.'*

'You always feared him, didn't you?'

'Feared and respected him. It was fear of him that made all this necessary. So, yes, I'm glad he's no longer in a position to threaten us. From what Brown told me, it appears things have been left so that Marshall will be the prime suspect for everything that's happened. The police will think he's taken his revenge, then done away with himself. All very neat and tidy. Everything carefully packaged for the police to wrap up with the minimum of effort. It even keeps the crime statistics looking right. They have the dead man, they have the motive. Once they find out who he is they'll know why he wanted Moran dead. Why should they bother looking elsewhere?'

'So that's all over with. I have to admit every time it happens I get a fresh set of quivers down my spine.'

'I'm afraid that's not quite it; would that life was that simple. I did mention that we need to dispense with the services of someone who's become a liability. It appears they seem to believe they are more important than is the case. They've become very greedy. Whatever the motive, they're a potential threat. We can't afford to have them threatening us, not when we're about to play for such high stakes.'

'What are we to do about it? Pay them off?'

'Would you trust them if we did? No, I've already made arrangements with Brown. It's absolutely vital that when we make our move, we do so without risk. We can use Brown to dispose of the danger they represent. Then we sacrifice him as planned.'

'Do we really have to do this?'

'I'm afraid so. Regard it as "natural wastage". I believe that's the current expression. Only in this case perhaps the term "unnatural wastage" would be more appropriate.'

'Won't it look odd if he uses the same disposal technique if the killer's supposedly dead?'

'It won't matter. What happens in North Yorkshire is unlikely to be connected to what goes on here.'

'Harry, you know I think the world of you but sometimes you scare me.'

chapter nine

Three Shires Building Society had several branches within Leeds city centre. Marshall chose the busiest, at lunchtime, when counter staff were taking breaks in rotation and customers formed long queues. The withdrawal went smoothly, even for so large an amount. Marshall was asked for proof of identity. The cashier, under pressure from the length of the queue, barely glanced at the documents he produced.

Marshall heaved a sigh of relief when he reached the open air of the shopping precinct and walked swiftly to his next destination: a branch of one of the big supermarkets. He claimed a trolley and selected several items from the clothing section. He wanted something inconspicuous. He began by picking some warm shirts, added jeans, socks, underwear and trainers to his collection. He finished with a zip-up quilted jacket. As an afterthought he selected a thick woollen scarf, ideal for wrapping up warm – and for covering part of his face. Everything was in dark, sombre colours, selected for anonymity. He headed off to collect other necessities: toiletries, and a pack of sterile dressings for his wound. He paused in front of a display of razors and blades and fingered his chin for a moment before turning away. If the police were looking for a clean-shaven Alan Charles Marshall, a few days' growth of beard might put them off the scent. Instead he went to the adjacent aisle, where he chose a barrel-shaped holdall.

When he had everything he needed he headed for the tills. On his way, a display at the end of one of the aisles caught his eye. He paused and read the features advertising the product on the stand; picked up the item and added it to his trolley.

Once he'd paid, Marshall walked across to the toilets. He

used the baby-changing table to open the holdall and place his purchases inside after removing the labels. He zipped the bag up and wandered out into the store. He was about to leave when he glanced across towards the restaurant. The dining area contained only about half a dozen customers. Most of them had ordered nothing more adventurous than tea, coffee or scones. From what he could see of the cafeteria Marshall reckoned there were more members of staff on duty than customers. That suited his purpose ideally. What he was looking for was a waitress of mature years with too little work to do and a propensity for gossip, one moreover who was well acquainted with Leeds.

Half an hour later Marshall was heading out of the super-market, his stomach lined with sausage, egg and chips. Scrawled on the back of his till receipt was the name and telephone number of a small private hotel in the suburb of Far Headingley. 'It belongs to my sister's husband's cousin and his wife. They run it together,' the waitress had told him. 'Although to be fair she does all the work. It's basic B&B, but the rooms are clean and the food's OK; you'll get a good breakfast. If you're here on business you'll not need much more than that, will you?'

Marshall returned to the foyer and crossed to the bank of public phones, dialled the number and within a couple of minutes had made a reservation. Once outside he paused, pondering whether to catch a bus or walk. He glanced up. Although the day was cloudy those clouds were high and he could see there was little chance of rain. He'd not set foot in Leeds for years. He decided to walk the four miles or so to his destination, familiarizing himself with the changes that had been wrought since he'd left. Time was not an issue, anonymity was, and Marshall still felt reluctant to be in an enclosed space. On a bus others would have the chance to study him or maybe compare him with a photograph in their paper, beneath some startlingly lurid headline.

He crossed the inner ring road and began the long gradual climb towards the university, then across the open area beyond to Hyde Park Corner. Crossing the road he walked up Otley

Road past the famous cricket ground. He saw the old Cottage cinema he'd attended as a boy, then swung left off the main road and was soon outside the Cardigan Hotel. The building was three storeys high, set in grounds that had been given to tarmac at the front to accommodate those guests with cars.

Marshall entered and identified himself to the proprietor. He completed the signing-in process after having undergone a cross-examination from the owner regarding his origin, reason for visiting Leeds and duration of stay. The story Marshall had concocted during his walk must have been credible. He was handed the key to room seven on the first floor. 'It's a double, I'm afraid. We only have three singles and they're all taken,' the proprietor told him. 'Breakfast starts at 7.30; goes on until 9.15.'

The room was at the back of the building, overlooking the garden. An effort had been made to keep the area attractive, but at that time of the year all gardens look sad. Marshall dumped his holdall on the bed and began hanging his clothes in the wardrobe. When the unpacking was done, he slid the additional item from the holdall and removed the blister pack. Having read the instructions he soon had it assembled and looked around for a socket to plug the charger in. He'd never used one before but according to the instructions it would be ready next day. When that time came he'd feel marginally less isolated. With the aid of his pay-as-you-go mobile phone, he'd be able to keep in contact with the Dickinsons and Lisa Andrews. His last act was to remove the sheath from his belt. So far the knife had been concealed by his coat, but Marshall knew one sight of it would be enough to raise suspicions. What would pass unnoticed in Layton Forest could cause panic in Leeds city centre. He carefully slid the forestry knife in the side pocket of the holdall and placed the bag in the wardrobe. He paused over the other item on his belt. Although it was a tool he found useful when he was shooting, there would be little call for it in Leeds. Nevertheless he decided not to part with it.

Getting an interview with Sir Maurice Winfield wasn't easy. Nash rang Winfield Manor only to be told to redirect his request via Special Branch. He eventually obtained permission to visit the manor next day.

He introduced himself and Lisa. 'I take it you're not as retired as rumour suggests, Sir Maurice?'

Winfield smiled but remained silent.

'I'd better explain why I'm here,' Nash continued.

'I imagine you want to talk to me about Alan Charles Marshall, aka Andrew Myers,' Winfield said calmly.

DC Andrews blinked in surprise.

'Come, come young lady. You don't think my staff would employ someone on my estate, without wanting to know everything about them. I knew all about Marshall before he was given the forester's job and about that horrendous miscarriage of justice when he was convicted.' Winfield leaned forward across the desk to emphasize his point. 'Over the last two years I've got to know Marshall reasonably well, and part of my job, as you're no doubt aware, concerns the ability to judge character. Marshall might be capable of killing someone, but I doubt if he killed these people. Any more than I think he murdered his wife. He might have killed Moran for revenge, but I'd look very carefully at the evidence before you rush to judge him. That happened before, with disastrous consequences.'

'Thank you, Sir Maurice. I had already come to that conclusion. I was more interested in your character assessment of the man.'

'Care to tell me why?'

Nash hesitated a second, before explaining about the waiter's uniform.

'That's good police work. Let me know if you need anything else. I'll leave instructions with my staff for any calls to be put through to me.'

Nash's eyes were drawn to a photograph on the dresser. When they left Winfield Manor Nash's doubts about Marshall's guilt had been reinforced by Sir Maurice's comments. But they had what they needed most: the photograph loaned by Sir Maurice of the Boxing Day shoot. The group included a cabinet minister, a prominent member of the House of Lords, a world-famous surgeon and a bishop. The only non-celebrity on the photo was Alan Marshall. Nash was about to change that.

'If you think Marshall's innocent, why put out his photo and say we want to question him?' Lisa asked on the journey back to Helmsdale.

'If Marshall's story is true, the person who attacked him might back off from having another go, if he thinks Marshall's going to be blamed for the Moran and Robertson murders. If we pick Marshall up, he's going to be a lot safer in our cells than out and about on his own.'

'If Marshall didn't kill them, what do you think the motive was?'

'That's the problem, Lisa. If it wasn't revenge and it wasn't robbery I've absolutely no idea.'

It was one thing finding a base, but Marshall was aware he had to conform to expected behaviour patterns to avoid drawing attention to himself. His first night in the hotel was not a good one. Despite his weariness his sleep was fitful. Every slight disturbance preyed on his heightened nerves. He awoke at every creaking floorboard, every flushed toilet, not to mention every cough, sneeze, belch or fart from the occupants of the rooms around him. The sounds carried through the lath-and-plaster-board walls with great clarity.

He was relieved when the display on the bedside radio read 7 a.m.; felt it would be safe to get up. There were sounds of movement from various parts of the hotel. Marshall tuned the radio to the local station and switched the TV on in time for the regional news report. He was relieved to find there was no mention of him, either under the name Marshall or Myers.

By 7.30 he was in the dining room, where several early risers were eating breakfast. It proved to be as good as the lady at the supermarket had promised. As he was eating, Marshall discreetly studied his fellow guests. A couple of them were obviously reps, their white shirts and ties giving them away. The rest seemed to be tradesmen judging by their more casual apparel and the logos on the vans in the hotel car park. Two of these had the names of a shop-fitting company on the side panels, a third bore the name and logo of a company that fitted drainage systems, whilst a fourth had a mildly smutty advert regarding scaffolding and the erection of it.

All of them would be out of the hotel by 8.15 to beat the Leeds rush hour. His aim should be to leave around the same time. If anyone asked, he could claim he was walking to the main road where a colleague had arranged to meet him. Thereafter the safe thing to do would be to walk into the city centre. There he could lose himself in the crowds thronging the pavements and shopping precincts, the office complexes and bars, pubs and clubs. There he would also have access to the public library. Inside, he could remain clear of the cold and any adverse weather; stay all day if he wanted without being disturbed. He could also use the time to read the local press to find out more about the Netherdale murders.

When Nash and Lisa arrived back at Helmsdale there was a message waiting. Nash stared at the name. It had featured heavily in the file he'd read on the Anna Marshall murder.

He dialled the number on the note. 'Superintendent Dundas, please.' He waited, curiosity building. Dundas had been the arresting officer. Nash had been puzzled by the single-minded way Dundas had gone after Marshall for his wife's murder. As far as Nash could make out, no other lines of enquiry had been pursued. Why was that?

'DI Nash?'

'You left a message for me.'

'Yes. I understand you've obtained the Marshall file. In view of the history I think my force should take over the investigation. As you must be aware Moran was a vital witness in securing Marshall's conviction. If it hadn't been for the stupidity of the Court of Appeal, Marshall would still be inside where he belongs. And Stuart Moran and the Robertson woman would still be alive. So I want you to send all the paperwork through to me, my team will take it from here.'

'Sorry, Superintendent. That isn't going to happen. The

murders took place on my patch where you have no jurisdiction. If, as you seem desperately keen to prove, Marshall did kill them, I've yet to be convinced about it. So my team will continue to run the enquiry.' Nash had been about to explain why he wasn't convinced of Marshall's guilt, but some sixth sense stopped him. He listened impassively as Dundas ranted and threatened for a few minutes. Eventually, wearied by the bluster, Nash said, 'Look, if you want to complain, phone Superintendent Edwards at Netherdale, or Chief Constable O'Donnell. Stop wasting my time.'

Nash shouted through to the CID office for Andrews. She appeared almost immediately, a mug of coffee in hand. As she set this on his desk, Nash asked, 'You've worked in Yorkshire Central. What do you know of a Superintendent Dundas?'

Lisa pulled a face. 'Nothing good, he's not popular with other officers. Well, most of them at any rate. He has one or two favourites. The remainder detest him.' She paused for a second. 'There are also a few rumours. Nothing specific, but they say his lifestyle's a bit rich for the money he gets. He's said to like the bright lights and isn't too choosy about the company he keeps. Why do you ask?'

Nash explained.

'Do you think there's something fishy about his desperation to convict Marshall?'

'Could be, it might equally be nothing more than over-zealousness. Either way I'm taking no chances. I'll make sure Ruth Edwards and the chief are primed.'

'Might Superintendent Edwards be tempted to recommend handing it over? Given that we're so short-handed?'

'I think I can convince her. In the meantime, I need to ask Professor Ramirez a question that's been bugging me.' He reached for his phone.

'Professor, Mike Nash here, sorry to disturb you. DC Andrews passed on your comment about the left-handed appearance of the injuries to Moran and his lady friend, I found it intriguing. Would you be able to tell the same about a murder committed several years ago?'

'You always disturb me, Nash. No, I'm afraid not. I'd need to examine the wound itself, not a photograph of it.'

'Thanks, it was just a thought.' He replaced the phone and turned to Lisa. 'Right, I want us to go through the file on Marshall's original conviction again. There's something buzzing at the back of my mind, but I can't think what it is.'

Nor could they find it, despite several hours reading the paperwork. It was much later before Nash worked it out.

Marshall read the words written about him in the morning paper with a curious mixture of concern and detachment. 'Alan Charles Marshall, the man police are anxious to interview in connection with the murders of Stuart Moran and Lesley Robertson on New Year's Day in The Golden Bear, Netherdale.' The statement went on to describe Marshall's earlier trial and conviction, the appeal and his life since then. The statement also mentioned that Marshall might be accompanied by a black Labrador. It described his Land Rover, quoting the registration number before adding the chilling final sentence: 'Members of the public are warned against approaching this man or challenging him in any way as police consider him to be highly dangerous.'

Marshall read the sentence about Nell again. The police didn't know about her, hadn't found the vehicle either. That meant he still had a chance. If people were looking for a car and a dog alongside him, he might be passed over. At least there wasn't a photograph.

'Is that Mr Brown?'

'Who's speaking?'

'Harry Jones. It would appear as if our congratulations were a little premature.'

'Yes, I've just been reading about it. What do you want me to do about it, Mr Jones?'

'I believe the situation can be put right.'

'Tell me how?'

'Continue with the new contract as discussed. Official attention can *then be guided in the right direction, if you take my meaning.'*

'Sorry, I'm not with you.'

'All you have to ensure is that you expedite delivery of the new contract before officialdom catches up with our mutual friend.'

'You wish me to proceed with the dispatch?'

'I do indeed.'

chapter ten

Barry and Shirley Dickinson read the report about Marshall. They were both shocked and saddened. They already knew the facts, but the implication in the statement was obvious. It had them questioning the wisdom of their decision to support him.

They were still discussing the report when the phone rang. Shirley picked up the kitchen handset and listened, pointing to the receiver with the index finger of her free hand. She mouthed the word 'Alan' to her husband. 'Yes,' Barry heard her say, 'we've just been reading it. To be honest, Alan, it frightened us.'

She listened for a moment or two and Barry saw her beginning to relax slightly. He could hear Marshall's voice but was unable to make out what he was saying. Then Shirley said, 'Yes, I'll try and find out for you, but I've something to tell you, Alan, something important. The morning you left I intercepted a letter for you.'

'Yes,' she continued after a second, 'for you. It was sent by registered post. The sender's name is on the back. It's from a firm of solicitors in Leeds: Carnforth and Lancaster. It's addressed to Woodbine Cottage, but listen to this, Alan. It isn't addressed to Andrew Myers. It's addressed to Alan C. Marshall. Do you want me to open it?'

Shirley nodded to her husband, then pointed to the envelope tucked behind the spice rack and made an opening gesture. 'Hang on a second, Alan, Barry's opening it.'

She waited as he carefully slit through the envelope with a kitchen knife. 'Sorry, what was that?' Barry heard her say. 'Oh yes, Nell's fine. She's missing you a bit, I think. She keeps lifting her head when she hears a car nearby, or when Barry comes through the door. Apart from that she's OK. Right, I've got the letter now. Are you ready?' Shirley paused. 'There's a covering note from a Mr Albert Carnforth stating that he's been instructed to send you the enclosed only in the event of Stuart Moran's sudden or violent death.' She turned the pages and said, 'The letter itself is signed by Stuart Moran. It's dated December 2008. Here goes:

'Dear Alan Marshall,

I hope you never get to read this letter. That's because of the conditions I attached to it when I lodged it for safe keeping. If you do read it, that will mean I am dead. I hope this letter may be of some use, if only to set your mind at rest regarding the past, or act in the nature of a warning. What follows is as close to a confession of my part in the events surrounding your wife's death and your conviction as you could get. But if you're reading this, my guilt will have been paid for. I'm so afraid of what will happen in the future that I had to write this down and keep it safe.

I did you a great wrong. Two great wrongs actually. I was party to a deception the result of which was to send you to prison for murder. A crime I knew you didn't commit. My so-called friends were anxious to get you convicted, in case you began asking questions about your wife's murder and stumbled across the conspiracy.

Anna was killed because she uncovered information that was dynamite then. It will be one hundred times more dangerous in the future. She wasn't prepared to look the other way, so she had to be disposed of. Every effort was made to incriminate you for her murder.

What Anna found out was one small part of a web of deceit and corruption involving business, local politics and the law. It was big then. It has since grown to massive propor- tions. Millions of pounds change hands every year to ensure the continuing success of the operation. No wonder Anna was expendable. Her decision to confront the men responsible instead of keeping quiet, signed her death warrant. I could have warned Anna she was in danger, but didn't. By the time I

85

plucked up courage it was too late, she'd disappeared.

I've been torn by guilt at my part in it all. I've had to live with that guilt. I've tried to disentangle myself from the mess, but I can't. The only decent thing I did was to pay for your appeal. Since your release I've kept tabs on you with the help of a private detective.

My part in the conspiracy was to ensure you were convicted and safely out of the way. They could simply have had you killed, but that wouldn't leave them with a ready-made culprit for Anna's murder. I used my influence with the police to ensure they got plenty of evidence to proceed against you. The detective in charge assembled all he could, including a lot that I had manufactured. Anything that might suggest your innocence got 'overlooked' in the process. My other role was to stand up in the witness box and lie.

I told the court Anna and I were lovers. That was a lie, a total and utter lie. I wouldn't have minded, but Anna would have nothing to do with me. I told the court she feared you'd found out; another lie. How could you? There was nothing to find. I told the court she had said you were insanely jealous. She never said anything of the kind. I also paid your neighbours to invent furious rows between you. I could see from your face as I stood there in court lying, that I was also destroying your belief in Anna.

Your expression, as you stood listening to my lies, has haunted my dreams ever since. That was why I paid for your appeal. That is why I've refused to have any more to do with the conspiracy. That refusal may cost me my life. If you're reading this, Alan, then it has.

My advice would be to stay buried in your country cottage and forget the past. The people behind this are absolutely ruthless, and developments mean they intend to play for even higher stakes. Trust no one; their network of contacts is so widespread. Anyone could be in their pay. And remember, if this letter gets to you, it means I know where you are. Others could find out equally easily.

Even now, when I know this letter will be lodged in a safe

place, I am too afraid to name any of those involved. But the strangest part is that you know more about the whole business and the people behind it than you realize. That knowledge is the reason they considered you, still consider you, to be such a danger.

That's all I have to tell you. Whether you seek retribution for your wife, or not, is up to you, but be very careful how you go about it if you do. I can't emphasize often enough how ruthless and deadly these people are. And how much they stand to lose.'

There was a long, dreadful silence after Shirley finished reading the letter. She heard what sounded like a sob at the other end of the phone. 'Alan, are you all right?'

After what seemed an age she heard his voice, low and toneless, devoid of any inflection. 'So it was all untrue. Anna wasn't unfaithful to me. She wasn't having an affair.' He paused again. 'She had a secret she couldn't share with me, and all I could think was that she was cheating on me. I let her down, Shirley. I let Anna down. I wasn't there when she needed me. That's why she died. Because she couldn't trust me.'

Shirley took a deep breath. This was bad, far worse than if Marshall had ranted and raved. 'Listen, Alan, stop wallowing in self pity. I can't speak for someone I didn't know, but what this letter shows is that Anna didn't tell you because she loved you. Do you realize how lucky that makes you? She died protecting you, and all you can do is moan about lack of trust. I tell you something, Alan: you're right in one respect, you didn't deserve her. She went to her death out of love for you. So what do you intend to do about it? Sit there moping and being a pathetic wimp until the police find you? The letter says you know something. Well, what is it? Think about it. Get out and find it; find Anna's murderer. Take your revenge for her, and for yourself. That's what I'd want you to do if I was Anna. I'd want a man, not a pathetic excuse for one.'

The silence was even longer before Marshall said, 'You're probably right, Shirley, but I'll have to think it over.'

She put the phone down and looked at her husband, her eyes

moist with unshed tears. She hadn't liked the defeated tone in Marshall's voice. 'I'm afraid, Barry. That letter seems to have knocked all the fight out of him. I can't see a way this will end, except in tragedy.'

Marshall sat on the edge of the bed staring sightlessly at the wall. For hours on end he remained in the same pose. The words from Moran's letter echoed ceaselessly in his brain. After the first pangs of distress abated, one phrase thrust repeatedly into his lamentation. 'The strangest part is that you know more about the whole business and the people behind it than you realize.' What had Moran meant? How would he have known the motive for Anna's murder? Did Moran believe Anna had confided some secret to him? Marshall wrestled with the idea all night, but the enigma remained unsolved.

'Is that Lisa? We haven't spoken before. My name's Shirley. We've a mutual acquaintance, one with scars on his arm and chest.'

'Right, I'm with you. What can I do for you?'

'Is it safe to talk? Our friend said you'd had one or two problems with others.'

'No, everything's fine.'

'Our friend was wondering if you'd had chance to do the research he asked you about? He's concerned about his security.'

'I understand, but I haven't been able to access the information yet,' Lisa lied. 'But with luck, I should have it soon.'

'I think he'll need luck. He's very down at the moment. I've had to tell him something which really upset him.' Shirley explained about the letter.

'Ask him if he wants me to tell my boss about that? I've some news that might cheer him up.' Lisa related the finding of the waiter's uniform. 'There's no way our friend could have worn it. He wouldn't even have been able to get into it. Tell him my boss is convinced he's innocent. If you can, try and persuade him to come to Helmsdale for his own sake. Either that, or make the phone call I suggested.'

'That's great,' Shirley said. 'He'll be delighted to hear it. And I'll try and persuade him. But it won't be easy.'

Marshall was in the library again. He picked up a copy of the local evening paper from the table and began reading. The double murder was still headline news. He was about to close the paper when a small item towards the bottom of the page caught his eye. 'Councillor Bob Starts Campaign', he read. 'Councillor Bob Jeffries opens his re-election campaign tonight with a meeting in Queens Hall at 7.30 p.m. All constituents and others welcome.'

Marshall remembered the name; remembered the man. He'd had a lot to do with Jeffries when he'd been working in the city. Jeffries had been a major force on the Yorkshire Central planning committee. It was a curious relationship, with Marshall spending company money purchasing small gifts for Jeffries. Tickets to Elland Road, seats for the Headingley Test and so on, whilst the councillor secured planning consent for projects Broadwood Construction wanted to build. It was no big thing; everyone in the construction industry did the same. Marshall decided to go to Councillor Jeffries' meeting.

There was little new in the fact that Councillor Robert (Call me Bob) Jeffries was up for re-election, but the count would be a formality, as with every election over the past twenty-five years. It was one of those wards. Nevertheless Bob didn't fall into the complacency trap by ignoring his electorate. Prior to every election he held a series of public meetings. These followed a familiar and successful formula, whereby one of his staff would open the meeting and harangue the gathering, much in the style of a warm-up comedian. Then Jeffries would enter accompanied by a regional or national party luminary. The guest speaker would deliver a short rousing speech on national issues, utter a few words of fulsome praise about Bob and his value to the party. Then it would be Bob's turn centre stage.

His routine had varied little over the years. He'd start by wishing every success to his worthy opponent. Actually he had changed that phrase a little, substituting 'worthy' with 'young' as a way of implying inexperience. He'd then proceed to demolish everything his opponent represented. He'd finish with a quick, but not too quick, embellished, but only slightly embellished, account of his achievements. Then a promise of what he'd be able to achieve in the future. He didn't go so far as to promise the earth, moon and stars, only that segment of them visible from within the ward. He'd end with a rousing exhortation for them to turn out on election day with the slogan: 'It's up to you. You know your job, Come Election Day, Vote for Bob.'

The hall was almost three-quarters full that night, for the guest was a man going places within the party. The first speaker was about to start when Marshall entered the hall. As he went to take a seat towards the back of the audience, the man in front stopped and turned round suddenly. Unable to stop, Marshall bumped into him. The hard point of the man's elbow struck Marshall in the chest. Immediately he felt a slight tear at the wound site. He knew what had happened. The gash had opened again. He could feel a warm sensation spreading across his shirt. Blood was seeping from the wound. Marshall cast a quick glance round the auditorium as the man he'd collided with mumbled an apology. He saw the sign for the toilets at the front, to the left of the stage. He knew he'd have to attempt some running repairs. The only place available was the privacy of a cubicle. The last thing Marshall wanted was to draw attention to himself.

The first piece of luck he had was when he saw the toilet was served by fabric roller towels rather than hand-driers. It was the work of seconds to force the towel cabinet and remove the roll of towelling. Marshall retired to the cubicle farthest from the door. Just in time to avoid being seen. As he swung the cubicle door closed behind him he heard the outer door open. This was swiftly followed by footsteps approaching the next compartment. Marshall listened. There were two unidentifiable sounds, a sort of gurgle, followed by a thump; then the sound of footsteps retreating. The outer door closed.

Marshall removed his coat and slowly lifted his shirt. The damage wasn't as bad as he feared. The collision had moved the dressing, allowing the wound to bleed unchecked. He mopped up as much as he could with the roller towel and replaced the dressing, tightening it as much as possible. He was about to replace his coat when he glanced down. A pool of liquid had appeared beneath the dividing wall. Marshall shrugged his coat on and went outside. He pushed the door of the next cubicle open. He stared in horror for a second. Then he turned to leave. As he reached the door he brushed past someone entering the toilets. The surprised man stared after him. Marshall headed for the exit. He had to get away as fast as he could.

'Where's Jeffries?' the party star waiting in the wings hissed. 'We're on in a couple of minutes.'

'He went to the loo,' the party agent replied. 'I'll go check he's OK.'

'Well hurry up about it!'

The agent almost collided with a man as he dashed into the gents. At first glance the lavatory appeared empty. One of the cubicle doors was almost closed. The agent glanced down. A thin stream of dark-coloured liquid had trickled across the tiled floor from within the cubicle. The agent pushed at the door. It resisted, blocked by something heavy. The agent pushed harder and the door flew open revealing the crumpled body of Councillor Robert Jeffries. Bob had always had a head for politics. Whoever slit his throat had all but severed that head from the body politic.

Getting out of the building wasn't as easy as entering had been. At least, getting out without drawing unwelcome attention. Marshall walked slowly down the aisle on the left of the seating. The audience was becoming restless. The opening speaker had finished and there was no sign of the succeeding ones. They were unprepared for this. One or two were shuffling in their seats. A hum of subdued conversation spread through the hall. Marshall had almost reached the rear of the auditorium, where the exits to the foyer were, when a body of stewards entered the hall. Some went down the trio of aisles; others remained at the rear standing menacingly in front of the door. That way was barred. Marshall turned hastily aside, as if looking for a seat. As he did so a fresh sound panicked him even more. Faintly, in the distance as yet, but distinct, the unmistakeable sound of sirens. Marshall knew where they were headed. Knew he'd to leave now. Knew the next two minutes were his only chance to escape. He saw a curtain halfway down the aisle at the far side of the hall where there was obviously a door. The luminous sign above read 'Fire Exit'. It was worth a try. Anything was worth a try. Any second now police would be entering the foyer. Marshall inched his way over towards the far side of the hall as if still looking for a vacant seat. His eyes scanned the auditorium constantly for movement that might signal the arrival of the police. He reached the emergency exit sign and looked quickly to his immediate right and left. He glanced cautiously over his shoulder to see a number of police officers entering the body of the hall as he slipped behind the curtain. Marshall slowly pushed the bar and the door opened a couple of inches. It led straight out on to the pavement. He carefully pushed the door wider, and slid through it, closing it gently behind him.

'Hey! You! What are you doing?'

Marshall turned, shock sending his legs momentarily into quivering jellies. Two large police officers were coming rapidly towards him. Their build suggested they might be rugby league prop forwards. Marshall turned to run and found himself confronted by a man in plain clothes. Recognition was instant and mutual, dislike almost as quick. It was the man who'd threatened Lisa in Netherdale. Obviously relishing the task, DS Donald Smailes began to speak, 'Alan Charles Marshall, I am arrest—'

That was as far as he got before Marshall came to his senses, came to realize the desperation of his plight. He reached for the object at his belt, swung it high and hard. Heard the loud crack as it made contact with the man's skull. Then he ran, with all the speed he could, from the collapsed figure on the pavement and the two officers lumbering after him. As he ran Marshall replaced the object on his belt. The eight-inch-long, lead-weighted cosh, used by anglers and shooters alike to dispatch wounded fish or animals. It was known as a 'priest', presumably because it administered the last rites. Marshall prayed it hadn't fulfilled that function on the detective he'd struck.

He got away more by good luck than management. His narrow escape left him shaken. The thought of what he'd left behind only increased his fear. Any chance of denying his involvement in the murders would soon be gone. The evidence was overwhelming. The councillor's body, his fingerprints close by. A towel soaked in his blood. His previous association with the dead man. If he'd been in a predicament before, his situation now was dire.

He risked catching a bus and got off at the stop nearest to the hotel and walked the intervening quarter of a mile. Caution was becoming more of a second nature now and he waited in the shadow of a tall chestnut tree, scanning the car park for strange vehicles; then examined cars parked in the street for people sitting inside. After fifteen minutes watching and waiting, when he was as certain as could be that it was safe, he walked swiftly across the road and into the building. The reception area was deserted, the reason becoming clear as he passed the resident's lounge. The big screen TV was on, a football match being broadcast, watched by almost every other resident and the hotel's proprietor. Marshall passed unnoticed and trotted up the flight of stairs to his room. He locked his room door behind him with some relief and went to switch the light on. He then had a second thought and crossed to the window instead. He stood in the shelter of the curtain for several minutes until a measure of night vision came to him and he was able to see the rear aspect of the hotel. Eventually he was satisfied that the shrubs and bushes were not concealing a posse of policemen. He closed the curtains before returning to the light switch. He flicked it on and examined the room carefully. Everything appeared to be as he had left it.

He waited for half an hour and by that time was reasonably certain he was safe, for that night at least. He picked up his mobile phone and rang the Dickinsons' number. Shirley answered. She sounded brighter than when he'd spoken to her last. She recounted her conversation with Lisa which cheered him immensely. He took the news of the delay in obtaining the car registration details in his stride, then explained how his evening had gone.

'What will you do? And what about this letter?' Shirley asked.

'To be honest I've no idea. I can't think why this is happening. My only thought is about that car and the owner. If I can find that out, it might give a clue as to who's behind all this. At the moment I seem to be blundering from one crisis to another and getting myself deeper in the mire. When I left Woodbine Cottage I was a suspect in two murders. Since then I've managed to avoid being arrested, committed an assault on a police officer and now I could be suspected of the Jeffries murder. The worst of it is, I can't think of anything positive to set against all that. I'm not sure how much longer this hotel will remain safe. All I can do is to sit tight, keep my head down and hope.'

'There is one other thing you could do.' Shirley's tone was diffident. She reminded him about Lisa's suggestion of contacting Nash.

'I don't know,' Marshall said. 'I keep thinking back to what Moran said, about not trusting anyone. How do I know this isn't a trick?'

'Phone from your mobile. There's no way they can trace you from that. What harm can it do? You're in that much trouble a phone call's not going to make things worse. They can't get any worse.'

'I'll give it some thought,' he promised.

After he rang off he sat for a long while, then crossed to the bedside and switched on the clock radio. He tuned into the local station and waited for a news report. It was 10 p.m. when the bulletin came on. The announcer's tone was grave as he described the finding of Councillor Jeffries with his throat slit in the lavatory of the hall where he was holding an election meeting. The newsreader went on to say the police had almost been successful in detaining the man they suspect committed the murder, but the man escaped after assaulting an officer.

Marshall switched off the radio and sat on the edge of his bed, deep in thought. The manhunt for him before this would have been as nothing compared to what it would be now. He looked round the room, assessing his position. Then he reached for his mobile.

chapter eleven

It was turned seven o'clock before Nash was about ready to leave the office, when the phone rang. It was Ruth. 'I'm just leaving Netherdale,' she told him. 'How do you fancy eating out? I'm paying.'

'I'll go for that, especially the last bit.'

'Spoken like a true Yorkshireman.'

'How long do you reckon before you're here?'

'Half an hour, tops.'

As he waited, Nash read the Marshall file again. He knew there was something in there he should have spotted before. An inconsistency. But he couldn't nail it. He'd closed the file, and as Ruth Edwards entered the CID suite, he realized what it was he'd missed.

'What is it, Mike?' Ruth could tell something was wrong by his expression.

'Bear with me a minute, Ruth.'

He reopened the file. He had to check his facts. If he was right, everything about the case, all their preconceived notions, went out of the window. He stared at the sheet of paper. He moved it to one side, hunting through the rest of the file until he located what he was looking for. 'There,' he said triumphantly. 'I knew it! I knew something was wrong.'

He looked up, saw Ruth's puzzled expression. He laid a hand on the folder. 'This is the file relating to Marshall's original conviction for the murder of his wife. Read that' – he pointed to a report – 'then read this statement. Look at the dates.'

She bent over the papers, her rich, auburn hair sweeping forward framing her face. After a few moments, she looked up. 'I'm sorry, Mike. I don't see the significance.'

Nash pointed to part of the statement. 'That's a transcript of the first interview with Marshall, right?' She nodded. 'Read that sentence there, and compare it with the report on the other piece of paper.'

Ruth read it once, then a second time; then realized what she was reading. She looked up, her expression one of shocked disbelief. 'That's not possible: totally impossible.'

Nash shook his head, his face grim. 'No it isn't. In one set of circumstances, it is perfectly possible. But the circumstances are almost unthinkable.'

'Explain it for me, please?'

'At the time of Marshall's first interview, Anna's body hadn't been found, only her car. Dundas was obviously trying to pressure Marshall into confessing. He asked him' – Nash glanced down at the file – '"isn't the truth that you slit your wife's throat and disposed of the body by tossing it into the sea?" At first, when I read that, I was dreadfully worried that Dundas might have been involved. How else could he have known precisely how Anna Marshall was murdered? But then I read this. . . .'

Nash turned the pages of the file until he reached the document he wanted. 'This is a transcript of Dundas's interview of Stuart Moran, the day *before* he questioned Marshall. In it, Dundas asked Moran, "What do you think happened to Mrs Marshall?" Moran's reply is very enlightening. "I believe Marshall slit her throat, drove to the coast and dumped her body in the sea. He had a ferocious temper, Anna told me that, and said he was insanely jealous. She told me they'd had terrible rows, and that she was so embarrassed about them she dreaded bumping into their neighbours." In those few sentences Moran planted the idea for Dundas that Marshall had murdered Anna, and even pointed the way for him to question the neighbours. Dundas would not have been aware of how Anna was killed, but Stuart Moran certainly knew, and his whole statement is a very clever attempt to frame Marshall. An attempt that succeeded. It probably sounded plausible to Dundas in view of the facts surrounding the finding of her car.'

'And you think the neighbours were bribed to say what they did?'

'Bribed, blackmailed or cajoled some way or other, yes. Reading the file, there were only two who said they'd heard these so-called rows. On its own, hardly overwhelming. But together with the other evidence, enough to build a successful prosecution on.'

'You realize I'll have to act on this?'

'Wearing your other hat, you mean? Your, Her Majesty's Inspectorate of Constabulary hat?'

'Exactly.'

'Hang on,' Nash warned. 'First of all, we've a killer to bring to justice. A man who's got away with his crimes for far too long. We can't afford to warn him by precipitate action. We know Marshall couldn't have killed the couple in The Golden Bear; not wearing that uniform. Now, we also have evidence that proves he's innocent of his wife's murder. As long as we remain in charge of the investigation we can afford to let the world continue to believe in his guilt for a while longer, giving us chance to try and find out who is behind this, and what their motive is.'

'Have you any idea how?'

'Yes, I think so. I'll tell you over dinner.'

They opted for a Mexican meal. Much of the time in the restaurant they spent conversing in low tones, barely above a whisper. Diners at surrounding tables would have assumed them to be lovers. The conversation would have startled them out of that belief. 'Somewhere out there is a killer with a penchant for slicing throats in as bloodthirsty a fashion as I've ever seen,' Nash stated.

'Agreed, and the problem we've got is, we haven't the remotest idea who it is. Could be any one of the adult population of the United Kingdom.'

Nash smiled. 'Actually, you're wrong, Ruth.'

She looked at him, curiously. He explained about Andrews and the car registration. 'Lisa checked it out. The car's registered to an address in York, not been reported stolen. I'm waiting to hear if the locals know anything of the owner.'

They were no sooner inside the flat than his mobile phone rang. 'Mike Nash. Who's this?' He listened. 'Mr Marshall – Alan. I'm glad you've rung me.'

'Where is he?' Ruth mouthed.

Nash shook his head. 'Listen, Alan. I've some more news for you.'

The conversation lasted almost half an hour. When it was over, Nash put the mobile down. 'Do you think we've done the right thing?'

Ruth thought about it. 'I don't see we'd much choice, given the circumstances. There's certainly nothing in regulations that comes close to covering them.'

'One thing for sure, Ruth, I'm glad you're here to back me up. Given your position.'

After another late shift, covering an assault in Netherdale following a rowdy birthday party that had got out of hand, resulting in several arrests, Lisa was exhausted. She found sleep impossible. She was more involved than she ought to be in the Marshall case and couldn't rest. At 6 a.m. she got out of bed and went into the kitchen to brew a cup of camomile tea. It did the trick. She wandered sleepily through to the bedroom and climbed back into bed. She was asleep within minutes. The ringing phone awoke her. The clock on her bedside cabinet showed 8.35 a.m. Lisa groaned and tried to ignore it, hoping whoever was phoning might get bored and ring off. Eventually, when the ringing continued Lisa thrust back the duvet. She stood up still marginally woozy from sleep and trudged reluctantly through to the hall.

'Yes,' she said testily without bothering to check the caller display.

'I wonder how interested your superiors would be in the identity of your new boyfriend.'

'What? Who is this? What do you want?'

'Consorting with a murderer; a man wanted by every police officer in the land. Watching him commit an assault on another officer without attempting to intervene. Conniving to help him escape. That would look really bad on your career record, wouldn't it?'

Lisa identified her former lover at last. 'Donald, what the hell are you talking about?'

'Your bloodthirsty, throat-slitting lover, Alan Marshall, that's who. Do you really expect me to say nothing whilst you help him? Of course, I might do just that for a small fee.'

'Donald, as usual you're full of shit. Marshall isn't my lover, he isn't a murderer and I've done nothing to be ashamed of. So why don't you take the message I've already given you several times. Why don't you piss off and go back to shagging Jackie, because you're not screwing me any longer. Not even for money. Blackmail's an ugly word, Donald, but it suits you because you've an ugly, dirty mind. So piss off and stay out of my life, you worthless cretin.' Lisa slammed the phone down to reinforce the message.

Unable to face the thought of trying for more sleep, she had a shower and was in the process of dressing when the phone rang again. She snatched the receiver up. 'What is it now?' she snapped, assuming it to be Smailes.

'Morning, Lisa, Mike Nash here.'

'Sorry, boss, I thought it was someone else.'

'Listen, I know you're not due in until this afternoon, but could you make it a bit earlier? Something's come up.'

Donald Smailes sat with the phone in his hand for a long time. He regretted the impulse that had caused him to take up with Jackie. She wasn't a patch on Lisa in bed, nor, as he was beginning to find out, was she as pleasant and loyal a companion. She blamed him for breaking up her friendship with Lisa. He felt bitter at the way things had gone, bitter and cheated. Although why he should have felt cheated only someone with as corrupt a mind as Smailes could have explained. In the end he dialled a number.

His phone call was handled with discretion, as was always the case. The nature of the work handled by the department he rang made it not only desirable, but in most cases essential.

'I have information concerning a serving officer, one of those involved in the Marshall enquiry. I think you should be aware that the officer has been aiding and abetting a fugitive escape from justice. The officer is DC Andrews from Netherdale and I believe she and Marshall may be lovers. She is in regular communication with him and I have reason to believe they've slept together on at least one occasion since he became a wanted man. Certainly she helped him escape arrest when there was a general warrant out for him.'

The listener replaced the handset and began to discuss the call with a colleague, who told him, 'We're bound to investigate such complaints, no matter what the motive behind them is. That's the function of this department.'

'I know, but that caller sounded so vindictive, how can we be sure it isn't someone merely being malicious?'

'I'm afraid the only way is by carrying out an investigation.'

'How do you want us to approach it?'

'We'll begin as normal with audio and visual surveillance of the young woman's residence. At the same time I'd like you to organize an inspection of everything she's been working on over the last three months. In particular, check whether she's been supplying the suspect with information or other assistance. That covers the first part of the allegation. As to the second assertion, that's not going to be as easy to establish. If DC Andrews has entered into a sexual relationship with the suspect that's an even more serious allegation, especially if she's slept with him since he was wanted for questioning. Quite how we're to prove or disprove that without catching them at it I'm not sure. For the time being, concentrate on setting up the surveillance.'

'What about listening to her phone calls?'

'Yes, I think so. Given the nature of the allegation and the fact that her alleged lover is a fugitive I consider it not only advisable, but essential. Particularly so, as the man Marshall seems rather successful at evading capture.'

Lisa had met Barry Dickinson briefly when he'd helped her with Marshall's Land Rover; this was the first time she'd met Shirley.

Before she could shake hands, Lisa had to greet an enthusiastic Labrador that was frisking around her. 'This is Nell, isn't it?' she asked.

'That's right. Come along in. When Nell will allow you to, that is.'

'I wondered what had happened to her.'

'He entrusted her to us. The poor thing's been fretting a bit. The two of them were rarely apart for long. I just hope this nightmare's over soon, for both their sakes.'

'I wanted to ask if you'd heard from Alan,' Lisa began, as she accepted a cup of coffee. 'Especially with what happened in Leeds last night.'

'Yes,' Barry replied. 'He rang us; spoke to Shirley. We didn't know what to do, other than advise him to phone your boss.'

'Don't worry, he did ring him, that's why I'm here.'

chapter twelve

Alan Marshall certainly hadn't slept easy in his bed. When morning came he rose before daybreak and slipped out of the hotel before any of his fellow guests were up and about. He went to a small café opposite the market for breakfast. It was an establishment that was constantly busy, so much so, the staff had no time to inspect their customers. If the staff were kept busy, the customers were too preoccupied with their own affairs to notice one another. It suited Marshall perfectly.

As soon as he'd eaten he moved on, spending all morning in the library where the high bookcases provided shelter from prying eyes. He read the morning paper which contained a full-page article on the Jeffries murder, a glowing eulogy on Councillor Robert Jeffries and a savage condemnation of his killer. It didn't quite go so far as to indict Marshall for the crime but if it fell short, it wasn't far short. Marshall noted the media conference scheduled for 11 a.m. and knew it would fuel the publicity surrounding him; the last thing he needed. He spent the remainder of the afternoon and early evening in the darkened anonymity of a multi-screen cinema before returning to the hotel after nightfall.

The reception area was deserted but as he walked towards the flight of stairs his gaze strayed to his right. The office used by the proprietor was unoccupied but the light was on. Marshall saw an open copy of the local evening paper lying on the desk next to the phone, revealing a photograph of Marshall under the single word headline: "KILLER".

The paper's proximity to the phone rang alarm bells. Even with his new growth of stubble Marshall was easily recognizable. He turned to head for the stairs, then, on impulse, turned

103

back and grabbed the paper before setting off for his room. He heard the distant sound of sirens. Somehow he knew exactly where they would be heading.

He pulled his holdall from the bottom of the wardrobe and stuffed his clothing and few possessions inside. He realized the front of the building was a no go area. Fortunately the fire escape ran past his window. Cautiously, he eased the window up, crawled through on to the steel platform and started down the iron rungs as fast as he could.

He'd got to within ten feet of the ground when he glanced down, in time to see a figure move away from the wall, little more than a darker shape in the darkness. 'Watch out, he's here,' a voice called out.

Marshall jumped. His feet and knees simultaneously hit the man in the midriff, who collapsed with a huge sigh, like a deflating balloon. As Marshall regained his balance a second man launched himself out of the shadows. Marshall swung the holdall and heard a cry of pain. Then he was off down the garden like a sprinter. He cleared the low hedge at the end like a steeplechaser and landed in the grounds of a terrace house in the road behind the hotel. The building, sub-divided into flats, had the garden area paved for car parking. Marshall sped across the tarmac and into the street beyond.

He heard sirens begin to wail and the screech of tyres as police vehicles set off in pursuit. He ran from the street into the back-alleyways amongst the maze of terraces surrounding Headingley's famous cricket ground. He dodged this way and that, following no defined pattern, sheltering where he could in back yards, gardens, gateways, and in porches as police cars zoomed past in their frantic efforts to locate him.

He kept on the move for over an hour, conscious all the time that around the next corner disaster could be lurking. At last the sirens became a faint echo in the distance. He needed to get clear of Leeds, but the bus and train stations would be highly dangerous now. Walking or hitching was equally unsafe. It was becoming impossible for him to move. Equally there was no future in remaining where he was.

As he reached a road junction Marshall's eye was drawn to a row of brightly lit signs on the buildings opposite. He had reached the edge of the student quarter of the city, pubs and café bars everywhere. He crossed the road, casting nervous glances to the right and left, and looked through the windows. He hesitated for a few moments, then decided to take the chance and slipped quietly through the door of the most dimly lit establishment he could see.

Inside, he ordered a coffee and settled down in a corner seat with a direct view of the door and window, sliding his holdall under the table. Around him, the incessant chatter of the students, too occupied with their plans for the evening to give him a second glance. He opened the paper he'd purloined from the hotel and began reading about his alleged misdeeds.

In the article there was a statement about him, his past, and time in Durham gaol. The journalist had quoted the source as Superintendent Richard Dundas of Yorkshire Central Task Force. Marshall remembered Dundas; remembered him only too well.

He needed a plan, but first of all he needed to get clear of the net that was closing in around him. He looked again at the article, memory stirring. Now he thought he knew a way, but it meant taking a chance. And doing something he'd vowed never to do again: taking someone on trust. From nowhere, or so it seemed, he recalled a conversation he'd had with the occupant of the next cell. The prisoner owed Marshall: big style. It had been Marshall's timely intervention that had saved his neighbour from death or serious injury at the hands of a trio of prisoners he'd angered. Recognizing the debt, he'd told Marshall, 'If you're ever in a jam and need help, get in touch.'

Marshall watched and waited until he was sure the coast was clear, then set off towards the city centre at a brisk walk, mobile in hand.

As soon as the call was answered, Marshall said, 'I used to live next door to you. You once promised to help me if I was in need of it.'

There was a long silence as he awaited the reply. 'Is that who

I think it is? Someone who has been making a lot of newspaper headlines?'

'You've got it. But you shouldn't believe everything you read. About the only thing they got right is my name. The question is, will you help me?'

'Depends what you want, but I'll do what I can.'

Marshall could sense some reluctance. Hardly surprising, as the man didn't know what the favour was. 'I'm taking you on trust,' he admitted, 'and I hope that boast you once made wasn't an idle one. You told me, with your contacts you were able to access information other people couldn't get. Is that still the case?'

'Pretty much.' The answer was immediate; the relief evident. 'What exactly are you after?'

'I have a car registration number. I know the make and model. What I need is the owner's name and address. Can you get that for me?'

'Piece of cake. I take it you need this as soon as possible?'

'Oh, no,' Marshall assured him, 'it's far more urgent than that.'

This time there was laughter in his contact's voice. 'Give me your phone number. I'll have the details for you by morning.'

Marshall rested in a shelter in a remote corner of a park; he was exhausted. The night was dark, moonless and the cloud cover was thick enough to threaten rain or snow. It was certainly cold enough for snow, but Marshall wasn't worried by that. As far as he was concerned the worse the weather, the better for him. He felt very much alone and depressed.

He awoke with a start, looked round alarmed: his mobile was ringing. He answered the call, committing the details of what he was told to memory. It was still dark. His holdall was still at his side. Marshall sighed with relief and rubbed at his arms, his legs, as he tried to get some feeling back into his numb body. He was frozen and hungry. He knew this was useless. Nowhere around here was safe. It was strange, he thought. At one time he'd been perfectly at home in a city; his city. Now, the place terrified him. Mind you, he hadn't been on the run then. After a lot of thought, he realized he had only one choice, dangerous though it might be. He knew where he had to go. But how to get there, that was the first problem.

'The audio-visual surveillance team is in place and the phone line has been tapped.'

'Good, keep me informed on the way things are moving, especially if there is anything positive to report.'

Had the various members of the Internal Affairs inquiry team inspected Lisa Andrews' file closely, they might have noticed that as part of her training she had attended a surveillance techniques course. They might have read the comments made on her report by the senior tutor. Sadly for them they failed to see either.

The tutor had been impressed by Andrews' ability to detect electronic chatter, the signature of all listening devices. He'd been so intrigued by this talent that he tried her with a variety of instruments from two-way radios to mobile phones. At the end of her course, he told her if she wanted to transfer into counter-espionage activities he would gladly recommend her for it.

Whether Lisa would have picked up the sound, had her alarm level not been heightened by Donald's threat of reprisals, is difficult to determine. When the phone rang she answered just in time to hear a faint but unmistakeably familiar click, then Shirley Dickinson's voice.

'Hello, Shirley,' Lisa answered. 'Listen, I've got a pan on the stove. Can I ring you back in five minutes or so? Right, I'll call you then.'

She waited for Shirley to disconnect, and immediately heard the same clicking sound before the dialling tone returned. 'Donald, you bastard,' she muttered as she wandered to the window in the lounge overlooking the street. She stared at the vehicles for a few minutes then closed the curtains. She was careful to leave a tiny gap between the two edges of the fabric. The curtains were heavy velvet, there was no way anyone standing behind them would be visible to the outside world. She was interested most in the occupants of the Ford Transit van she could see.

She went back to the phone and lifted the receiver. Once again she heard the slight click before the dialling tone kicked in. She smiled and replaced the receiver. She went back into the lounge and switched the TV on. She turned the volume up, then tapped Shirley's number into her mobile.

'Shirley, I'm sorry about the noise but I think I'm being watched, that probably means the phone's tapped. I can't even trust my mobile for long. Do you have a mobile?'

'No, but my husband does,' Shirley replied.

'Do you have caller display on this phone?'

'Yes we do. Why?'

'Write my mobile number down then send me a text so I can get yours. It saves repeating it aloud. I'll send you a text in reply. I'm not going to say any more, OK?'

Five minutes later Lisa received a text which read, 'Haven't heard from our friend, worried. You take care'. She replied immediately. 'Will contact tomorrow'.

Lisa was about to go to bed when she remembered the parked van. She walked over to the lounge window and peered through the gap. It was still there. Lisa went round the flat turning the lights off one by one, then entered her bedroom where she switched the bedside light on and closed the curtains. She sat on the bed for ten minutes then switched off the lamp. Anyone watching would assume she'd gone to bed.

She walked cautiously back through to the lounge and across to the window. She stood watching. Her patience was rewarded when the rear door of the vehicle opened and a man climbed out. He turned as if to close the door but held it for a moment peering into the interior. It was impossible to be certain at that range and in darkness, but from his posture Lisa guessed he was talking to someone.

The man closed the door and set off to walk towards the town centre. Lisa continued to watch. It was some twenty minutes later when she spotted him returning, carrying a plastic bag. He knocked on the van door which opened immediately. Instead of climbing in he delved into the carrier and began passing small containers inside. Lisa smiled, obviously a takeaway. With a little luck she might be able to gain the advantage. She took her mobile, dialled 999 and specified police assistance.

'There's men watching from a van outside. I'm scared. They've been there hours. I daren't go to bed.' Lisa gabbled the words in a breathless whisper, panting nervously to further disjoint the delivery.

'Could I have your name and address please?' the police operator asked patiently.

'What? Oh, er, yes. My name, er, Jackie Reynolds,' Lisa continued to whisper. 'I live at seventeen, Wharfedale Close, Flat D. They might be burglars or worse. Please, will you send someone?'

'How long has the vehicle been parked there, madam?' the operator asked.

'It's miss, not madam. It's been there hours. I don't know exactly how long. Before dark, because I know it's blue.'

Lisa paused. Then injecting a degree of panic into her voice went on. 'There's a man getting out of the van. He's walking over towards the building. Oh please send someone as fast as—' She pressed the button to end the call.

The operator rang back three times, each time Lisa ignored the call. She wondered how sensitive the surveillance equipment might be. Whether the team had gained access to the flat itself and placed bugs inside? There was no sign of movement. Obviously her little charade hadn't been picked up. Five minutes later, a police car drew to a halt across the front of the van.

Lisa watched. Her interest turned to amusement as the two officers from the patrol car began inspecting the van. One of them tried the rear door which opened easily. He shone his torch inside. In a whirl of activity he stepped clear as a trio of men emerged. There was a heated conversation lasting several minutes, towards the end of which documentation was produced.

The men's explanation must have satisfied the officers, for they moved away from the trio and began walking towards the flats. Lisa watched as the three men stood for a few moments obviously debating the events and their significance. Several glances were cast up towards her windows before the trio climbed into the front of the van and drove away. As they departed Lisa heard the faint sound of a doorbell ringing somewhere in the building. She glanced at her watch, it was 2.15 a.m. Lisa remembered how upset Jackie got when her sleep was disturbed. She smiled with satisfaction as she wandered through to her bedroom. It might only have been a small triumph, but it was enjoyable nonetheless.

The senior internal investigations officer listened to the report. 'When the officers went to the flats to reassure the woman who'd rung, she knew nothing of the complaint. We checked the number of the caller. It was a mobile phone. The woman they spoke to doesn't possess a mobile.'

'I take it you're assuming DC Andrews has become aware of our activities and taken retaliatory measures?'

'I think it's a reasonable assumption.'

'I wonder how she found out?'

'According to her file, she was extremely talented at spotting telephone bugging during her training course.'

'Her response seems to have been highly effective. She's got rid of the team watching her home. She's stopped using the phone in her flat and we can't bug her mobile unless we can get hold of it. I'd say she's winning hands down.'

'It seemed sensible to withdraw the surveillance team as soon as their cover was blown. I've given instruction for another unit to be deployed as soon as is practicable.'

'Marvellous.' There was no doubting the sarcasm in the senior officer's voice. 'Be sure to let me know when plan B is in operation. Do you think you can manage to search her flat for evidence without her noticing? If you find Marshall's fingerprints for instance, then I can contact her senior officer.'

chapter thirteen

Marshall boarded the first available train next morning. He'd waited until it was due to leave, saw there was one compartment without passengers and headed for it. Given the early hour and that there were only a couple of stations en route, he hoped it would stay that way. He opened the paper he'd bought at the newsagents in the station concourse. The only reason he'd chosen that one was that it was a broadsheet. Useful for hiding behind. Almost immediately, an item caught his attention. It was a profile of one of the parliamentary candidates standing at a forthcoming by-election. Marshall had little or no interest in politics but remembered the conversation he'd overheard at Sir Maurice Winfield's shoot. The man they'd talked about was obviously the one interviewed here. After the first sentence Marshall's interest was well and truly caught. With considerable surprise he realized he knew the subject of the article.

FORMER PILOT NOW A HIGH FLYER
When Julian Corps left the RAF to take over the ailing family business few people guessed he would one day become one of the leading figures in the construction industry. Even fewer would have suggested he might become a powerful force in parliamentary politics. Yet twenty years later, Corps heads Coningsby Developments, one of the two major players in the construction and civil engineering industries. Although not yet elected to Westminster, the by-election looks to be a foregone conclusion, and many political pundits are predicting a rapid rise for Corps through the party ranks. Some have even gone so far as to suggest him as a future Prime Minister.

Corps himself was one of those early doubters. Stressing

that his name is pronounced like an army unit rather than a dead body, the prospective MP explained, 'My first priority was to get the company on to a sound footing. My father was a great engineer but less talented as a businessman. I was too concerned with the day to day running of the firm to think of much else.' When asked how he'd gone about performing the rescue act, Corps smiled. 'It took a lot of bloody hard work for little reward. It meant long hours of solid graft, day in, day out. First priority was to make sure all the bills got paid. Then cross my fingers and hope we had enough left to pay the wages. If there was anything left in the kitty after that, it got split between building up a reserve and paying myself a wage.'

'What if there wasn't enough?'

Corps smiled again. 'Then I had to do without. It's a good discipline being hungry.'

'When did you think the company was beginning to turn the corner?'

'I don't remember there being a defining moment. It was more a gradual process. After a while I felt confident enough to tender for bigger, more lucrative contracts. I suppose it was when we'd serviced one or two of them successfully, that I began to think we were making real progress.'

'Nowadays Coningsby has only one serious rival. How do you compete with Broadwood Construction?'

'They're a tough bunch, that's for sure. So we have to be as tough, as competitive, and if we're lucky we win out. Harry Rourke's another who's built a company from nothing. As such, I respect him enormously. That isn't to say I wouldn't cut his throat as soon as look at him. Just the same as he'd do to me. In a business sense, that is.'

'So what of the future? What exactly are your political ambitions?'

'My approach to politics is modelled on the way I ran Coningsby, or CBC as it was then, in the early days, when survival was my greatest ambition. I know quite a lot's been said and written about me, but to be honest I try to ignore all that. What concerns me at the moment is winning the by-election.

Anything beyond that will have to wait. Only when it's over will I start to think of what follows.'

Despite the modesty of his stated ambitions I think it will be only a matter of time before Julian Corps is MP for Central Yorkshire constituency. After that, who knows? Maybe we do have a future Prime Minister in our midst. One thing is for sure. At least he won't have to worry about getting a wage at the end of the week.

Marshall whistled aloud with surprise, then glanced around nervously. The compartment was still empty. He relaxed and considered the facts he'd just read. It was another face, another name from the past. He didn't think there was a connection with what had happened to him, but then, after what he'd just read, nothing would surprise him.

The difficulty he had was trying to reconcile the profile in the paper with the man he remembered. Corps hadn't been much more than a front man with a salesman's demeanour. Certainly not a business heavyweight. And certainly not capable of slugging it out with the likes of Harry Rourke. So how had he turned himself into the tycoon described in the article?

Nash had travelled to York for a meeting and was waiting in his car for his contact to arrive. He was approached; the newcomer introduced himself. 'DI Russell, Charlie to my friends. What's this all about? And why the need for secrecy?'

Nash explained. There was a moment's silence before Russell responded. 'If you're convinced the man's innocent, why is his face splashed over all the papers, and why the hue and cry after him?'

Nash's face was grim as he replied, 'Mainly for his own protection. There are things happening with regard to our investigation that I'd rather not go into, certainly not at this stage. But let's say the successful appeal against Marshall's original conviction was a triumph for justice.'

'You're saying this man Marshall was framed?'

'I'm afraid so.'

'Then I can understand the need for discretion. What you've told me about the case tallies with certain information I've been able to dig out about the man who lives at the address you gave me.' The officer paused. 'Although information's a bit too strong a word.'

'You know something about him?'

'John Brown? That isn't his real name by the way. But I reckon you've probably already guessed that. When I said information was too strong a word, I meant that there's nothing concrete against him. Nothing worse than a couple of parking tickets. However, there are lots of rumours. Highly unsavoury rumours at that.'

He saw Nash's quizzical expression. 'Let's just say he's suspected of being "for hire". No proof, obviously, but the word on the street is that if you want somebody disposing of, and you've plenty of money to spare, Brown's the man to contact. He's far from cheap, but he's supposed to be highly efficient. His speciality's the knife, unless you want the event to look like an accident, which he can also arrange quite easily.'

'The knife bit tallies with what's happened to the victims in our case,' Nash pointed out.

'Again, I'm going on hearsay, and third-hand hearsay at that. I've a colleague in the murder squad who got most of this from an informant. He'd to do a lot of talking and make a few threats before the man could be persuaded to say a word. That's how much Brown's feared. Anyway, the man said Brown's such an artist with the knife, he sets up his own defence. If anybody challenges him, or if he's ever accused of the crime, he makes it look impossible for him to have done it.'

'How can he do that?'

'I have to admit there's a touch of genius about it. He makes the crimes appear as if they've been committed by a left-hander.'

'How do you mean?'

Russell demonstrated. 'If a right-handed killer went up to his victim from behind, you'd expect him to cut the throat from the victim's left side, across to the right. What Brown does is cut from right to left. A sort of backhand action.'

'A back-slash? That's interesting.' Nash remembered Mexican Pete's words. 'Our pathologist thought at first the two victims in the hotel had been killed by a left-handed person, but when he examined them closer, he wasn't as convinced. I'm still waiting for him to come back to me with a final opinion. But, from what you say, Brown could have done it, and made it look like a left-hander, simply by using a back-slash.'

'Maybe. But like I say, everything you've just heard is little more than rumour. But now that they know about it, our murder guys are more than keen to see how things develop. They reckon if we can nail Brown, we can clear up quite a few unsolved murders of our own.'

'Then let's make a start. Let's go talk to Mr Brown.'

They walked across the gravel towards the front door. It was one of those dark mid-winter days where it barely seems to get light all day. A PIR light sprang to life, disturbed by their movement. Apart from that, the building appeared to be in total darkness. Nash rang the bell. There was no response, so, after trying a second and third time, he tried the door. It was locked. 'Let's have a look round the back,' Russell suggested.

They found the parking area empty of cars. 'Looks as if we've drawn a blank.' Nash sighed. 'I've had a long drive for nothing.' He walked across to the back door and reached for the handle. He didn't need to turn it, the door opened at his touch. He glanced back at his colleague. 'Something's not right.'

'We'd better have a look inside,' his companion agreed.

They were about to enter the building when they heard the sound of a siren. It was close and rapidly getting nearer. Neither of them associated the sound with themselves until a squad car, lights blazing, skidded round the gravel sweep and pulled to an abrupt halt alongside them. Fortunately the officers knew the local detective. After some confused explanations, the driver of the patrol car told them, 'One of the residents in that block' – he pointed to an adjacent building – 'saw somebody lurking suspiciously near the dustbins a couple of hours back. By the time they rang us and we got here there was no sign of life. We rang

115

the doorbell, but couldn't get any reply.'

'Did you try this door?' Nash asked.

The uniformed officer nodded. 'It was all secure then, both this one and the front.'

'That means, if anything did happen here, it happened after your visit,' Nash said thoughtfully, as much to himself as to the others. 'Were there any cars about?'

The officer shook his head. 'The thing is, there's been a spate of burglaries around here recently, all committed during the daytime. We reckon it's the time of year. After Christmas, somebody short of cash, need to pay the bills before the end of January.'

'I think we should have a look inside, there's obviously a problem here,' Nash said. 'Especially now we've got back-up.'

All appeared well as they ventured up the stairs but at the top they could see the door to Brown's flat had been forced open. Charlie Russell handed out disposable gloves. The first room was a living room. They could tell at a glance that the place had been ransacked. 'Yes, this place has been done over, but there doesn't appear to be anything missing. The TV and electrical stuff's still here.'

'Maybe he got disturbed, sir,' one of the officers suggested.

Russell shrugged and indicated the doors to the left. 'Check those out. I'll have a look in here.' He pointed to a third door.

Left to his own devices, Nash wandered over to the far side of the living room, where a small office had been created from a desk and computer workstation. An open filing cabinet stood alongside; a bunch of keys hanging from the lock. He called to Russell, who hurried back into the room with the constables. 'There are two Yale keys on here,' Nash pointed to the key-ring. 'And that fob, it's the same make of car as Brown's. I reckon these are Brown's spare keys. Let's see what's so interesting in these.' He gestured to the dining-table where the files had been spread out. Nash began examining the folders as he spoke. 'There are bank accounts with virtually every bank and building society you can think of. They're all in different names, small deposits in each one on similar dates over the years.'

'That's a professional's work, to avoid suspicion of money laundering. Very clever. How long have the accounts been open?'

'Twenty years at least judging from the statements.'

'That would explain it. The regulations only came into being piecemeal, so if the account was already open, Brown was safe.'

Nash found an even more revelatory file. At first glance it seemed to contain nothing more than a handful of press cuttings. He lifted it clear for inspection. Each news report concerned a murder or sudden violent death. Some of the cuttings were old, the pages yellowed. The earliest was dated 1983. After flicking over one or two Nash stopped. 'Look at that!' Nash pointed to the cutting. 'I think that confirms who killed Anna Marshall.'

Russell turned to the officers. 'I think we should make a thorough examination of this flat. You two make a start. In the meantime we'll have a look at these.'

'There are cuttings on Moran and Robertson as well,' Nash continued. 'I think we should have a closer look, try to spot a link with any other deaths.' Nash pulled the file towards him.

While they were still reading, the officers came out of the bedrooms. 'Anything?' Russell asked.

'Yes, in one of the wardrobes there's a boiler suit wrapped in a bin liner. There are a lot of stains on it. I'm willing to bet they're bloodstains.'

Nash looked up. 'I'll be interested to read the forensics on those. We know the killer of the couple in the hotel wore a waiter's livery when he slashed their throats. If our suspicions about Brown are correct, I reckon I can guess the identity of the owner of the blood on those overalls.'

'Are you going to share this with us?' Charlie Russell asked.

'I'd guess it will match that of Councillor Jeffries, the councillor who was murdered in Leeds two nights ago.'

'We may have answered a few questions, but there are still a couple of big ones remaining,' Russell said. 'Number one: who was the suspicious character reported near the back of the building earlier, and second: what's happened to Brown?'

'That,' Nash said, 'is the million-dollar question.'

chapter fourteen

The following morning, when Nash walked into the CID suite, Andrews was already there. He signalled to her to follow him. They'd barely reached his office when Jack Binns called out, 'Mike? I've got Superintendent Dundas of Yorkshire Central for you on the phone. He sounds like a boiler about to explode.'

Nash studied a moment. 'Tell him I'm in a meeting and can't be disturbed. Join us as soon as you can, Jack.'

After he'd explained the events of the previous day to them, he sighed. 'I need time to think all this through. I'll have to take it to the chief. We might have identified the killer of the couple from The Golden Bear, and a connection to the Jeffries murder. However, the rest of the news is far from good. Marshall seems to have an uncanny knack of being in the wrong place at the wrong time. I'm only guessing, but he may be in serious danger. May even be dead by now.'

'I hope not, he's a nice bloke. I told you what happened at my flat when my ex turned up?' She went on to explain about the surveillance and her suspicions of Smailes.

'Sounds as if you did the right thing, ditching him. Don't worry about the internal guys. I'll get the chief to sort that. With what's in here' – he tapped his files – 'that won't be difficult.' He paused for a second or two. 'Although, it might be better if things took their course. From an outsider's point of view at least.'

'I don't understand?'

'We now know Marshall's innocent. It might be to our advantage to let those who really are responsible for the killings believe we still think he's guilty, and that we're still hunting him. If they see you've been suspended following investigation, it would further the illusion.'

Lisa stared at him in disbelief. 'You mean to say you're going to let them ruin my career? But I haven't done—'

'Don't worry about it,' Nash interrupted. 'I'll see you're OK. I'm going through to Netherdale. I'm meeting Superintendent Edwards and then we're taking all this to the chief. Jack, anybody rings for me I'll be back late this afternoon.'

'What about Superintendent Dundas?' Jack asked.

'Particularly him. If anyone from Internal Affairs rings, tell them where I am. No one else though.'

The chief constable was predictably shocked by Nash's news. He produced the file and pointed out the relevant parts. O'Donnell sat back in her chair. 'How do you want to play it, Mike?'

'I've been thinking about that on the way over. Obviously we can't have Dundas investigating the Jeffries case or anything where Alan Marshall's a supposed suspect. On the other hand, we don't want to alert the real killer to the fact that he's been rumbled. One way would be to combine operations, with us taking charge, but the way we are on manpower that's also a non-runner. All I can think is to let Yorkshire Central continue with the Jeffries enquiry but keep them clear of the Moran/ Robertson case.'

'You're absolutely convinced Marshall's innocent?'

'Oh yes, without a doubt. I'm not sure exactly what happened with the Jeffries murder, but I'm inclined to believe Marshall's version of events. As to the others, I was unhappy about the original conviction when I read the file you've just looked at. As to Moran, well, if you look at the photo of Marshall and imagine him trying to get into that waiter's uniform it'd make you laugh. There's also this letter.' Nash placed it on the chief's desk. 'Moran arranged for it to be sent to Marshall in the event of anything happening to him. Obviously, Moran had done something that made him fear for his own life and wanted to put things right. It clears Marshall completely. It does more than that, though. It suggests the motive for Anna Marshall's murder lies in Marshall's own past. What that might be, I've no idea.

Nor will I have until I can get to talk to him, providing he hasn't become a victim as well. And that's a real possibility. Forensics has found traces of blood on the knife from Marshall's cottage matching both Moran's and Robertson's, besides his.'

Nash explained what had happened in York. 'My only hope is that Marshall has managed to steer well clear of Brown and gone to ground somewhere. If so, he's alive and well. But if he encountered Brown, then I think we must assume that Marshall's dead. The local DI told me Brown's reputation is horrific. Unfortunately none of the information is provable, except for what we found in Brown's flat.'

Nash told her about the paperwork. 'That in itself is damning, but it might not be enough to secure a conviction on its own. However, there's more.' Nash related the finding of the blood-stained boiler suit. 'If the blood turns out to be that of Councillor Jeffries, we've a cast-iron case.'

'There've been no sightings of Marshall, then?'

'None whatsoever. That worries me, worries me a lot. The only thing is, there's been no sign of Brown returning to his flat either. I find that rather strange. He'd no knowledge that we'd been there or that there'd been an intruder, I assume. No reason to think there was anything amiss. York CID has somebody watching the place, and Brown's not been near. Nor have there been any visitors.'

'We must hope Marshall turns up, then. I don't see we can do any other.' The chief constable glanced at Ruth Edwards, who nodded agreement.

'There's one other thing I need to discuss though. It's to do with DC Andrews.' Nash explained about the surveillance. 'I'm concerned about her,' he admitted.

'I can get that quashed easily enough,' the chief said. 'I imagine that's what you want, manpower being as it is?'

'Not exactly,' Nash said. He glanced at Edwards. 'Ruth and I have a different plan, but we need you to sanction it.'

Nash outlined what they had in mind. At the end of it, O'Donnell leaned back in her chair. 'You do realize it's totally unorthodox.' She studied both Nash and Edwards. 'OK, but as long as Ruth's involved and ensures everything is documented, I think it could just work.'

'Thanks, ma'am,' Nash said as he stood up to leave.

'Ruth, would you mind? I'd like a word with Mike before he bolts back to Helmsdale.'

'Certainly, Chief,' Ruth turned to Nash. 'Do you want me to ring Dundas for you?'

'That would be great, thanks.'

When Ruth had left, O'Donnell smiled. 'You're a devious son of a bitch sometimes, Mike. We'll play it your way. Now, can I ask about your domestic arrangements?'

'Sorry, ma'am, I'm not with you.'

'It seems your seductive charm has reached the rank of superintendent, I don't want you to get ideas that it could reach any higher.'

'Hang on,' Nash objected. 'Ruth's only staying at my place because she couldn't get a hotel room. Nothing more than that.'

'Really? OK, I'll believe you, this once. I did wonder, but then I got to thinking about this man Marshall. Perhaps the reason you're so keen to prove him innocent is you've something in common.'

Nash frowned. 'Sorry, I'm not with you.'

'Marshall's wife was murdered, and by the sound of it, he's never got over that. And much the same thing happened to you. There's your common bond.'

'I guess so, ma'am.'

'Right, in that case I'll say no more about it.'

'Yes, ma'am.'

'Now, I'll have to think up some tale for the Chief Constable of Yorkshire Central.'

'Can you manage not to tell him anything, ma'am? Not yet at any rate. Not until we've more proof.'

O'Donnell considered this. 'I'm not in favour of all this secrecy,' she sighed. 'But sadly, given the circumstances, I don't see how it can be avoided. But, Mike, please try and get this cleared up as quickly as possible. With such an exceptional situation, I'm even prepared to tolerate some unconventional methods, as long as it gets the job done. You understand what I mean?'

When Nash emerged from the meeting, Ruth was waiting. 'How did it go?'

Nash smiled. 'Carte blanche.'

All the way back to Helmsdale and long afterwards, Nash remembered the chief constable's words. Was it true? Was that why he was so prejudiced in favour of a man he'd never met, had only spoken to on the phone once? And although he convinced himself time after time that he'd got over what happened to Stella, perhaps that sort of thing never truly goes away.

The wind that blew across Roundhay Park seemed to be coming directly from the Arctic. Scudding grey clouds threatened rain, or possibly snow. It was no day for walkers and the park was all but deserted. The two figures who met by one of the benches alongside the footpath were muffled tight against the weather. It had the added advantage of making them virtually unrecognizable.

'Are you sure all this was necessary?'

'Absolutely. Stop worrying. Everything's going according to plan.'

'That's easy for you to say. You're not the one who'll be in the lime-light if it goes pear-shaped.'

'It won't go pear-shaped. That's why we've taken such stringent precautions.'

'The latest event is drawing a lot of attention.'

'We're playing for high stakes, far higher than before. You know the consequences if we fail. Think about that and compare the risk against the potential rewards.'

'But was it necessary?'

'It was prudent housekeeping.'

'For fuck's sake, Harry, you make it sound so normal. We're talking about murder in case you've forgotten.'

'Listen, we've both been in the construction industry a long time. If I were to tell you what the bridge supports on the M1 contain for example you wouldn't be so fucking squeamish about a few slit throats.'

'It still makes me nervous.'

'If it eases your political conscience, it should be over now. We've achieved almost everything we planned. Once the election and the takeover are done with, we'll be free and clear. Then the way will be open for us to really clean up.'

'What if somebody ties us in to those murders?'

'Who's going to do that? The point of the whole exercise was to dispose of anybody who could blow the whistle on us. Now they're out of the way. Nobody else knows anything except the paymaster and he's too deeply involved to harm us without harming himself. Besides, I've enough on him to scare him shitless. He doesn't even know what's been going on yet. But he soon will.'

'Won't the people we're paying panic?'

'It'll act as a timely warning for them not to step out of line.'

'What about Brown?'

'I have my own plan for dealing with Brown. I'll tell you about it soon.'

'I sometimes wonder if there's anything you're not capable of to get your own way?'

'You're happy enough to go along with it, you've never complained about the end results.'

'Yes, and that frightens me too.'

'I suggest you continue with your campaign, leave the rest to me.'

The ranks of the party faithful attending their candidate's first public meeting were swelled by a large press contingent. As by-elections go the result was a foregone conclusion, the only speculation being the size of the majority. There was considerably more interest in the candidate, for he was regarded as something special. Political editors have an instinct second to none for such matters, and there'd been whispers.

The meeting wasn't much out of the ordinary but the candidate was certainly impressive. The pressmen, more interested in style than content, watched keenly. He gave a short speech, starting with what was becoming a likely catchphrase: 'Let me begin with my surname. It is pronounced like a body of men, not a man's body.' This was obviously intended as an ice-breaker before inviting his audience to ask questions. Abandoning the stage, and with the aid of a roving microphone, he took to the body of the hall. He sat on a chair facing his questioners. There, at the same level as the audience, he answered their queries about his background. He told them how he'd started in the construction industry, how he'd built up Coningsby Developments, and imparted some of his philosophy along with his biography.

There was little new in what he said, nor, to be fair was that the issue. It was the candidate who was being judged, by both the party members and the press. Neither was disappointed.

The passengers felt the change as soon as the aircraft touched down. The contrast between England and Barbados in January was stark. Even with the terminal building to protect them, they shivered from the cold.

Having queued with typical British patience at passport control, they formed a massive discontented scrum around the carousels of baggage. There is something about the reluctance of these devices to disgorge luggage that brings out the worst in people. The Barbados passengers were no exception. Eventually, with the safe recovery of their cases completed, they got through customs clearance into the spartan surroundings of the arrivals hall.

Such is the nature of British holidaymakers that the first things they require on returning home are a newspaper and a cup of tea. Nor were the Barbados passengers about to break this tradition.

One of the passengers walked purposefully across to the kiosk and queued for a paper. Having bought one of the tabloids he returned to his wife who was standing sentinel over their luggage. On his way he glanced idly at the paper's front page, then stopped dead. He skim-read the text, muttered, 'Good God!' and continued to the baggage guardian. 'What do you say we go get the car and head straight home?'

'Why, Chris, is something wrong?'

'No. But the car will be warm, the house will be warm and this place is bloody freezing.'

Even after long years of marriage Julie Davidson was never sure when Chris was lying. There surely couldn't be anything in the lurid headlines to upset him?

'We'll have to stop somewhere to buy milk.'

'No problem. Let's get out of here.'

As he drove, Davidson couldn't get the newspaper's front page out of his mind. The sooner he got to a telephone the better.

'Hello, boss. It's Chris Davidson.'

'*I thought you might be in touch today. I take it you've read the papers?*'

'Yes, boss. They gave me one hell of a shock.'

'*I can imagine. I would have forewarned you, but you will go swanning off on these fancy holidays.*'

'Is there going to be trouble?'

'*No, why should there be? The action we took was precisely to avoid any trouble.*'

'I don't like it, boss. It makes me nervous.'

'*Relax, Chris, it's over now. That side of the operation at least. There's plenty more to do in other areas. We can start moving now there's nobody in a position to pose a threat.*'

'What about my contacts? They're going to be as twitchy as hell.'

'*That won't do any harm, so long as they twitch in silence. Make sure you get that message over to them. That's your first priority. Tell them what's happened is a result of people twitching. Make them aware that if anyone breaks ranks we'll deal with them. That should keep the twitching unobtrusive. You might also remind them what they stand to lose: their liberty, for example.*'

'Yes, boss, but I must say I'm still nervous.'

'*I don't have to remind you what you have to lose, do I? They tell me your sort get a rough time of it inside. The other prisoners make sure of that. I don't need to remind you exactly what evidence I have, do I?*'

'No, boss.'

'*I'm so glad about that. It would have been an added burden to replace you at this stage of proceedings.*'

chapter fifteen

Lisa was in Helmsdale CID suite before anyone else arrived and began reading through the files. The phone rang.

'There's a man on the phone insisting he speaks to someone in CID,' the community support officer told her.

'DC Andrews speaking. Can I help you?'

He identified himself before stating, 'I'm a private detective. I was covered by client confidentiality, but that no longer applies. I can tell you that Alan Marshall has been living at Woodbine Cottage on the Winfield Estate since his release from prison. I was asked to keep an eye on him.'

'Thank you, but we are already aware of that.' She smiled as she replaced the phone and looked up, startled. She'd been so engrossed she hadn't noticed Superintendent Edwards enter.

Ruth smiled. 'You're still wondering what's going on, I'll bet?'

Lisa nodded.

'OK, let me fill you in with a few details. You're going to be rather surprised. Particularly when I tell you what has happened, and what's going to happen. You know a fair amount already, but there's more to it than that: much, much, more.'

Later, Nash received copies of the documents removed from Brown's flat. Attached to them was a note from Charlie Russell asking Nash to ring him.

'That was a very interesting flat,' Charlie said when Nash reached him. 'And there are a set of prints on the documents belonging to, of all people, Alan Marshall.'

'Really! The thought did cross my mind, but I dismissed it.'

'We're still waiting for the analysis of the boiler suit, but it has been confirmed that the stains are human blood. Apart from that, we found an array of weapons in a secret compartment at the back of a wardrobe. These included seven knives and three automatic pistols. Ballistics confirms that two of the pistols match ones used in unsolved murders here, believed to have been contracts. I'll let you know more ASAP.'

Nash sat pondering the new information. How had Marshall known where to go? Had Brown returned and caught him? Now, they had both disappeared. So where were they?

A week later it was a question being asked by others. It was being asked by Barry and Shirley Dickinson and by Lisa Andrews, by Superintendent Dundas and DS Smailes as well as those who were paying Brown. Friend and foe alike were equally baffled. Marshall hadn't phoned, nor had he communicated in any way with his allies. Nor had they been able to contact him. Lisa had tried, Barry Dickinson had tried, but Marshall's mobile remained unanswered. They scanned the papers, listened to news bulletins expecting to hear news of his arrest. Day succeeded day with no news as their concern grew. It seemed Marshall had performed a disappearing trick worthy of Houdini himself. If Nash had asked the right question of the right person he would have known. But the thought didn't occur to him until it was almost too late.

Marshall had been both lucky and unlucky. On his return to the station he spotted a police car parked on the forecourt. He considered catching a bus, but felt the danger of being recognized and trapped was too great. Nor would his cash run to the expense of a taxi, besides which that was almost as dangerous. There was no alternative but to risk walking, at least for the first part of the journey.

His luck changed once he was clear of the city. He knew the centre of York well, from when he and Anna had spent much of their leisure time there. The ancient city had hardly changed, and by using a complicated series of back street short cuts he was able to avoid contact with much of the pedestrian traffic until he reached the outer ring road. Beyond that his luck was definitely in the ascendency as he reached a small transport café.

It was one much frequented by lorry drivers. There was risk involved in going inside, but he was hungry, and had just made up his mind to brave the danger when he was approached by the driver of an HGV that had just pulled into the parking area. 'Excuse,' the driver's English was heavily accented, 'you are of local area perhaps?'

Marshall looked past the man at the lettering on the curtain-sided truck. 'Certainly nearer than Warsaw,' he suggested, then saw the man's puzzled frown. 'Yes, I'm a local,' he added.

'I am trying,' the man held up a clipboard for Marshall to read, 'to reach a place called Helmisdale. Do you know of such?'

Marshall stared at the sheet in disbelief. 'Helmsdale,' he corrected automatically. 'Yes, I know Helmsdale very well. In fact, that's where I'm going. If you give me a ride there, I'll show you the best way; take you right where you need to be.'

The driver smiled. 'Then today is my fortunate day.'

'You and me both,' Marshall agreed.

After the driver dropped him off at the junction of the Helmsdale to Kirk Bolton road, Marshall tried the Dickinsons' phone, but with no success. From there, he would have to walk. He glanced at his watch. The time he'd gained by getting the lift meant he should reach his destination before dark, even with the short hours of daylight at that time of year. He wondered briefly if the police would have maintained a presence at Woodbine Cottage; then remembered something Lisa Andrews had told him, about how short-staffed they were due to the flu epidemic.

It was curious, he reflected, that he'd started thinking of her as Lisa, rather than DC Andrews. She was a very pretty girl, and if circumstances had been different. . . . That in itself was strange, because Marshall hadn't thought of a woman in that way for a long, long time. She knew the worst about him, but that hadn't seemed to deter her. Was that because she found him attractive? Marshall took himself to task. No way would a girl like Lisa be interested in someone like him. She was merely being kind-hearted.

*

Almost before he realized it, Marshall reached the lane leading to the cottage. If things had been normal, he would have headed straight down the lane. Instead, he pushed his way through a gap in the hedge, skirted the field, where the ruts caused by the tractor contained puddles that were beginning to ice over. It was going to be a bitterly cold night, no weather to be out in the open. His breath was already forming a slight mist in front of him as he walked. He reached the edge of the field where it bordered a strip of woodland. The wood stretched all the way to the cottage and beyond. To anyone less familiar with the area, the dense entanglement of briar and bracken would have presented a formidable obstacle, but Marshall knew them well; knew where to find the narrow deer paths; knew which routes to follow that would enable him to reach the cottage without being seen. Moreover, he knew the vantage points from which he'd be able to spot anyone waiting in or around the cottage.

Brown was annoyed. More than that, he was cold and uncomfortable. He hated the countryside. He was used to cities, with all their hustle and bustle of activity. Out here in the wilds, the silence was eerie. Worse still, just as he was becoming accustomed to the silence, some creature or other would let loose an unnerving screech or yelp. For a cold-blooded killer, Brown was close to fear, something he was more used to inspiring in his victims. Despite that, he'd a job to do. His orders were to dispose of Alan Marshall. He felt certain sooner or later Marshall would return here, and when he did, Brown would be waiting. His certainty was based on one stark fact. With police forces throughout the land searching for him, the fugitive had nowhere else to go. Brown sneered at the thought that the police hadn't the sense to work that out. He had, and when he completed his work he would be well paid for it. The sum he'd demanded was a huge one, but he knew his employer was extremely wealthy. Men like Harry wouldn't flinch at the price. That was how they got where they were.

Brown examined his surroundings and wondered how

Marshall could stand living here, could stand the silence and the solitude. The place was little more than a hovel by Brown's standards. No TV, none of what he would class as luxuries. Very few necessities even. No modern conveniences; how on earth did Marshall manage? And how did he amuse himself, out here alone on those long winter evenings? Sure, there were books; plenty of them, although the titles of most of them were incomprehensible to Brown. And there was a good quality hi-fi, but when Brown turned his attention to the CD collection, he found they were of music he'd never heard of. Almost all of them seemed to be classical.

It was as he was examining the discs that Brown felt a faint draught. He turned and glanced towards the front door, his hand reaching automatically for his knife. He slid the weapon, with its wickedly long, wickedly sharp blade, out of its sheath. The front door was closed. The draught hadn't come from there. He looked to his right, from where he could see through into the kitchen. That room too was deserted, but he thought the kitchen door might be slightly ajar.

Brown felt that familiar sensation that gripped him before he went into action; the clawing of nervous tension in his stomach. He moved slowly, cautiously towards the kitchen, slid almost sideways through the door, the knife held out in front of him, ready to strike. The room was empty. He frowned, certain he'd closed the door. So, how had it come open? He crossed the floor in three lithe strides and slammed the door shut. He reached forward and tugged at the handle. The door came open. He repeated the manoeuvre a second and third time. Obviously the catch wasn't engaging properly. Like everything else in this tumbledown ruin, he thought. He closed it and slid the bolt across. Now, no stray gust of wind could cause it to open accidentally. Had Brown known more of the countryside, or possessed a little fieldcraft, he would have realized that on a still, frost-laden afternoon, the door would not have opened of its own volition.

He returned to the sitting room and sank into the solitary armchair. This place was really getting on his nerves. Before long he'd get in his car and drive back home, he'd been away too long. Sod Marshall, sod Harry. The job could wait another day. He'd give it until dusk. After that, bollocks to it. He'd been sitting there for a few minutes before he heard a noise. It was very faint, a sort of scratching sound. What the hell was it? And where the hell was it coming from? Within the cottage, that was certain. Not the kitchen, he could tell by the direction. He listened again. It must be coming from the bedroom; that, or the bathroom.

Brown got to his feet, slipped the knife from its sheath again, and started towards the door. He flung it open and entered the bedroom. Empty. He inched his way to the bathroom. Flung that door wide and stepped quickly through, too quickly for anyone lying in wait. Empty again. He turned back into the bedroom. As he did so, he heard the sound again. He stopped. It was close now. But where?

Suddenly, the sound changed, became a creak. At the same time, he saw a vague shadow moving to his left. Brown struck out with his knife. It jarred against something hard, with a teeth-grating screech. The knife had hit the mirror on the inside of the wardrobe door. He stared at his own reflection. This bloody dump of a house! Doors opening all on their own; things grating and screeching. In the mirror, Brown saw the shadow of something move behind him. He turned and struck out. The knife plunged into something soft. Brown drove it home with all his strength, pulling it upward at the same time in a flesh-tearing wrench. At the same moment he felt something strike him hard on his temple.

Marshall stood in front of the open wardrobe looking at the prone figure on the floor. He kicked the knife away, before glancing ruefully at the ruined pillow in his hand. Feathers from it were drifting down towards the unconscious man in a tiny blizzard. He tossed the pillow on to the bed, causing another snowstorm; then untied the string he'd attached to the doorknob. The device had worked a treat, distracting Brown and giving Marshall time to get into position to strike. As had the trick of opening the kitchen door, then scooting round to the front, where he'd waited until he heard the sound of the kitchen door slamming.

He reached down and started winding the string round the killer's wrists. To ensure he didn't try and free himself, Marshall twined the loose end round the man's neck. If he struggled too hard, all he'd do was strangle himself. Now, what to do with him? The sensible thing would be to hand him over to the police. But that would only achieve half a result. It wouldn't give Marshall what he wanted: the name of the man who'd employed Brown. The man who'd paid to have Anna killed. Or the motive for her murder. Only Brown could give him those answers, or some of them at least.

He reached into the wardrobe and removed a leather belt from a pair of jeans. He strapped it tightly round Brown's ankles, grabbed the man's shirt collar and dragged him unceremoniously out of the bedroom into the lounge. He barely noticed the twinge of pain in his arm. He certainly noticed Brown's head hitting the doorframe, but if it bothered him, he didn't show it.

He dumped the killer, who showed no sign of coming to, in the middle of the floor, wondering briefly if he'd overdone it: hit him too hard. He gave a mental shrug; what the hell, if he was dead, so what. He left the comatose figure and began rummaging through the cupboards, removing every item he would need. Every so often he glanced through into the lounge. His prisoner was still showing no sign of life. Marshall turned his attention to the freezer. He took out only those items he could cook simply.

He knew he couldn't stay here. At any point the police might come along and arrest him. Marshall wasn't going to allow that to happen. Certainly not until he'd spent some time alone with his prisoner. Time during which, Marshall felt sure, he'd be able to persuade Brown to tell him everything he knew.

During his time in prison Marshall had made few acquaintances. Given his fearsome reputation, most prisoners had steered well clear of him. Only his neighbour, however, had become as close as you could get to a friend in such a place. And from him, Marshall had learned one or two tricks. Tricks he'd never thought he'd need to employ. One of them had been how to dislocate a man's shoulder. Another was supposedly guaranteed to make even the toughest man talk. And Marshall felt sure his prisoner wasn't that tough.

chapter sixteen

Tara examined herself carefully in the bedroom mirror. She inspected her appearance critically, although she knew she was at the peak of her attractive best. It wasn't vanity; she knew she was more than pretty, she was stunningly beautiful. She passed a brush thoughtfully through her long blonde hair, pausing to inspect her carefully manicured and expertly enamelled nails. Satisfied, she stood straight, allowing the sheer negligee to fall open. Her figure was close to perfection but even then Tara wasn't satisfied. She swung round, brushing the negligee to one side. She craned her neck to inspect her posterior. No sagging: the result of a rigorous exercise routine devised by her personal trainer.

Harry was happy to pay for anything to retain and enhance Tara's desirability. And Harry did desire her. Tara smiled at the thought. When they had met two years earlier, he'd wasted no time in making her aware of his feelings. It was at a cocktail party; she was married, he was twice divorced. He'd walked across to her and smiled. 'I'm Harry Rourke and I want to go to bed with you.'

Tara hadn't known whether to slap his face or walk out. In the end she'd done neither. There was something appealing in the boldness of the statement, the roguish smile that accompanied it. 'What about my husband?' she'd objected.

'No thanks, just you.'

The following day, shortly after her husband left for work, a huge bouquet of flowers arrived. The card accompanying them reiterated the message. She hid the card, put the wrapping paper in the bin and told her husband she'd bought the flowers. Within a month she and Harry had become lovers. Within six months she moved into his mansion on the western outskirts of Leeds. Harry had an appetite for her that was close to insatiable. Tara found no difficulty with this, indeed she enjoyed his attention. It wasn't until well into their relationship that she realized how wealthy and powerful her lover was.

Recently however, Harry had been less demanding. That worried Tara. Was he tiring of her? She knew she was nowhere near his intellectual equal. Would he weary of her beauty, hanker for something more? Tara wasn't used to being ignored. She knew he'd a lot on his plate running his massive business, and she was aware that he had some extra problems at work. Tara couldn't help him with these but realized he worked better when he was relaxed and content. She could think of only one way to help him achieve relaxation and contentment.

Although it was Sunday morning, Harry would be at his computer. For Harry the working week didn't stop on Friday evening. It was how he'd achieved success. It was the only formula he knew for retaining it. This was all very well, but Tara wanted him. She wanted the Harry she'd met, the Harry who had swept her off her feet. The Harry she had difficulty in matching for the energy of his lovemaking.

Tara stripped off the negligee and removed her bra and pants. She went across to Harry's wardrobe and selected one of his shirts. She knew this would get him aroused if anything could.

Harry Rourke was sitting staring at his computer screen, exactly as Tara had predicted. He hated these damned things. He was a practical man, a man used to dealing with problems on the ground, not on a screen. There was something impersonal about working through a computer. Harry solved problems best when he could be on site and look into a man's eyes. Check the materials were as they should be, that the work was being done as he'd ordered it. That was what construction was about, not a row of figures on a screen. He knew he'd have to get to grips with this technology. It was the only way to handle all he was now being pressured to take on.

Tara appeared by his side. She gently eased his chair away from the desk, swivelling it so he was forced to look at her, not at the screen. 'Harry,' her voice was little more than a whisper, 'Harry, how many excavators do you own?'

He blinked in surprise at the unexpected question. 'Twenty-six.'

'Is that enough to cope with the work you have on?'

'More than enough.' He grimaced. 'I could do with another couple of contracts to keep them busy, thanks to this bloody recession.'

Tara leaned forward slightly. The shirt gaped open. 'Well, in that case, darling.' She straddled his knees with her thighs. The shirt rode up almost to her waist. 'Do you think you could spare some time to make the earth move for me?'

Much later, as they were sitting in easy companionship in the conservatory, Tara asked him what the problem was. 'I know it's to do with work and I probably won't understand, but maybe just talking about it will help.'

'I'm sorry I haven't been my usual self recently. Business is slack and we're not getting the contracts we should. The problem is I can't see what we're doing wrong.'

'If you're not getting them, who is?'

'Coningsby mainly, though it's not just them.'

'What do you intend doing about it?'

'I've already taken steps to remedy matters. Very painful decisions have had to be made and I can't expect others to make them for me. It means dispensing with a lot of people, some I've worked with for years.'

'I've received the writ from the returning officer. The election date's set for April 27th.'

'That's one part of the operation under way. I had a phone call from Darren Cowan. He's sending the draft offer document for the takeover through.'

'We'll have to time it right, or we might have to pay too much.'

'I don't see that as a problem.'

'How come you're so confident?'

'Leave it to me.'

'We could do with more work. Contracts aren't that plentiful.

Having said that, I got the figures from the auditors today. Last year's results will look terrific.'

'So will ours. The rivalry has done both companies good. When we put them together we'll do even better. The dip in work looks to be no more than a seasonal thing, but it'll help make the price look reasonable.'

'Where do you think we should pitch the bid?'

'Somewhere around twenty-five per cent of the valuation Cowan comes up with.'

'Will we get away with as little as that?'

'By the time I've finished we will.'

'I'll be glad when it's over. For one thing, it'll make a change to meet in more civilized surroundings than a rain-sodden park.'

Darren Cowan was a manipulator. In some this would be a shortcoming. In Darren's case it was an asset. He worked in the City and his career was studded with deals he'd pulled off for clients, sometimes against the odds, invariably using his manipulative skills. Recently these had been less in demand than in the heyday of the nineties, but Darren was usually able to keep one or two projects in hand. A new prospect had recently landed on his desk and although the takeover market had been quiet of late this was a deal worth his undivided attention. A hostile takeover bid of one construction company by another would grab the headlines. Not only in the City columns, but also on the front pages of the nationals. It would be Darren's name that would be associated with it. There were problems, but Darren was well capable of handling them. The deal had taken a while to put together. Secrecy was essential. There had been the added snag of obtaining the necessary information. Both predator and victim were private companies which made the job harder. With public companies it was easy. They had to divulge information by law. Private companies weren't bound by those restrictions.

The problems were more than offset by the potential rewards. Darren knew he'd get a massive commission if the bid succeeded. Equally important, he'd recently learned it was likely to give him considerable favour in political circles. The head of the bidding company was a by-election candidate and Darren had discovered that once the man was returned to Parliament he would be in the ascendancy. Darren loved power. The power he could wield himself, and association with others who could command higher levels of influence. If Darren pulled the deal off he'd be able to swing considerable weight in Westminster. He wasn't about to risk losing the opportunity of grasping at the coat tails of someone on their way up. He'd bent his not inconsiderable talents to consideration of the bid details with renewed enthusiasm.

Acting on his client's instructions he'd put together a bid based on a conservative estimate of the target company's worth and sent them for approval. He'd been expecting his client to agree an offer price in excess of that. Now he stared at the figures in disbelief. What on earth was the client thinking of? There was no way the bid could be successful on the terms they'd suggested. Whatever Darren thought his client's reaction would be, he'd not been expecting a bid price set below the basic market valuation; and certainly not as low as this. He knew he'd have to check that the bidder hadn't made a mistake before he authorized the typing of an offer document.

Darren wondered how his client, a shrewd businessman, had justified arriving at such a low figure. He was used to the wheeling and dealing that accompanied takeovers; was used to the strategies that went along with them. He couldn't make sense of the reasoning and logic behind this one. He reached for the telephone.

The early morning light filtered round the edges of the curtains. Harry Rourke lay on his back wide awake. Tara's head was on his shoulder, her hair tickling him slightly. She stirred in her sleep and her leg brushed against his in an unconsciously erotic movement.

Harry was unable to resist. To be fair, he didn't make much effort. He turned and began to caress the smooth curve of her waist. Tara muttered something, low and unintelligible. A protest? If so he ignored it. Seconds later he realized it hadn't been a protest.

Later, when he'd left the bedroom, the phone rang. Tara answered it. 'No,' she told the caller, 'he's taking a shower.' She listened. 'OK, I'll tell him the minute he comes out.'

'Sid Robinson wants you to ring him on his mobile,' she told Harry when he emerged. 'Said it was more than urgent. He sounded to be in a panic. Who is he?'

'He's the site supervisor for our Wakefield contract. It's not like him to panic. I wonder why the mobile, there's a landline on site.' Harry reached for the phone. 'Sid, what's the problem?'

He listened for what seemed an age. 'Oh shit, no. How the fuck did that happen? You're joking! Bastards! Send the men to that café down the road until we find out what's going on. Set up a meeting with whoever's in charge. I'll be there as fast as I can.'

He put the phone down and stared unseeingly at her. Tara had never seen such an expression on his face. Not so much bleak as ruthless. 'What's gone wrong?'

'Sid got a call-out half an hour ago. The site cabin's been gutted. Police and fire brigade reckon its arson.'

Building sites aren't the tidiest of places. When Harry Rourke pulled his BMW as close as he was allowed, he saw the extent of the damage immediately. He identified himself to the police officer and ducked under the incident tape. Sid Robinson hurried over with a senior fire officer and a uniformed policeman at his heels. He introduced them. The fire chief took over. 'We believe somebody opened the tap on the diesel tank, let the fuel flow towards the cabin, then torched it. The first thing to go up was the tank, but the cabin wasn't far behind.'

'What a bloody mess. And because it's arson the insurance won't pay out, so we'll have to stand the loss,' Harry said grimly.

'Mr Rourke, have you any idea who might have a grudge against you?' the police officer asked.

'How long a list do you want? I'm running a business. I make enemies. People I've fired, competitors, environmental objectors to construction; you name them, I've upset them.'

'Anybody specific, that you've crossed swords with recently? Anybody who's made any threats against you personally, or the company?'

'No one in particular,' Harry answered. 'How did they get access to the site? It should have been secured overnight.'

'I can answer that.' Robinson pointed across the site. 'They cut a hole in the security fence behind those bushes. Must have used a big pair of wire cutters, took out a six-foot section.'

'That doesn't sound like kids or chance vandals,' Rourke said. 'How long before we can get back on site and start trying to tidy this bloody mess up?'

'The forensic people will want to be in as soon as the site's safe and the temperature round the cabin and the tank has cooled. They'll need a fair amount of time. I reckon you'll be looking at the day after tomorrow.'

Rourke groaned. 'More expensive delay.' He turned to Robinson. 'Right, I'll organize a new cabin, another tank and set delivery for the day after tomorrow. In the meantime I want that fence securing. Properly mind, not a patched-up job. Then I want the whole site checked over, every inch, and I want you to organize site security. Get on to the phone people and have their engineers here for the day after tomorrow. I want this site up and running by lunchtime. Any problems, call me at the office.'

An incident involving an arson attack on a site operated by Alan Marshall's former employers might have seemed significant if the CID team had made the connection. However, the report didn't reach any of the officers who were familiar with the Marshall case.

chapter seventeen

Extra pressure had been caused by the arson attack. If Harry Rourke's hopes were for an improvement, they were dashed by another phone call. The call came from Sheffield where another Broadwood Construction site was due to start operating. The site manager was almost incoherent with rage and mortification as he reported the calamity.

'We brought the machinery down from Leeds as you ordered. We had the two excavators, the loading shovel and the dump trucks ready to start work tomorrow. I got a call from the police an hour ago. I'm at the site now. Somebody cut the fuel lines on all the machines and torched the lot. All that's left is a pile of twisted metal, fit only for scrap.'

'Oh fucking hell, not another. If I get hold of the bastard who's doing this I'll bloody kill him. I'm on my way. Make sure the police and fire people are still there. I'll be with you in about an hour.'

'What is it this time?' Tara asked.

Harry seethed as he told her. 'One,' he added, 'I could have put down as a random act of vandalism, two looks like a deliberate campaign.'

'Will it cost a lot?'

Harry grimaced. 'I don't want to think about it. We're talking six figures for the damage at Wakefield alone. Fuck knows what this will cost. I can't go on losing money like this.'

Broadwood Construction's head office personnel were dreading another incident. Harry Rourke's volatile temper was on continuous fast boil these days. Business was tight anyway and the company had missed out on several massive contracts. They were contracts Harry had been confident of getting. To lose out to their main rivals Coningsby was especially galling. As if all that wasn't bad enough, the vandalism was the last straw.

Even Freddie, Harry Rourke's trusted right hand man, had been unable to placate him and if Freddie couldn't, nobody could. When news filtered through of the third and most violent attack to date many of those working in Broadwood's impressive head office building began wishing they'd chosen a less stressful occupation, such as a Formula One racing driver.

'They've really done it this time.' Harry slammed the phone down.

'Go on, Harry, tell me the worst,' Tara said quietly.

'If I could get my hands on the bastards I'd kill them. They've only rammed a fucking excavator into the sodding wall of Kirkbridge Shopping Centre, that's all.'

'Oh God, is it badly damaged?'

'I don't bloody well know until I get there. The site manager reckons the wall will have to be completely rebuilt. That's going to cost a mint. Apart from that, the centre's due to open in two months. There's fat chance of that happening, which means we'll incur penalties for late completion. The bill could run into millions.'

If Harry Rourke had been angry, now he appeared depressed. He'd spent the last two days poring over the figures Freddie had collated, figures that represented the potential cost of the attacks on their sites. To add to the estimates of the physical damage, which no insurance company would cover, was the consequential loss amount in contract delays and penalty clauses. To add insult to injury, Harry had been forced to authorize the expenditure of extremely large sums for a security firm to undertake round the clock patrolling of every Broadwood site.

The bottom line figure was the cause of Harry's depression. The noughts, neatly typed in, leapt from the page as if they were in 3D. Within a matter of weeks his personal wealth had been more than halved. Although Broadwood Construction was a limited company, Harry was the sole shareholder. The loss to the company was mirrored by the loss to Harry.

Tara looked across the dining table at her lover. 'Harry, talk to me. Tell me about it. Don't just keep staring at your plate and pushing your food around. That won't help. Neither will bottling it up, you have to talk about it.'

Harry looked up and smiled but it was a pale imitation of the smile that had captivated her. 'I'm bloody bad company, sorry love,' he told her. 'This vandalism business has brought us damned close to ruin and that's a fact.'

'Go on, tell me,' she urged.

'Where to start, that's the problem. There's so much.'

Slowly she coaxed the bad news out of him. 'That's appalling,' she sympathized. 'Will you be able to survive, keep the company afloat?'

'What's matter? Worried about your lifestyle?' he snapped. Then he saw the hurt expression on her face. 'I'm sorry, that wasn't fair.'

'Harry, I love you, not your money. I didn't ask for any of this.' Tara gestured at their opulent surroundings. 'If it all goes, and we finish up in a one bedroom flat I don't care. I only care about you, Harry.'

'I don't deserve you, Tara. I'm sorry I said that, but I was so pissed off I wasn't thinking straight.'

'Who did this? Who hates you that much?'

'Don't think I haven't asked myself that time and again. The answer is I've not got a clue. I've done some dodgy things in my time. You can't get to the top in this industry and remain a saint. Off the cuff, I can't think of anyone alive who hates me that much.'

Tara tried to lighten his mood. 'Well, if it isn't anybody alive we've really got a problem. Mind you, I've yet to hear of a ghost capable of setting fires and ramming walls with excavators,' she added thoughtfully.

His smile was a little brighter; the worried frown a little less noticeable. Tara stood up and walked round the table. She stood directly in front of him, one arm on his shoulder. 'Let's leave the dinner plates. I can sort them in the morning. I can think of something that will cheer you up.' Some tactics have never been known to fail, Tara thought later; much later.

'I have a concern.'

'What's wrong?'

'I haven't been able to contact Brown.'

'Is that important?'

'Not in itself no, however, I would like to know where he is so I can arrange for him to tell the police everything he knows.'

'What? You must be mad.'

'Not in the slightest. It isn't madness to want Brown to tell the police everything. I'm not just hoping for it. I'm counting on it.'

'I'm sorry. You've lost me.'

'If Brown tells the police everything, that'll include the identity of the person who's paying him.'

'What! Oh yes, now I've got it. That's absolute bloody genius.'

'Thank you. But if Brown isn't available we have a bit of a problem.'

'Yes, I can see that. How will you get round it?'

'I'm not sure yet. I've been ringing his number for the last couple of days, but there's been no reply. He doesn't have voice mail, and I wouldn't use it in any case. I'll just have to keep trying. If the worst comes to the worst we have our fallback.'

'You mean the man the police are seeking so strenuously?'

'Yes, but without success. I rather wish he was out of the equation. He still worries me.'

'Why should he worry you after all this time?'

'He always did. Call it fate, superstition, whatever you want. From the moment I met him, I had the notion he'd ruin everything.'

'He can't harm us now. He'll be caught soon, you'll see. Then they'll put him away for life.'

'They did that once before and look what happened. I'd be far happier if Brown gets to him first.'

'Maybe he already has. Maybe that's why you can't get hold of Brown. Because he's dealing with our other problem.'

'Anyway, with or without that being resolved, I think it's time we exerted more pressure. I've got all the evidence together. All we need to do now is post it off.'

Miles away, in Helmsdale CID suite, Mike Nash was also concerned about Marshall's fate. If, as Nash was now certain, Marshall had discovered Brown's flat and confronted him, what were the chances that Marshall would still be alive? And if he was alive, how had he managed to avoid recognition and capture, given that his face was on the front page of every newspaper, on TV screens during every news bulletin, and that every police officer in the country was on the lookout for him? As he waited for DC Andrews to report the result of her disciplinary interview, Nash sat at his desk, pondering the likely chain of events. Where would Marshall have gone? Where would he have felt safe? Safe, not only from the police, but more important, from the hired assassin, Brown, who was also missing. Although Russell and his colleagues had conducted surveillance at Brown's flat, he hadn't returned.

Brown would also be searching for Marshall, of that Nash was certain, aware that the killer wanted the bounty Nash felt sure there must be on Marshall's head. After a few moments' thought, the solution came to him. Of course: it was obvious. He smiled, wryly. How come it had taken so long? One man would be able to confirm the accuracy of his theory. He reached for the phone and his filofax simultaneously. He thumbed through the address section until he came to the letter W. Then he began to dial.

For the first part Lisa's interrogators had been fair, courteous and relaxed. They'd asked about Marshall, what her relationship with him had been, but only politely. Soon, however, things changed dramatically.

'How long have you and Marshall been lovers? How long have you been sleeping with him? Have you been to bed with him since he became a wanted man?'

'That's all lies,' she insisted angrily. 'I've only met Marshall a few times. I've never been to bed with him. I'm not even a friend of his.'

'We think differently, Andrews. If you're not in a relationship how come his fingerprints were found in your flat?'

145

'How the hell did you find them? You can't do that sort of thing. It's not legal.'

'You should read your procedures manual more closely. You'll find that when it comes to investigating misconduct, there is very little we can't do. So would you answer my question?'

'He visited my flat once to ask a favour.'

'When you knew he was wanted for the murders of Stuart Moran and Lesley Robertson?'

To the astonishment of both officers Andrews started to laugh.

'I'm glad you consider it funny,' the senior of them said angrily.

'Marshall couldn't possibly have murdered Moran and the woman. But everybody seems hell-bent on pursuing him for a crime he didn't commit instead of looking for the real murderer.'

'Very impressive.' The officer's drawl was bitingly sarcastic. 'And can you explain what your "friend" Marshall was doing in Leeds? Can you explain that, Andrews? Because unless you can and make it damned convincing, when you walk out of this office you'll be suspended from duty pending a full investigation. An enquiry that will seek to prove you should be dismissed from the force and face criminal charges as an accessory to murder. I suggest you do some fast talking, and some even faster thinking.'

If he'd expected to intimidate Andrews he misjudged her. Lisa stared at him and then leaned forward slightly, threateningly. 'I know nothing of what happened in Leeds. If you want to toss me out of the force; then go ahead. What you can't do is get me on a charge of being an accessory to murders that Marshall didn't commit.'

'You seem mighty sure of yourself, young lady.' The other investigator broke in. 'Would you mind telling us what makes you so certain these crimes weren't committed by Marshall when everyone else is convinced to the contrary?'

'Don't call me young lady again,' Lisa snarled. 'It's Detective Constable Andrews to you. That's number one. Number two: if I answer you, will you forgo the suspension? I don't think so. In that case we'll leave things as they stand. That's with you and all the other great detectives convincing themselves Alan Marshall's a mass murderer, when I know for a fact he's innocent. I rather like the thought of that. It will be such fun watching you all make arseholes of yourselves. So you'd better get on with it and do your worst.'

Twenty minutes later, her warrant card handed in, Miss Lisa Andrews walked out of Netherdale police station. She walked out with her head held high and a dangerous glint in her eye. She'd vented the heat of her temper on the investigators. What remained was an icy cold rage.

She reached Helmsdale and stalked into the CID suite, her face like thunder. Once inside, she stopped, her shoulders relaxed and a smile spread across her face. Nash and Binns had been looking at the paperwork. 'How did it go?'

'Like a dream. I'm now officially suspended, if you know what I mean. How's it going here?'

'I thought about where Marshall might have headed for, if he'd wanted to go to ground. Where better than the area he knows best? You've seen that forestry. You could search for someone in those woods for months without even coming close to them, unless you had heat-seeking sensors or whatever fancy gadgetry they use.'

'I take your point, Mike, but how will we find out if he's in there?'

'Well you can't sit about in your flat, that's for sure, so I'd like you to go find Alan Marshall.' Nash held out an envelope. 'These are copies of all the stuff we got from York. Ask Marshall to go through them and give me a call. Not on the station phone, though. He's got my mobile number.'

'But how? I mean, how will I find him?'

'Work it out, Lisa.'

'I'm sorry, Mike,' Andrews said after a while. 'Not everybody's got your brilliant mind.'

Nash grinned. 'Clara usually says devious, so brilliant makes a pleasant change. I suggest you go see his friend Barry Dickinson.'

'How do you know he can help? I mean how can you be sure?'

'Because I'm a detective. That's what detectives do. Barry Dickinson might know Marshall's there, or he might not, but I've just been talking to Sir Maurice Winfield. When I explained that I needed to talk to Marshall, he was most helpful. Tell Dickinson to ask Sir Maurice to put you in touch.'

'You mean Sir Maurice knows where Marshall is?'

'Not exactly, but he and some members of his staff know he's close by. Sir Maurice is convinced Marshall's innocent. As sure of it as we are. Given that conviction, and the fact that he doesn't answer to anyone, not even us, he was the logical choice for someone to help Marshall. How else has he survived all this time? He'd have to get supplies from somewhere.'

Shirley Dickinson was washing up when a car drove across the gravel yard and screeched to a halt opposite her window. She paused, staring out in astonishment, until a trickle of water up her forearm reminded her she was still holding a part-washed utensil.

She dropped the item back into the sink and looked round for a towel. As she peered outside she saw Lisa Andrews erupt from the car. The driver's door was hurled back into the frame with a resounding crash before she marched across the yard.

Shirley hurried to the back door to rescue it from Lisa's furious assault before the glass panes caved in. She opened it as wide as she could and stood in its shelter, half-expecting Lisa to stalk straight past her.

Instead Lisa looked at her, her face a mixture of emotions as anger vied with distress. She screwed up her nose and eyes in a fierce effort to control herself. She gave a hiccuping sob. 'I've been sacked,' she declared dramatically. 'I'm suspended from duty.'

Shirley took her hand and guided her inside. As she closed the door Lisa straightened up. 'I haven't really. That's just a ruse. I'll explain in a bit. That was just acting in case anyone was watching.'

'Do you think they might be?' Shirley's alarm was apparent.

'Probably. But don't worry. You're not in danger. Now, let me tell you what's going on. At least the part I know.'

Lisa had barely begun telling her tale when Barry returned from Winfield Manor. 'What's going on, Lisa?' Barry asked as he came in. 'Sir Maurice told me to make sure I was in the house tonight, at all costs. What does that mean?'

Lisa just smiled. 'I'm not sure, but I think it means that Alan will try to contact us tonight. We'll have to wait and see. The thing is, my flat has been bugged along with my phone, so I can't do much from there. I don't like to impose, but do you think I could use your spare room?'

'No problem at all. If we are being watched, I'll feel safer with someone else here when Barry's out. Added to that, you want to be on hand if and when Alan does get in touch. Besides, Nell's glad you're here,' Shirley told her. She looked across the room to where the Labrador was lying, her head between her paws and a soulful expression on her face. 'She's quiet now, that's because she's hoping some leftovers might fall into her bowl, but she's been extremely restless over the last few days. Normally you hardly notice she's here, but lately she's been unable to settle. She prowls up and down the house for hour after hour, and when Barry takes her out he has no end of trouble even though he keeps her on the lead.'

'Shirley's right,' Barry confirmed. 'I've never known her behave like this. Usually, she's the most placid of animals. I think she's pining for Alan. In fact I'm sure she is.'

'Maybe you could take her for a walk?' Shirley suggested.

Lisa opened the back door, slipped the lead over the dog's head and guided her towards the lane. The dog seemed bent on heading in the opposite direction. Even when she had completed her comfort break the Labrador continued to pull against the restraining leash towards the woods.

The afternoon was cold, cold and grey enough for Lisa to wonder if it might snow. The first impression she got of the forest was of sound. There was a gentle breeze blowing, stirring what few leaves were left on the trees. There had been a frost overnight, sharp enough to penetrate even where the woodland provided shelter. Lisa heard the grass crackling with every step.

Their passage disturbed a variety of game. More than once a woodcock rose with a squawk of alarm before hurtling into zigzag flight away from them.

As they crossed one of the rides Lisa became aware of Nell's increased agitation. The dog was almost impossible to control and Lisa realized the sheer physical strength of the Labrador. At the same time she got the strange sensation that she was being watched. Several times she stopped and looked round. On two occasions she actually back-tracked a few paces so strong was the feeling, but she was unable to identify the cause for her concern.

It was after the second of these forays that disaster struck. Lisa caught her foot in a tangle of roots that tripped her and sent her sprawling headlong on to the woodland floor. As she fell her grip on the lead slackened. The Labrador, seizing the moment, shot from her grasp. Lisa watched helplessly as the dog hurtled forward into the thickest part of the wood, heedless of Lisa's despairing and anguished cries of, 'Nell, Nell. Come back, Nell.'

Lisa scrambled to her feet and dashed after the dog. With scant regard to the clinging, scratching thorns and briars she plunged into the undergrowth. She chased the dog for more than five minutes before she realized the futility of her efforts. She stopped and looked around. High banks of dense, seemingly impenetrable shrubs surrounded her on all sides. There was absolutely no trace of the path Lisa had left in her pursuit of the dog. No indication even of what direction to go in search of it. Lisa's heart didn't sink but that was only because her dejection was already absolute. She didn't know whether to swear or cry. In the end she did both.

She felt marginally calmer when she'd vented her feelings. She was lost. She'd lost Marshall's dog, the dog he loved. The only living thing he cared for. The day was becoming colder, the sky darker, the woods seemed suddenly more menacing. How could things get any worse? Lisa felt something brush gently against her face. She touched her cheek with her hand and it came away wet. To add to her misery it had started to snow. Things had just got worse.

chapter eighteen

'We have listening devices in place within her flat, in every room to be precise. In addition we have her telephone line and her mobile phone tapped, and we have a surveillance team in place watching her every movement.'

'What have they reported so far?'

'She left here and went to Netherdale to collect her belongings. She then drove to Helmsdale police station and on to Kirk Bolton to a cottage on the Winfield Estate, the one occupied by the gamekeeper and his wife. Their names are Barry and Shirley Dickinson. They're Marshall's closest friends. Andrews is still there. She hasn't used either her landline or her mobile.'

'It would be foolish to underestimate either the intelligence or the resourcefulness of this young woman. She knows we can't plant any listening device on the Dickinson house, nor can we tap their telephones, not without a warrant. All we have available is physical surveillance, and I would guess even that might be tricky, given the location.'

'That's absolutely right. We're doing what we can, but there are great difficulties in avoiding being detected. We have one man stationed in the woods close to the cottage. That's as much as we dare do. The car is parked a couple of hundred yards from the cottage towards the Netherdale road. We can't risk getting it closer.'

'Have they reported anything significant yet?'

'Not really. Andrews has gone for a walk in the woods with a dog. Because of the nature of the terrain it was impossible for our man to follow. All he can do is wait for her to return.'

The gentle soft light of the winter afternoon had become a harsh blurred white mass of dancing flakes. These had started small but now they were substantial, warning Lisa of the danger of her predicament.

The snow was settling, rendering the forest featureless. The frost-hardened ground assured that. Even if Lisa managed to force her way out of this morass of tangled undergrowth back to the ride, she had no idea which direction led to safety. She might finish up deeper in this enormous forest instead of escaping from it.

She became aware of another strange sensation, that of silence. Before the snow started the woods had seemed alive with sound, now there was none. No leaf rustled, no pheasant croaked its rusty yelp. 'Oh God, what have I done?' Lisa was overwhelmed by a sudden panic attack. 'How the hell am I going to get out of here?'

She heard a soft sound behind her. Not a cry or a growl, more like a clearing of the throat. She turned swiftly, staring into a pair of steadfast brown eyes. 'Nell,' she cried overjoyed. 'Where have you been? How are we going to get out of this mess?'

The Labrador loped easily across in front of Lisa and went into the narrowest possible gap in the briars. Lisa followed and found the going marginally easier. Ten minutes later they emerged into a ride Lisa assumed to be the one she'd left. She turned to her right and began to stride confidently towards where she thought the cottage lay. A single bark caused her to stop. She turned and looked back. The dog, which was now covered with snowflakes and had the appearance of an inside-out Dalmatian, turned and set off in the opposite direction.

Lisa was totally humiliated. As she meekly followed the dog she noticed that Nell had somehow slipped her lead. Although the snow was now at their backs, which made visibility a little better, conditions underfoot were worsening rapidly. It was with considerable relief that Lisa saw, some twenty minutes later, the edge of the wood appear as they turned a bend in the ride.

As she strode towards it Lisa realized another strange thing. Nell was ambling easily alongside her. All her earlier agitation had vanished. They reached the edge of the woods and Lisa paused, taking in the welcome sight of the Dickinsons' cottage. As she looked she noticed something blue draped over the back door handle. She walked across the snow-covered gravel and picked it up. She stared at the object in disbelief. It was Nell's lead.

Barry and Shirley listened with astonishment to Lisa's misadventure. Neither of them could offer an explanation. 'I know Nell's intelligent but I doubt if she could have managed that,' Barry stated as Shirley made coffee. She used the last of the milk from the bottle in the fridge. 'Barry, do me a favour. Pop out to the stable and get another six-pint carton of milk from the fridge. Bring a loaf out of the freezer at the same time.'

Barry returned five minutes later with the milk and bread. 'That's the last of the milk and there's no more bread,' he told Shirley as he placed them on the worktop.

'Nonsense, there were two cartons of milk in the fridge and another loaf in the freezer.'

'No, there aren't, I checked the fridge and looked inside every drawer in the freezer, but these are the last.'

Shirley had to inspect the evidence before she believed him. She stared at Barry and Lisa in perplexity. 'What on earth's going on? Apart from the bread and milk I'm certain there's a packet of sausages and one of bacon missing. We're going to have to start locking the outbuildings. I never thought we'd be burgled out here.'

The phone rang as Shirley was speaking. As Barry went through to the hall to answer it, Lisa asked Shirley, 'Who do you think might be responsible?'

'I don't know; some vagrant probably. Though to be fair we don't get many of them round here; certainly not at this time of the year.'

'Barry Dickinson speaking.'

Barry heard the voice, low, tense and barely more than a whisper. He didn't recognize the speaker. 'You've a lot of grey squirrels, especially in those silver birches to the west of the house. If I was you I'd go out right now and shoot one or two. If you do, be careful not to shoot the man standing beneath them: the one watching the house.' Then the line went dead.

Barry stared at the receiver for several seconds as if he'd never seen one before. He replaced it on the cradle and walked thoughtfully back into the kitchen.

'Who was on the phone?' Shirley asked.

Barry stared at her, then at Lisa. He glanced outside before replying. 'I haven't the foggiest idea.'

He repeated the strange message. 'Do you think it was someone trying to disguise their voice?' Lisa asked.

'I'm not sure. If it was they did a damned good job of it.'

'What are you going to do?' Shirley asked.

'I'm going to do what he said. Apart from the way I feel about squirrels, I want to know if someone is watching the house, and why. I'm going to take my .22 and go out of the french window in the lounge. That way I can get into the woods without being seen and come round from behind. You two stay in the kitchen.'

'Be careful,' Lisa cautioned him. 'Remember there must be two people watching the house.' She saw his surprised look and added, 'Whoever phoned must be watching too, or he wouldn't be able to pinpoint the other one.'

'I hadn't thought of that.'

He crossed to the gun cabinet and unlocked the door. He took out one of his rifles and fastened the telescopic sight to it. 'Don't panic if you hear gunshots,' he told them. 'I'll be aiming at squirrels.' He paused before adding, 'You only need worry if someone fires back.'

Barry walked through to the lounge. Silence descended on the house as they waited in trepidation.

It was a matter of no more than twenty yards to the edge of the wood. Once he'd gained the shelter of a bank of Scots pine, Barry glanced up. He noted that smoke from the chimney was drifting towards him, away from where the watcher was allegedly standing. He'd be able to get close without being scented or heard. He set off to get further into the forest under deeper cover.

Less than a quarter of a mile away the watcher stood in

abject misery. He was cold, he was wet and his legs ached from standing in one position for so long. He glanced at his watch and wondered if it needed regulating. He couldn't believe he still had forty-five minutes before his replacement arrived and he could get back into the warmth and comfort of the car.

He stamped his feet, although he had long since lost all feeling in them. He thought of the horror stories he'd been told of people contracting frostbite, then gangrene. As a boy he'd watched the film *Scott of the Antarctic* and remembered the heroic but doomed figure of Captain Oates. His morbid train of thought switched tracks. If he survived without getting frostbite he might catch pneumonia. The cold, damp conditions would be a fertile breeding ground for the disease. If not, he'd probably get the dreaded flu bug.

He shuddered and huddled deeper into the inadequate protection of his padded jacket. He'd imagined the garment would be sufficient for his needs. It wasn't. He felt sure the day could get no worse. Snow dropped from a branch overhead and landed with icy venom on his head and his shoulders, then slid down his neck inside the collar of his coat.

He revised his thoughts. The day had got worse. If he'd glanced upwards he would probably have seen the bright beady eye of the miscreant that had caused his discomfort. The grey squirrel peered down at the strange apparition below, before moving cautiously further out along the branch. Unaware of the scrutiny from above, the watcher had another problem to concern him. At least this was one discomfort he would be able to deal with.

No one likes being spied on. It creates a sense of outrage. That feeling overcame Barry as he saw the watcher standing in the exact position indicated by the caller. He scanned the surrounding area. The intruder appeared to be alone. He glanced up at the trees and was able to see at least three squirrels. Again the caller had been accurate. He was about to line up a shot at one of the squirrels when the watcher began to move.

Barry waited, then smiled when he saw what the man was doing. When he was certain the watcher was fully engaged, he shot the nearest squirrel. It fell to the ground no more than two feet from the watcher. The rifle shot, fired from no more than thirty yards away, caused instant panic. The falling corpse merely intensified the man's fear. He was trapped, unwilling to remain, temporarily unable to move. He called out. 'Help, don't shoot, please don't shoot.'

Barry moved from under cover. He saw with considerable satisfaction the large damp stain on the man's trousers that owed nothing to the weather. 'What the hell are you doing here?' he demanded. 'This is private land. You've no right to be here. You're trespassing.'

The watcher fastened his trousers up. The fleeting warmth on his legs was more than offset by the damp and humiliation. He knew there was nothing for it but to tell the truth. 'I'm a police officer,' he told Barry with an attempt at defiance. 'Put that gun down.'

Barry laughed. 'No way, Jose.'

The gun remained pointed at the watcher. 'If you're a police officer, which I very much doubt, you'll have no trouble explaining what you're doing in the middle of Sir Maurice Winfield's estate.'

'I'm not allowed to reveal any operational details.'

'Sorry.' Barry lifted the rifle. 'Wrong answer. I'm Sir Maurice's gamekeeper. All poachers and those trespassing on his land with the object of taking game are classed as vermin in my eyes. You've seen how we deal with vermin. If you need reminding, just take a glance down.'

The watcher was no longer cold, he was sweating profusely. 'Look, I can prove I'm a police officer. Let me show you my warrant card.' He moved his hand towards his pocket.

'Stop!' Barry said loudly. 'Absolutely still. Don't even think of moving.' He moved closer until they were no more than ten feet apart. He studied the watcher whose lips were moving as if in silent prayer. 'Turn round very slowly, keeping your hands where I can see them. No sudden movements. Is that clear?'

They emerged from the wood into the lane. The officer stumbled back to the main road, uncomfortably aware of the gun at his back, and Barry's warning ringing in his ears, 'Tell whoever you're working for, Sir Maurice will hear of this.'

Back in the car, his partner listened as his mobile crackled with the sound of their superior's displeasure as he tried to explain. 'I'm sorry, sir; there was nothing I could do. It's all very well saying that, but if you like to test it out I'll willingly point a rifle at your chest and see what sort of snappy answers you come up with.' He paused, then went on, 'We're cold, wet and tired and I've to change my clothing. Our cover here has been well and truly blown and we will serve no useful purpose by remaining. I should also warn you that the gamekeeper has threatened to report us to his employer. He said the name might mean something: Sir Maurice Winfield.'

At the end of the call he turned and grinned at his colleague. 'It seems we're in excellent company, but whereas I only pissed myself, our superiors are now shitting themselves uncontrollably.'

'Why's that?'

'Apparently our aggressive gamekeeper's employer is only head of MI5!'

In the kitchen, Shirley and Lisa waited in anxious silence. Barry seemed to have been gone an age. The cottage was quiet, unnaturally so. The snow had muffled all but the loudest sounds. Into this quiet the ticking of the kitchen clock sounded abnormally loud.

After a long agonized wait, the women heard the sound of a single gunshot. Then silence. No matter that they'd been expecting it, it still made them jump. They looked at one another, a flock of unspoken questions flooding their thoughts, neither willing to voice their anxiety. The Labrador lifted her head at the sound of the shot. She looked from one to the other, as if seeking guidance. Receiving none she returned to lying with her head between her paws, listening as intently as were the two women.

The minutes dragged slowly. Eventually Shirley could stand the suspense no longer. 'Something's wrong,' she said. 'Barry should have been back by now. Suppose that phone call was a trap to get him out of the house?'

'Why would anyone want to do that?'

'I don't know.' As Shirley spoke they heard a sound from the direction of the lounge. It was a gentle thump, as of a door closing, closely followed by a click. Nell stood up immediately. She was moving towards the hall when the back door opened and her husband walked in, a broad smile on his face.

'Barry,' Shirley exclaimed. 'We thought you'd come in through the lounge.'

'What, and dirty the carpet? More than my life's worth. What made you think I'd come in that way?'

'We heard the door, a second or two before you walked in. That means there's somebody else in the house.'

Lisa pointed to the dog. 'Look at Nell.'

The Labrador was standing as close as she could get to the hall door, sniffing along the gap below the door, her tail wagging furiously. Barry brought his rifle up to his shoulder. 'Keep clear of the line of fire.' They waited, watching with horrified fascination as the door handle began to turn.

Lisa snatched up a poker from by the Aga. Shirley armed herself with a long-handled broom. Barry levelled the rifle at the door, aiming chest high. The door gradually opened, inch by inch. Nell's tail went into overdrive, as she hopped from foot to foot with impatience. As soon as she could, she inserted her muzzle into the gap and pushed the door wide.

The bearded man in the doorway blinked in surprise at the rifle, the poker and the broom. 'Hello,' he said quietly. 'Here's a nice friendly welcome.'

He bent over the Labrador, who was bashing his shins with her tail in rapture, and stroked her. 'At least you're pleased to see me, Nell.'

Barry lowered the rifle and Lisa put the poker back in the companion set. 'What do you expect when you come sneaking into the house that way? When folk don't know whether you're alive or dead and they've been worried sick about you,' Shirley told him severely.

'Yes, Alan, where the hell have you been?' Barry chimed in.

'I'm sorry, I haven't been able to contact you, but I've been a bit busy. Besides which I wasn't sure how safe it was until today. I've been babysitting a murderer. That was the main reason. I wasn't sure which phones might be safe. I was waiting for something else as well. I was waiting for the man to tell me everything he knows.'

'Sit down and explain,' Barry ordered.

'I'm not sure how much Lisa ought to hear,' Marshall said with an apologetic smile.

'Don't worry about that.' Lisa explained about her 'suspension'.

'Alan, what's this about a murderer?' Shirley asked.

'That's the problem I faced. I needed to find out who's paying him.' Marshall continued to stroke his dog. 'I'm convinced John Brown killed Jeffries, Moran and Lesley Robertson. Brown also killed Anna.'

'I think you're right,' Lisa interrupted. 'I've been given some documents I think you'll be interested in. I'll tell you about it later.'

'I've been hoping Brown will confirm it. I've been trying to persuade him, but without any luck – so far. I'm going to have to resort to some fairly unorthodox tactics. He's a professional killer; I believe the term is 'hitman'. So I make no apologies for what I'm going to do to him. I've had to convince Brown that he will tell me in the end, if it's the last thing he does. Which it may be, if he doesn't talk.'

'Alan,' Shirley ordered him, 'for God's sake. Do as Barry says and sit down. I'll make you a cup of tea and you can try to tell us a straight tale.'

Marshall sat at the kitchen table, flanked on either side by Barry and Shirley with Lisa Andrews sitting opposite him. Nell found it comfortable to lean against his left leg, her head on his thigh. Marshall laid his left hand on her head, stroking her gently. He described everything that had happened from when Barry had dropped him off at Netherdale railway station. There were no interruptions. Even when Shirley made a second pot of tea she urged Marshall to continue his tale.

'I didn't know what the hell to do. He was in my house, obviously there to finish me off. I had no gun, nothing I could think of to match the bloody knife he carried. But then I remembered the priest.'

'The what?' Lisa was baffled.

Marshall pulled the cosh from out of his coat. 'It's used for dispatching wounded birds,' he explained. 'I hit him with this. At first, I thought I might have overdone it. Anyway, I tied him up and took him off into the woods, along with some basic supplies.'

'Don't tell me you've been camping out in this weather?'

'Not exactly camping out. I'm a guest of Sir Maurice. Not at the house, of course; in the woodman's hut, over in the big plantation. But Brown won't talk.' Marshall's face darkened slightly. 'So in the end I decided to call on some techniques I learned from someone who knows a bit more about interrogation than I do. I haven't much choice. Every copper in the land' – he looked up and smiled at Lisa – 'with maybe one or two exceptions is on the lookout for me, convinced I was a latter-day Mack the Knife. I've followed the case in the paper.' Marshall saw the look of surprise on his listeners' faces and laughed. 'Shirley puts the paper out for recycling the day after you've read it. I simply came along and recycled it.'

Barry nodded. 'If you've been wandering about outside, it explains why Nell's been so restless.'

'Have you been nicking food out of the fridge-freezer in the outhouse as well?' Shirley demanded.

'Guilty, but I was only borrowing it. I needed milk most of all. It was too far to go to the Manor sometimes. Most of it I can replace now I can get to my cottage. Now that you've scared off the watchers, for the time being at least. But I suspect they'll be back?' He looked to Lisa for confirmation. She nodded.

They were interrupted when the mobile in Lisa's pocket rang. She answered, listened for a while, before saying, 'Yes, but not all of it. I'll call you back, shall I? I think he might do.'

She ended the call. 'That was Inspector Nash. He wanted to tell me he's had a phone call from York CID. They confirmed the blood on the boiler suit in Brown's flat is that of Councillor Jeffries. What he wants to know is, have you managed to get any information from Brown, mainly, do you know who's paying him?'

Marshall gasped. 'How did he know all that? Did Sir Maurice give me away?'

Lisa shook her head. 'He worked it out. Worked out you must have Brown. Worked out where you'd run to, worked out Sir Maurice must know, rang him and got confirmation. Worked out that there's only one reason you'd bury yourself away with the man who was paid to kill your wife, and that reason was, to get information. He wanted to know whether you've succeeded.'

'Blimey!' Barry exclaimed, 'That's close to genius.' He frowned. 'But if he's as clever as all that, what about that phone call? Surely, if you're under surveillance, your mobile will be compromised?'

Lisa nodded. 'It might well be.' She held up the phone. 'But this is a cheap pay-as-you-go mobile Jack Binns got for me, not mine.'

chapter nineteen

Lisa took the opportunity to explain what was happening. 'Mike Nash set up the spoof suspension. Superintendent Edwards and the chief constable both know all about it, and they know we can prove your innocence, not only of your wife's murder, but the others too. Mike did it so that the people who hired Brown will be fooled into thinking we're still chasing you. I've got copies of the papers they found in Brown's flat. He wants you to look through the press cuttings, see if you can spot anything relevant, any names that might ring a bell. He said the likeliest source of information regarding a motive is you.'

'That's more or less what Moran said in his letter,' Marshall agreed. 'Though what it was remains a mystery to me. Anyway, let's have a look. I've seen them before, but I only got a cursory look. I saw the clipping about Moran, and Anna's report. But we might glean something more. I've been too concerned with babysitting Brown to give any thought to much else.'

Barry looked puzzled. 'How have you seen these papers?'

'I had a day out to York and tried another of my new skills. I'm not very good at burglary though. I got into Brown's flat, but the police arrived. Luckily, I'd locked the outer door behind me when I went in but I was that spooked I ran like hell the minute they left.'

It was obvious from the papers that Brown had been in great demand. Lisa pulled two of them to one side. 'Both these might be relevant.'

'What have you got?' Marshall asked. He leaned over to study the cuttings. 'This isn't a murder. It's about a road accident.' Marshall picked up the paper. It was dated eighteen years earlier. It reported the death of a local councillor, killed in a head-on collision with a truck on the Leeds ring road. The inquest recorded accidental death after a police mechanic gave evidence that the politician's car had a fault on the steering. 'I'm sorry. I fail to see the significance.'

'Any report in Brown's cuttings indicates it was probably foul play. Look at the responsibilities the councillor had,' Lisa prompted.

Marshall read that section of the cutting again. 'He was chairman of the planning committee.'

'Exactly!' Lisa reached across the table and plucked another cutting from the pile. 'Councillor Jeffries became chairman of the planning committee straight after the previous chairman was killed in a road accident. I don't think that's a coincidence, do you?'

'It certainly seems suspicious.'

'Remember what Moran wrote about you knowing more than you realize. What if this is to do with your work rather than Anna's? Or, a combination of the two perhaps? Remember the victims, a solicitor plus his assistant, and two members of a planning committee. What does that suggest?'

'The construction industry.'

'Exactly!' Lisa repeated again triumphantly. She paused. 'What was the name of the firm you worked for?'

'Broadwood Construction.'

She pulled another cutting from the pile. 'Read this.'

Marshall read the report aloud. '"Officials from the Health and Safety Executive will today begin investigations into the death of Gary Watson, the Leeds construction worker who fell from the seventh floor of a building site two days ago. Watson's employers, Broadwood Construction refused to comment ahead of the inquiry. Watson, a thirty-one-year-old married man, was found by colleagues when they arrived for work at the prestigious waterfront office development. It is believed he fell to his death whilst checking for damage following the recent gales"'.'

'That's yet another connection. How many people has this butcher slaughtered?'

'Do you mean Brown, or the man paying him?' Barry asked.

'Whoever it is, they won't be short of money,' Lisa said quietly.

Marshall looked at her enquiringly.

'Ordering a hit isn't exactly cheap,' she told him. 'I don't know what the going rate is, but you can work it out from the bank statements. This guy's paid for three within the last month, as if he was ordering a pizza to go.'

'What now?' Shirley asked when they finished examining the documents.

'I'm going to have another word with Mr Brown. I'm going to get as much information from him as I can.'

'How will you do that?' Lisa asked.

'When I was inside, one bloke in particular taught me a lot. That trick with the guy outside your flat was one. Getting information from someone was another. I've no experience, but I'm sure it will work.'

'If you're going to see Brown, mind if I tag along?' Lisa asked.

'I think it would be better if you stay here. It might be unpleasant. Very unpleasant. Certainly not for the squeamish.'

Marshall was looking at Lisa as he spoke, or rather, as she realized later, he was looking through her. The expression in his eyes made her shiver.

In the end, Barry volunteered to help. 'I'll tell you what we're going to do,' Marshall instructed him as they walked through the forest. 'I've got a tape recorder; your job begins when I switch it on. I want you to recite names from that list I made from those press cuttings. Pick any at random. Just the name, the year and the method. Say that, and no more. Then wait until I give you the nod and do it again. OK, is that clear?'

'Absolutely.'

'Keep all emotion out of your voice.'

'I'll do my best.'

'There's one other thing you should know. It won't be pleasant. It won't look pleasant. It won't sound pleasant and in all probability it won't smell pleasant. If it gets to you remember one thing. That screaming, bleeding, shitting prisoner's the same ruthless bastard who slit my wife's throat. He did it for a few lousy quid.

He's the man who came to kill me. He's the enemy. He put me in Durham gaol. He's ruined most of my life. He's taken away my career, my youth and my happiness. What's more, if someone paid him, he'd do exactly the same to you. Get it?'

'Got it.'

'He doesn't look happy, does he?' Marshall pointed forward as they approached. Brown was standing on the points of his toes. His hands were roped over the branch of an oak tree and his ankles tied to the trunk. He was stark naked.

'What's the reasoning behind that?'

'It humiliates him. It makes him cold and it stops him trying to get away. Even if he managed to escape from the ropes, he'd not make it far in bare feet. Not through the bramble, briar and thorn.'

Barry was mildly shocked. Not by Brown's miserable state, but by Marshall's obvious satisfaction. Then he remembered the roll of victims this man had slaughtered. And that one of them had been Marshall's wife.

Brown wasn't happy. He'd never been so unhappy. For the last week he'd survived imprisonment without problem, even though he'd been tied up and interrogated. The last twenty-four hours had been different. He'd been stripped naked, blind-folded, and humiliated. His misery was partly physical, mostly mental.

'After we get what we want, I'm going to cut him free,' Marshall said. 'Otherwise we're in danger of him losing his hands and feet.'

'Cut him free? Won't that be dangerous?'

'He won't be going anywhere. Are you ready?'

Marshall produced a tape recorder from his pocket. As they neared the prisoner, he picked up a bamboo cane that was lying close to the trussed man. Brown heard them approaching. At least he heard something, he wasn't sure what. Then he heard the whistling, *John Brown's Body*. He hated the whistling. Then he heard the voice. He hated the voice, even more than the whistling.

He not only hated the sound of the voice. He hated his surroundings. He hated his own wretched soiled state. He hated the man holding him captive, and he hated the man who'd paid him. The man who'd caused his torment.

'Now, Mister Brown.' Brown's head came up with a jerk. 'You've been very naughty, Mister Brown, very naughty indeed. And you're a long way from home, aren't you? What's the matter? Don't you like the countryside? Prefer your comfortable flat in York? I bet you wish you were back there, don't you?'

On and on, the hated voice continued tormenting him until he could have screamed. Eventually he heard the man ask him a question. 'So, Mister Brown, what do you have to say for yourself, you naughty, naughty man?'

Brown remained silent, a mistake. He heard a sharp swishing sound followed almost at once by an excruciating pain to his testicles. This time he did scream. The tears started to his eyes. He urinated, feeling the shame as the warm fluid trickled down his legs. 'Speak when you're spoken to. Those are the rules round here. Now, I'll ask you once more. What do you have to say for yourself? Be careful how you answer, you know the penalty for giving the wrong answer.'

'I've got nothing to say,' Brown stated defiantly.

'Wrong answer!' Swish, pain, scream. 'Try again. You don't seem to be getting the hang of this speaking business. This is how it works. I ask you a question and you answer it. Do you understand?'

Silence. Swish, pain, scream. Silence.

Brown knew he couldn't stand much more. There was a fierce, wrenching, constant pain from his stomach downwards. His genitals felt as if they were on fire. He was sure they were bleeding. Where was his tormentor? Brown listened. It was all he could do. Silence. Not a sound. He waited, wishing he could at least see. The silence seemed to go on and on. Had his captor gone away? Or was he there, waiting? Dreaming up some other way of inflicting pain?

'It really is a shame you won't cooperate.' The tormentor hadn't left. 'That means you'll be able to help me with a little experiment. You would like to help me, wouldn't you, Mister Brown? I'm sure you would. Now what do you say?'

'Go fuck yourself.' Brown winced expecting the retaliation his words would provoke. Instead he heard his tormentor's voice once more.

'Now that wasn't a nice thing to say. But at least you haven't lost your voice. That's good; because I'm sure you're going to be using it in the very near future. However, to ensure you don't frighten any of the wild animals round here . . .' Brown felt a sharp prod to his solar plexus that drove the wind out of his lungs. As his mouth opened, a rough piece of cloth was thrust none too gently inside. 'I'm going to gag you,' the voice said.

'Now, Mister Brown, this is your final chance to avoid a very unpleasant experience. All you have to do at any time is to nod your head twice. What could be simpler than that? As you can't speak at the moment perhaps you would indicate by nodding your head?' Brown remained stock still. 'I said, nod. Like this.' Brown's hair was grabbed tightly and his head forcibly pulled backwards and forwards as his chin hit his chest. 'Now do you understand?' Brown nodded.

'Good, now to business. Like I say, any time you want me to stop all you have to do is nod twice. If I see you, I'll stop straight away. If not, you might have to keep nodding. I'm sure to see you in the end. Oh, I almost forgot. I was going to tell you what I'm going to do to you. Actually I'll let you into a little secret. I don't think it sounds very painful, not to a strong man like you. However, a friend of mine assures me it works every time. I'm told it's the worst pain in the world. You'll be able to tell me soon, won't you? I'm going to take a knife. It's nowhere near as sharp as yours, but it'll have to do. Then I'm going to slice down the front of your leg. Right down to the shinbone. Then I'm going to pull the flesh away from the bone. Once the bone's exposed I shall take the knife and scrape it along the bone. Now that's the painful bit, or so I'm told. But you'll be able to tell me yourself, won't you, Mister Brown?

'All you have to do to avoid this is to tell me what I want to know. Now doesn't that sound simple? I can't understand why you're so shy. Tell me what I want to hear and you can avoid all that pain. I'm going to tell you what we want you to talk about, or rather, my colleague will.'

Marshall nodded to Barry, who cleared his throat and began to call the roll.

'Simon Dale, October 1983, strangled.' Brown heard the words with a shock. It was so long ago he could barely remember it. He waited. Silence. Followed by more silence.

'James Edwards, February 1984, shot dead.' Brown remembered that one only too well. He'd nearly been caught, and had been forced to lie low for a while.

'Liam O'Grady, May 1984, throat slit.' The list went on remorselessly, interspersed with the silence until Brown wasn't certain which was worse. He wasn't sure, but the silences seemed to be getting longer. He wasn't to know that Marshall was carefully orchestrating the roll call. After what seemed an age he heard one final name. 'Anna Marshall, November 1999, throat slit.'

Brown felt himself thrust violently against the trunk of the tree from which he was suspended. 'That was my wife, Mister Brown.' The voice hissed in his ear. 'I'm sure you're aware by now just how much trouble you're in. I could slit your throat and bury you in these woods. Your body would never be found. I will do, too, unless you tell me what I need to know. So, why don't you consider your options, whilst I go fetch my knife?'

Brown attempted to make one last defiant gesture by urinating on his tormentor. Unfortunately for him the gesture was as empty as his bladder.

Marshall released his captive from the tree and watched him crumple to the floor. Brambles were growing there and Brown felt every thorn in a thousand small pinpricks of pain. Then he felt his leg grasped. Then he felt the knife point against his skin. Then he felt the point scratching away at his skin. Then below the skin. The agony increased. The nerves shrieked protest to his brain as the tissues of his flesh separated. When the pain became intolerable he began to nod, and nod and nod and nod.

Half an hour later, Marshall walked away. Towards the end

of Brown's confession he'd heard what he needed to know. He'd heard the name of the man who paid Brown to murder Anna. He'd heard it, but did not believe it.

There was a council of war that evening at the Dickinsons' cottage. The only item on the agenda was Brown's confession. After the tape recording had been played several times everyone was convinced Brown had told all he knew. Everyone apart from Marshall.

'Look, Alan,' Barry insisted. 'What Brown said was real. I was there, remember. Do you need to hear the tape again?'

Lisa shuddered. 'Barry's right, Alan. Why would Brown say it if it wasn't true?'

'Brown's got no chance of escaping. Nobody's coming to his rescue. What option has he but to tell the truth,' Shirley backed her. 'I know loyalty's admirable, but don't you think you're carrying it too far?'

All three stared at him, willing him to admit the inevitable. 'I'm sorry, but it's not right. I hear what you say, but I don't accept it.'

'Why would Brown lie?' Barry asked.

'I'm not saying Brown's lying.'

'You are. You keep saying it, over and over. You've just said you don't believe what Brown said was true.'

'That's not quite the same. You don't get the point do you? Maybe he believed it, but that doesn't mean it was true.'

'I'm sorry, Alan, I don't follow.'

'OK. Try this. Lisa, tell everyone what happened after you took me to hospital.'

Lisa looked blank for a moment, whilst the others looked totally nonplussed. 'I went back the following day and they told me the name I'd been given for you was wrong. What's this got to do with Brown's confession?'

'I'd told everyone my name was Andrew Myers. I hadn't been asked to prove it. Everyone accepted it. Don't you see? That's the weakness in Brown's confession. Do you honestly believe whoever paid Brown would give their right name? Brown got his money, so he wouldn't be bothered. He wouldn't care if the bloke said his name was Mickey Mouse. If the cheques had bounced he'd have been a whole lot keener. Failing that, Brown's not going to worry who paid him.'

'That's all very well, but you keep saying you don't believe this man Harry's the culprit. The evidence still points to him. Brown named him and you haven't offered an alternative,' Barry insisted.

'That's true. But I can't think of a motive. Why would Harry have Anna killed? Harry's capable of many things, lots of them underhand, some of them illegal. But not murder. I can't picture him as a killer and I've one advantage over you. I know the man.'

'What if Anna discovered something about Harry,' suggested Shirley. 'Something so bad he had to order her killing? Something that bad it made him desperate.'

'Shirley's right. Men do things out of desperation they'd be horrified by in normal circumstances; look what you've just done to Brown. Why do you persist in being so obstinate? Harry's the only one connected to you, to Anna, to the construction industry, to Jeffries and the others. What about the man Brown pushed off the building? He worked for Harry. It was one of Harry's buildings he fell from. How much of a connection is that? Why not accept it and stop being so bloody stubborn?' Barry was becoming exasperated.

Marshall remained unconvinced. 'There was a time when everything pointed to me, when nobody believed me innocent. A few days ago the police thought I was a multi-murderer. Majority of them still do. I was convicted on far stronger evidence than you've got for saying Harry Rourke's guilty. Perhaps that's why I don't believe it. I need a hell of a sight more to convince me, than the word of a killer desperate to save his skin.'

Towards the end of their argument Lisa had come round towards Marshall's viewpoint, but the others were still sure he was wrong.

'I've had an idea.' Marshall announced.

'What is it?' Lisa asked.

When he told them, Lisa was shocked, angry and dismayed. Barry looked at him with something approaching respect.

'Surely the police will have done it already?'

'Maybe, Lisa, but they'd be at a disadvantage. They wouldn't recognize the significance. Remember the words in Moran's letter? "Marshall knows more about this than he realizes." I might find out what the police couldn't.'

All attempts to dissuade him proved fruitless. If he'd appeared stubborn before, now he was intractable. Lisa turned to Barry for support. He shrugged. 'It could be dangerous. But how else is Alan going to get at the truth? And if he doesn't, it'll keep festering away inside him.'

Lisa stared at Alan. 'You believe you owe Anna this, don't you?'

'Yes. But I have to do it for my own sake. I have to know the truth.'

'All right. Go ahead with this stupid scheme of yours. God help me. I must be crazy to even consider going along with it.' She shook her head in resignation.

'Hang on. You don't have to join in.'

'I must be as mad as you to even think about it.'

'We have to dispose of Brown first. We can't do anything until he's out of the way,' Barry reminded them.

'Don't tell me,' Lisa rounded on Marshall. 'I suppose you've had a stroke of genius about that as well? What do you intend to do, stick bananas in his mouth to suffocate him and drop him down a mine shaft?'

'Not quite.' He smiled. 'But I think I know how to get rid of him. Now he's told me all he can, he's more of a nuisance than anything.'

Lisa sighed with relief. Half her concern had been that Marshall might be tempted to do something silly. Understandable, given that he was holding prisoner the man who had murdered his wife. But the outcome would have been that he would again be arrested for murder; and this time with justification. She listened as Marshall outlined the scheme.

'That's about all you can do with him, as far as I can see,' she agreed. 'My only concern is that they react quickly enough. I know you're not worried about Brown, but I'm a police officer, even though I'm currently under suspension, and if he dies, and people got to know that I was aware of his situation, that would be curtains for my career. It would also put you back in the dock, for manslaughter at the very least.'

Marshall shrugged. 'Better that he doesn't expire, I suppose. Not that I care, one way or the other.'

chapter twenty

Within five minutes of Rourke's arrival at his office the staff at Broadwood Construction knew they were in for a rough day. At first they were convinced there must have been another attack of vandalism. The only person brave enough to enter Rourke's office was Freddie. He lasted only five minutes, and the sound of Rourke's voice told the listeners that whatever Freddie was saying to try to placate his boss was having little, if any, effect. When Freddie emerged he was ashen-faced. 'I wouldn't go in there today,' he told Rourke's secretary and anyone else within earshot. 'Not unless he asks you to. Even then I'd think twice.'

'What's wrong, Freddie?' Harry's secretary asked.

Freddie shook his head. 'That's the problem. I've absolutely no idea.'

Tara heard Harry's car long before he entered their drive. Normally he treated the car gently. Today it was being subjected to severe cruelty. Even after he pulled to a screeching halt and yanked the handbrake on, the abuse continued. The violence with which Harry slammed the driver's door and then the rear passenger door would have caused considerable damage had the car been less sturdy. Once he'd finished with his car, Rourke attacked the front door. Had that not been solid oak, it would probably have finished up as matchwood under his assault.

He marched across the hall and flung open his study door with such violence that it crashed into the wall. When Tara entered the room he was standing by the drinks cabinet with his back towards her. 'If we do have to sell the house wouldn't it be better in one piece?' Tara suggested calmly.

Harry swung round. The whisky tumbler in his hand was

full but there was little evidence of ice or water in the glass. Tara lifted one eyebrow. 'A bit early for that, isn't it?'

Harry glared at her. 'I don't care. I need it after the day I've had.'

'More vandalism?'

'Worse than that. I'll show you.'

Rourke reached into his brief case. 'Come and look at this. I've had an offer for the company.'

Sergeant Binns was ending a phone call as Nash arrived next morning. 'Morning, Mike. I've just had a call from Dickinson. Murderer Marshall's mate.'

Nash concealed a smile. 'Go on.'

'He rang to report they've had poachers roaming the woods. He thinks they might be after deer and wanted to ask if we can send a patrol car.'

'I'm sure we can do that easily enough.'

'It depends on what manpower we have. We've a couple more uniforms but still not enough. Ideally I'd suggest we stake the woods out, but the expense wouldn't be justifiable.'

'I'm sure I can leave it to you.'

Nash's phone rang, it was DS Mironova. 'How are you feeling?' was his first response.

'Awful, but I've decided not to die. I've just seen my doctor and I've asked to come back to work.'

'Are you sure you're fit enough?'

'I think I can manage, but reading the papers isn't doing me any good. Sounds like you're stretched to the limit. I can't sit here while you run yourself ragged chasing a triple murderer. I don't suppose Viv's back?'

'No, he's going to be off another week or so.'

'That's because he's got man-flu, I've only had flu!'

'Listen, I'll tell you what, I need back-up over in Netherdale. Tom Pratt's still off and they're running at half strength, there's only two DCs there. I've got Jack Binns, and a couple of uniforms are back on duty. Would you go to Netherdale and help there, if you feel up to it?'

'No problem, at least I'll be doing something. I'll be there tomorrow.'

'Thanks, Clara, I owe you a pint. I'll be through at some point and bring you up to speed.'

After he'd put the phone down Nash sat for a few moments, reflecting on the conversation. It was typical of Clara's dedication that she wanted to return to work, although her voice suggested she was far from one hundred per cent fit. And it would be good to have her back. He missed being able to bounce ideas around with her and Pearce. Andrews was proving very capable, but he'd got used to relying on the members of their small team.

He also missed Tom Pratt. The superintendent had shouldered all those tasks that Nash hated, the routine administration job, the mountains of paperwork that went along with policing. It was only in the months following Tom's heart attack that Nash realized exactly how much Tom had taken off his shoulders. Sadly, the longer he was absent, the more unlikely it seemed that he would return at all.

The phone call was from a mobile. The harassed civilian drafted in from Netherdale took the call in between typing reports and custody sheets.

'I wish to report an abandoned vehicle,' the woman told her.

'Can I have your name, please?'

The request went unanswered. 'It looks as if it might have been stolen by joy riders or something. It's in a lonely spot, and the keys are in the ignition. I tried the driver's door but I think it's locked. It's parked on the western edge of Layton Woods, at the end of Woodbine Lane.'

The civilian receptionist repeated her request for the woman to identify herself, but with no more success than previously. 'There's one more thing,' the caller's voice was no more animated than if she'd been ordering a takeaway pizza. 'There's a man's body on the back seat. I knocked on the window, but got no response. I think he might be dead. His hands are tied together with that tape they use on parcels.' She gave the registration number, then immediately ended the call.

The receptionist was left staring at the hastily scribbled note on her pad. 'What's wrong?' Binns asked her.

The woman explained. 'The caller wouldn't give her name. All she said was she'd found a car and there's a body on the back seat. The odd thing is, although she wouldn't give her name, she insisted on telling me the registration number.'

'I'll get Nash to look into it. It'll have to be Mike and me. There is no one else. What's so special about the registration number, I wonder?'

The receptionist glanced down at her pad and repeated it.

'What!' Binns exclaimed. 'That's the car belonging to that missing bloke from York. What the hell is it doing up there? I only hope the body inside isn't whose I think it might be.'

As he was speaking, Marshall looked across the table. Shirley and Lisa were sitting next to one another. They were alike in many ways. Their build was similar; their hair colour almost identical. The sight of them together suggested a refinement to Marshall's plans. He sat back and thought about it for a few minutes. The others noted his distraction. Shirley glanced at Lisa. 'Is he all right?' she asked with mock concern.

Lisa grimaced. 'He might be, but I'm beginning to recognize that expression. He's planning something, and that means trouble. Not for him but the rest of us. Just you wait.'

'Big Issue. Get the Big Issue here. Plenty to read in the Big Issue, only one-forty for the Big Issue.'

'You're new, aren't you?' The bank clerk hunted amongst the change in her purse before finding a £2 coin lurking inside.

'I'm not new, but I'm in very good condition. Low mileage and one careful lady owner,' replied the vendor with a grin.

The clerk laughed. 'You'll do all right with chat-up lines like that.' She handed over the coin in exchange for the paper. She smiled at the vendor. 'Keep the change. See you again.'

'I'll look forward to that. Thank you for buying the Big Issue.'

She smiled again and departed, clutching her copy and her salad sandwich. 'Low mileage, one careful lady owner' indeed; he deserved to succeed. She wouldn't leave the paper lying around. She'd read it and then take it home. That way the other girls in the bank would have no excuse when the vendor approached them.

The vendor watched her go. 'Big Issue,' he called out. He decided to try a new slogan, 'The sun ain't out, the sky is grey, but buy the Big Issue today. Come and get it, only one-forty for the Big Issue.'

The call brought a couple more buyers, part of the army of scurrying office workers dashing to and fro on any number of secret missions they must complete in their short lunch break. Like giant ants they dashed purposefully across the broad pedestrian precinct. The vendor frowned and concentrated on the reason for being there. 'Plenty to read in the Big Issue, only one-forty for the Big Issue.' This time the call yielded five customers.

Pleased with his success, the vendor wandered further along the precinct, passing between new buildings and renovated ones. 'Big Issue. Get the Big Issue here,' got him another three customers. This was proving a good site. So it should with plenty of well-heeled customers anxious to salve their social conscience by paying something towards the homeless. There were banks and solicitors, insurance companies and accountants as well as the shops. All full of workers emerging only for lunch. Every journey outside their building represented a sales opportunity for him.

The pitch had been profitable so far. He'd done so well during the week that there was the temptation not to bother on Saturday. There wouldn't be the office workers moving around. On the other hand, town would be busy with shoppers, particularly as Leeds United had an away game. He decided to give it a go. You never knew who might be out shopping.

The Internal Affairs officer was embarrassed. 'It was a natural mistake to have made.'

'Tell me, what went wrong?'

'The car belonged to Lisa Andrews. The woman driving it

looked like Lisa Andrews. She was wearing an identical silver quilted jacket. Our surveillance team followed the car as soon as it came out of the Dickinsons' drive. They followed it all the way into Netherdale and hung back until they saw the woman park and go into the supermarket. One of them followed her inside. He thought she might be using it to meet Marshall. It wasn't until he caught a glimpse of her face that he realized they'd been following Shirley Dickinson, not Lisa Andrews.'

'Bloody brilliant.'

The team leader stiffened with resentment, suspecting sarcasm. His superior continued, 'A superb decoy operation. It was a natural assumption to have made. Andrews' car, Andrews' coat and so on. We can't even prove it was intended to mislead us.'

'So what do we do?'

'That's a bloody good question. Let me think a minute.'

After a silence lasting much longer, the head of the investigation unit said, 'If the idea was to distract us from Lisa Andrews' real destination, that suggests she's going to meet Marshall. We know Marshall hasn't contacted her direct, so he must have done it through the Dickinsons. What we don't know is if she's set off yet. The best bet would be to go back to the cottage and check to see if Mrs Dickinson's car's still there. If it is, Andrews will still be at the cottage and we won't have lost anything. Get the team back there as fast as you can. We can't afford to lose a minute.'

Twenty minutes later the squad reported in. 'Mrs Dickinson's car is still there. As is her husband's Land Rover. If anyone's left here, they went on foot.'

The team leader and his superior sighed with relief. They hadn't been fooled. All they had to do now was sit and wait for Lisa Andrews to emerge. Follow her and she would then lead them to Marshall.

It was a natural assumption to make. It was also disastrously wrong. It failed to take into account Marshall's ingenuity.

chapter twenty-one

As Barry and Lisa headed for Leeds, he explained how the deception had worked. 'I parked Alan's Land Rover so it's impossible to read the number plate, except from inside the woods. After their recent experiences I don't think the police will be too keen to venture in there. In any event, once they get the "anonymous phone call,"' – he glanced at his watch – 'which should be in half an hour or so, they won't have time to worry about us.'

As they got nearer to Leeds city centre Barry started manoeuvring the vehicle towards one of the multi-storey car parks. 'Not that one,' Lisa said sharply. 'Go further south towards the river.'

Something in her tone made Barry glance at her. 'Why not that one?' he asked.

She explained. 'I read the reports on the file, remember. That car park was where Anna Marshall was killed. I don't think it would be a lucky omen. Besides, the other ones will be closer to where we want to be.'

'Got you. Good point.'

Barry drove into the car park and collected a ticket. He found a bay, and parked. 'This is going to be a long, boring wait for you, Lisa.'

'Don't worry about that. Do you understand where you've to go?'

'I've to walk along that new precinct by the river and wait for Alan to find me. Then I've to check everything's OK for tonight and ask him if he has any instructions. Is that it?'

'That's right. I'll see you back here when you've finished.'

'Is there anything I can bring you?'

'A coffee, if you can manage it.'

'That shouldn't be a problem.'

'*Big Issue*, get the *Big Issue*.'

Barry shook his head and made to walk on, but the seller wouldn't take no for an answer.

'Plenty to read in the *Big Issue*. You can read it over your coffee in that nice café across the way,' the vendor continued persuasively.

Barry stared at the persistent salesman. He certainly looked the part. From the baseball cap to the untidy beard. From the threadbare padded anorak, to the designer slit jeans and ancient trainers. He was the archetypal *Big Issue* seller. 'Oh, very well then,' he said, dragging the money from his pocket.

The coffee was welcome, hot and tasty, a suitable antidote to the biting wind outside that seemed to be funnelled by the city streets.

'Not reading the *Big Issue*, Mister?' The vendor sat down.

'Hell's bells, Alan,' Barry greeted him. 'That disguise is good, you had me completely fooled. How did you get the job?'

'Simple enough. I found the real vendor and bought him a square meal; then I put the proposition to him. I told him I was doing research for a new TV programme. I gave him £100 to take over his pitch for a week. In addition he gets the takings. He'll be upset when the week's over, because I'm selling more than he does.'

'What have you been able to find out?'

'It's going to be dead easy getting in. I reckon five minutes from start to finish. All these big buildings have gone in for numerically coded locks. Somebody must have done a great selling job on them, because they fondly believe they represent good security. Getting round them is a doddle.'

'How will you do that?'

'I chose the easiest way. Learning the code.'

'How did you get it?'

'I started with the street door. I waited for the first person to arrive in the morning. I was sheltering in their doorway as it was raining. I asked him for the time. Then I pretended to adjust my watch whilst he was punching the numbers in. Just to be on the safe side I did the same routine a little later the next morning and that confirmed they don't change the code. Probably because they're too dim to remember a new one. Security, I tell you, it's a joke. They're so confident the doors will keep intruders out they haven't even bothered with motion-sensitive burglar alarms. I'm surprised their insurance company allows them to get away with it. Mind you, being solicitors and accountants, they probably own the insurance company.'

'What about the internal door?'

'I had a bit more trouble with that, but in the end I got lucky. I bought one of those cheap desk-top shredders, parcelled it up and addressed it for the attention of the office manager. Then I posed as a delivery man and waited in the corridor until one of the staff came back from lunch. I waited for her to punch the numbers in then delivered my package. As soon as I could, I wrote the number down.' Marshall chuckled.

'What's so funny?'

'I have this picture of the office manager tearing her hair out trying to find out who bought a shredder without going through the usual ordering process.'

'You said lucky. I think that was clever. When do we go in?' Barry asked.

'This evening would be best, Saturday night in Leeds? Who's going to pay attention to us? The police will have enough on their plate with the druggies and drunks and the boisterous clubbers to worry about anything else. Unless an alarm goes off. And it won't, because we've got the numbers to disable it. With nobody at work tomorrow, we can take all night over the job if we want.'

'I'll have to move the car at some stage. The car park we're in closes at 7 p.m.'

'Just be sure not to park within range of a CCTV camera.'

'Is there anything else?'

'One more thing, can you call at a chemist's before they close?'

'Whatever for?'

'We need a packet of surgical gloves. We don't want to leave fingerprints all over the place.'

'That makes sense. I'll stop and get them whilst you take Lisa the coffee I promised her, that way you get out of sight. No point pushing our luck.'

Shortly before 8 p.m. Marshall and Barry Dickinson left Lisa in the car, which was parked in a dimly lit side street, and wandered towards the main road. By the time they reached the precinct it had started to rain. 'We're lucky with the weather. Nobody will be rushing outdoors in this.' Marshall glanced to the right and the left. The street was deserted. 'Follow me and once we're inside don't move until I give the word.'

He stepped up to the door. Barry heard the electronic tones as Marshall pressed the numbers on the keypad. The door yielded obediently to his touch. 'Come on.' Their first objective had been achieved in less than thirty seconds.

Marshall ensured the door was fully closed and they heard the lock engage. 'We don't want any zealous copper finding the door unlocked,' he explained. 'Right, now follow me to the stairs.'

Marshall opened the door to the stairwell. Once it had swung to behind them he flicked his torch on. 'We can't be seen from outside. The stairs are in the middle of the building but I'll have to switch it off when we get to the first floor.'

Less than two minutes later they were standing outside the glass door leading to their objective. Marshall switched on his torch to see the numerical display. It illuminated the name of the company picked out in gold lettering; Hobbs & Hirst Solicitors. Hobbs & Hirst, whose senior partner had been murdered six weeks ago. The company that had also employed his secretary and mistress, Lesley Robertson. Hobbs & Hirst; where Anna Marshall had worked.

'We're in.' Marshall opened the door. They moved cautiously into the large reception area. 'Where do we start?' Barry asked.

'Moran's office, I think. From memory, it should be this way,'

Marshall pointed to the right. 'His files would be the ones most likely to contain what we're looking for.' As they passed through the outer office Barry pointed to a four-drawer filing cabinet on the wall near the desk. 'That might be worth checking as well.'

'I agree,' Marshall replied. 'In fact, I think we should look everywhere until we find what we came for. After all, they can only lock us up once.'

There were three filing cabinets across one wall of Moran's office, but their contents proved disappointing. There were only a few suspense files hanging from the rails, a fact that briefly puzzled the searchers. Marshall relocked the cabinets with the keys obligingly left in the locks. 'Security, hah, what did I tell you?'

The filing cabinet in Lesley Robertson's office proved similarly unrewarding. It also contained only a few files. 'I bet Moran's office has been reallocated to a new partner,' Barry whispered. 'All his files would be taken out to make way for the new man. I shouldn't wonder if they've been placed in the filing system in the general office.'

'That sounds logical. But why are you whispering?' Marshall grinned.

They entered the general office, a large, open plan room to the left of reception. Barry groaned as he saw a bank of a dozen filing cabinets lined up against the wall opposite them. A similar row lined the wall to their right. 'It's a good thing we've got all weekend,' he remarked.

'The only good thing is that this office is in the middle of the building with no windows. That means we can switch the lights on without being seen from outside.' Marshall pressed the switch and they stood blinking for a moment at the brightness of a dozen fluorescent lights.

'Where shall we start?' Barry asked.

'Let's do it the simple way. Start at the far end, take a cabinet each, then work our way round the room.'

They'd anticipated an element of risk, been nervous about it. What they now experienced was tedium. Each file had to be examined, each cabinet cross-checked, before they could move on to the next. Occasional distractions delayed their task, but provided lighter moments. Finding documents dating back over a century was one. Another came from the salacious but highly entertaining evidence in a libel case concerning a judge, a prostitute and various items of household equipment produced in evidence.

By the time they'd searched the first bank of cabinets it was after midnight, and they were still only halfway through their task. They set about the second set of cabinets with weary determination. 'These legal papers with their weird and wonderful phrases and antiquated wording are making me go cross-eyed.' Barry complained.

'Me too. If you want to make the task a bit more exciting let's start at the left-hand set of cabinets and work to the right this time.'

It was twenty minutes after they recommenced searching that Marshall came across a file labelled CBC. Curiosity caused him to remove it from the drawer. He looked inside and took it to the nearest desk. 'Corps Building Corporation. That name rings a bell,' he muttered.

He turned over a few of the papers, without finding anything to enlighten him. As he went to lift it off the desk, one of the suspension hooks caught against the coils of the phone cable. Marshall pulled, and the receiver came clattering off its rest. Several of the file's documents cascaded on to the floor. 'Shush!' Barry's chiding merged with Marshall's own, 'Damn and blast!'

He replaced the receiver and bent to pick up the documents. A name on the heading of one of the sheets caught his eye. He scanned the rest of the page. He groped behind him until he found the chair, sat down and reopened the file. It was five minutes before Barry realized that he'd neither moved, uttered a sound, nor replaced the file. 'Alan?' he said. 'Have you found something?'

There was a long moment of silence. 'Have you seen a file for Coningsby Developments?'

'Yes, it's in here, I think.' Barry delved into a drawer, found the folder and passed it to Marshall.

He flicked through the contents, then settled on one document. He stared at it for some time. 'I've found it. I've found out why Anna was murdered. Why all the others were killed. Why they framed me, and why they want to kill me now. The problem is I'm still trying to make sense of it. I need time. It's too complicated to take in at one go. I also need to check something Brown said. Before we leave, I'm going to use their photocopier. I want to make a copy of everything in this file.'

It was a few minutes after 2 a.m. when they left the building. They found Lisa in the Land Rover, almost frantic with worry. 'I daren't move, in case I missed you, but there've been sirens going, left, right and centre. I felt sure you'd be locked up by now. How did it go?'

'Like a dream,' Marshall reassured her. 'What's more, we got what we came for. I'll show you when we get back.'

As they reached the outskirts of the city they relaxed slightly. They'd committed an outrageous act of burglary and compounded this with the theft of copier paper and an envelope. There would probably be a case for them to answer in the use of copier cartridge ink. But they didn't care.

They spoke very little on the journey. For the most part Marshall pondered the implications of the papers. Once they left the ring road, he spoke. 'You appreciate this isn't by any means the end.'

'No, I don't suppose so.' Lisa was concerned what Marshall would do, now the truth about Anna's death was emerging.

'You could say it's only the beginning,' he told her. 'I'll have to think it through very carefully.'

'What will you do with the information?'

'I wish I knew. Once, I only wanted revenge, now I'm not so sure. It's just another problem to sort out.'

'Will those files give you all you need?'

'Yes, but there are a lot of loose ends to tie up: pieces of the jigsaw to put into place.'

'Have you any idea how to do it?'

'Not yet. It's far from straightforward.'

'No matter what you learn, no matter how horrible it

becomes, you must remember one thing?'

'What's that?'

'If you do anything rash, it could land you back in Durham. This time with justification, I don't think Anna would want that.'

'Is that the police officer talking, or the concerned friend?'

'The concerned friend.'

'I'm glad. At one time I hadn't a concerned friend in the world. Then, I'd have found these bastards and killed them. I'd have done it because I owed it to Anna. Now everything's different. You're right; I don't think Anna would want me to put my future in jeopardy. I've been concentrating so hard on keeping out of the police's way; I haven't given a thought about what happens afterwards.'

Barry phoned Shirley from his mobile. 'We'll be another half an hour. No, stop fretting, we're OK. You get to bed. Leave the french window in the lounge unlocked. We'll hide the Land Rover and take a short cut over Sir Maurice's kitchen garden to the woods. If the police are still watching they won't see us come in that way.'

chapter twenty-two

Barry decided he needed a few hours' sleep before Alan told him exactly what he'd discovered. 'I'll try and make sense of everything. At the moment it's pure speculation. I need to go through both sets of files. Those we've just got and Brown's. I'll tell you what I find in the morning. It'll be easier to explain the whole thing instead of parts of it.'

Only the repeated stimulation of more coffee kept Marshall and Lisa awake, reading the file documents over and over, whilst Marshall made copious notes. He suggested they listen to Brown's taped confession again.

'It was someone called Jones, it was part of the code, Smith or Jones. I never knew their names.'

'That's not good enough, Mr Brown. Jones tells us nothing. Tell us who paid you to kill Anna Marshall.' Silence.

'Tell us who paid you to kill Stuart Moran.' Silence.

'Tell us who paid you to kill Councillor Jeffries.' Still silence.

'If you want to be a tough guy I'll have to do it the hard way.'

'No, no, don't do that, I'll tell you, I'll tell you,' the voice was close to screaming.

'Go on then. Who paid you?'

'His name's Harry, Harry Rourke.'

'How do you know?'

'He told me.' Now the voice was agitated.

'He told you his name was Harry Rourke?'

'As good as.'

'What does that mean?'

'When I asked him, he told me. '"Just think of me as Harry,"' that's what he said.'

'I thought you told me that when you talked with customers

you used Smith and Jones?'

'That's just our code. I always insist on another name as well, one that will help me identify them. I have more than one customer, you know.' Now there was a little bravado returning.

'How do you know this "Harry" is Harry Rourke?'

'Because he's careless. Most customers use withheld numbers, but he didn't bother. I used 1571 and ring-back. When the receptionist answered she said, "Broadwood Construction". I looked them up and found out their managing director's name is Harry Rourke.'

Lisa switched the tape off. 'Was he right? Is it Harry who's been paying for the murders?'

'Oh yes, it's Harry all right.' Marshall started to laugh.

Lisa stared at him curiously as the Dickinsons entered the kitchen. Shirley headed for the stove. 'I'll get some breakfast started. You two must be starving.'

When they'd eaten Lisa demanded, 'Now, would you mind explaining?'

Marshall looked at his notes. 'OK, I'll tell you as much as I've been able to piece together.' He tapped the papers. 'A lot of it is gleaned from these. The rest is informed guesswork. There are still a few gaps.

'A long time ago two men served together in the RAF. They became friends and when they left the service they kept in touch. One of them took over the running of the family business. A small building company, doing original works and some renovation. The other went to work for a much bigger concern. Somewhere along the line the two old comrades got together and hatched a plot that involved a huge risk, but would yield massive rewards.'

'What sort of plot?' Barry asked.

'A fraud of gigantic proportions. If it had been discovered they would both have got long prison sentences. Set against that, the fraud must have earned them millions over the years. The small family business, which was called Corps Building Corporation, grew and prospered. It took on larger, more valuable contracts and began to tender for public works. As it got bigger, the company name was changed to Coningsby Developments. The managing director, Julian Corps, became a well-known and respected figure in the industry.

'Eventually Corps was approached to stand for parliament. He was offered the candidature of a safe seat that was coming up at a by-election.' Marshall paused. 'I gleaned the next bit of information when I was picking up at a shoot last month. Apparently, Corps has made such a good impression within his party that he's already being talked of as a future leader.

'All very laudable: except for one thing. What no one knew was that Corps hadn't succeeded on his own merits. He succeeded because his company tendered for, and got, contracts due to influence exerted by the chairman of the local planning committee. Councillor Bob Jeffries. Who was, I have no doubt, well rewarded for his services.'

Marshall paused, 'I remember Corps from my own time in the construction industry. He was a nonentity without much business ability. I actually convinced myself I'd got the wrong man. Either I'd got the name wrong or it was another bloke called Corps.'

'So Corps wasn't the leading light in the fraud?' Lisa asked. 'Shame about that, I was going to make a feeble joke about Corps producing corpses, but maybe I'd better not.'

Marshall groaned. 'Definitely better not. In fact Corps was a non-starter compared to the man I'd worked for. Harry Rourke had more business acumen in his little finger than Corps had in his whole body. It just didn't make sense that he could compete successfully with Rourke.

'When I realized Corps was indeed the same man, my first thought was, how did he manage to find out which contracts were up for grabs? Let alone win them against such stiff opposition. Now I know the full story, winning them was easy. Councillor Jeffries saw to that. Finding them was just as easy, because Corps didn't find them. He simply stole them. Or to be precise, his secret partner did. That alone wouldn't have been enough. Corps needed somebody behind him, because he couldn't think his way out of a paper bag, not in a business sense that is. So there had to be another figure guiding him, a sleeping partner. But one who would have been ruined if his identity became known.

'The need for secrecy was essential, but Corps's benefactor also needed security. He needed paperwork that would ensure he could claim his just deserts. However, that agreement also had to be kept totally secret.'

Marshall stood up and began pacing round the room. 'So they approached Stuart Moran, a junior partner in Hobbs and Hirst, and asked him to draw up an agreement to satisfy both needs. Moran came up with a deal that would ensure the eventual sale of Corps Building Corporation, later known as Coningsby Developments to a further company, Leconfield Holdings. Leconfield had two shareholders, each with a fifty per cent stake in the company. Because of the need for secrecy, Leconfield had to remain a dormant company until the time was right. That way the shareholders' names never appeared. It didn't have to file accounts. It just lay on the shelf gathering dust.'

Marshall's pacing, Lisa noticed had become somewhat more agitated and she thought she knew why.

'Unfortunately, Moran's security wasn't as tight as it should have been. Somehow, Anna got to know of the conspiracy and the name of the man behind it.' Marshall paused again. 'You'll understand, I'm speculating here. Anna was a no-nonsense and confrontational sort of person. She also had a strict code of ethics. If I hadn't been fed a load of lies about her, I might have guessed she would never have countenanced such wrongdoing.'

Marshall paused in his walking tour and rested his hands on the chair back. He leaned forward. 'The irony is, that if anyone else in Hobbs and Hirst had seen that name it would have meant nothing to them, but because Anna was married to me she recognized it immediately. My bet is, she told Moran that unless the scam was finished and the agreement torn up, she'd tell me. They couldn't risk that, and they certainly weren't prepared to drop their lucrative scheme.'

He straightened up and began to wander again. 'Killing Anna wasn't enough. They needed to frame me for her murder, for two reasons. One was to get me out of the way so I wouldn't ask awkward questions. Also, if the police were satisfied I'd killed her, they wouldn't look for anyone else. From that moment the ground rules were laid. If anyone got in their way, they were disposed of. Originally, they were doing quite nicely stealing contracts from Broadwood, but that wasn't enough. They weren't getting the success their greed demanded. So they got Brown to organize a road accident involving the chairman of the planning committee. Once he was out of the way, they waited to see who was elected in his place. Step forward, Councillor Robert 'Call me Bob' Jeffries, long-time political hack, well and truly on their payroll. Once they had the chairman of the planning committee in their pocket, Coningsby Developments never looked back.

'You might think they'd be satisfied with that, but their ambition was growing all the time, or was it their greed? They wanted the lot. The only way was to get rid of the opposition. That meant buying out Broadwood Construction. The only problem was that Broadwood is a very wealthy company. Going by what I've been reading in the press recently, my guess is they arranged a series of very expensive accidents to equipment they knew would be uninsured. The result was to reduce the value of Broadwood. Again I'm guessing, but I reckon that was only the first phase of their final push to get control.'

Marshall ceased his walkabout and sat down at the table. He took a mouthful of fresh coffee. 'The vandalism was working well, but they needed more to push Rourke into selling. They launched a bid based on a ridiculously low offer price. A copy of the offer document is in the Coningsby Developments file at Hobbs and Hirst and I'd love to have heard Harry Rourke's language when it landed on his desk.' Marshall held the photocopied document up. 'They wanted to push Harry into a position where he'd be forced to sell, even at their price. They were certain he'd reject the bid unless they could put him into a position where he'd no alternative.

191

'The whole focus of the bid was based on an old tactic; one that had worked well before. They would remove Rourke by having him framed for murder. They had some murders to commit, they had Brown to commit them and they had the means to set Harry up for the role of fall guy. If you were able to trace the money back from Brown's bank accounts my bet is you would find Brown was paid by Valley Services, a subsidiary of Coningsby, and by all appearances a company which has no obvious *raison d'être*. My guess is that Valley Services invoiced Broadwood Construction for the amount of Brown's fee. Their next step would have been to blow the whistle on Brown. When he was arrested, he'd tell everything he knew. As we've heard, that someone called Harry from Broadwood Construction had paid him to commit the murders. Harry Rourke would be arrested, Broadwood Construction would collapse and Coningsby Developments would buy it at their own price.'

'If they decided to frame Rourke for the murders, why involve you?' Shirley asked.

'That was quite clever. They thought they could pin Moran's murder on me. Make it look like revenge. Then have me killed and make it look like suicide. I might have saved them the trouble if I'd caught up with Moran before Lisa stopped me. Once Brown had served his purpose they'd throw him to the wolves. They were sure he'd confess and implicate Harry.

'As I say, they already had a precedent to work from, it was the same as they used on me. Once Harry was out of the way they'd have a clear field, with a power base to tender for national contracts the like of which they'd only dreamed of. They'd be able to rely on influence from Westminster too; Julian Corps, MP, would see to that.'

'But why kill Moran and Jeffries?' Shirley asked.

'Difficult to be sure, but I can guess. Moran had already had twinges of conscience. He funded my appeal. My guess would be that Councillor Jeffries was getting too greedy.'

'I asked you if Harry was behind all this. I take it that isn't true?' Lisa asked.

'Oh yes it is. Perfectly true.' Marshall lifted some papers

from out of the file. 'This is an agreement for the purchase of Coningsby Developments and all its subsidiaries by Leconfield Holdings.' Marshall pointed to one of the documents. 'And these, are the Memorandum and Articles of Association of Leconfield Holdings.

'Leconfield Holdings has only got two shareholders, each with a fifty per cent stake in the company. One of the shareholders is Julian Corps and the other is his old RAF comrade, Frederick John Harrison. Harry Rourke's trusted right hand man: Deputy managing director of Broadwood Construction. When he left the RAF and joined Broadwood he had to drop his old nickname because it was causing too much confusion: Freddie Harrison, previously known to one and all, as Harry.

'He has to be the architect of the whole scheme. Left to his own devices Corps would have failed. He's too lightweight. Freddie, by comparison, is the ideal candidate. A man in a privileged position able to pass tenders to Corps almost before the ink was dry. The man who is able to sign off invoices to Valley Services and probably even sign the cheques for, and on behalf of, Broadwood Construction. The man who will emerge from the shadows, as a fifty per cent shareholder in Leconfield Holdings, which would by then own both Coningsby Developments and Broadwood Construction. With Harrison running the group, and Corps using his Westminster influence, the rewards they'd previously achieved would pale into insignificance by comparison with what lies ahead.'

The silence was broken only by the ticking of the kitchen clock. Eventually Barry spoke. 'Now you know. What will you do?'

Marshall shrugged. 'I'm still thinking it over.'

'Why not just take this evidence to the police?' Barry asked. 'Surely that's the most sensible thing to do?'

'It would be under normal circumstances. The problem is we don't know how widespread the corruption is. For all we know they might have police officers on their payroll. So who do we trust?' Marshall smiled. 'Apart from Lisa.'

'And DI Nash,' Lisa reminded him.

Marshall looked at her for a second. 'Yes, but how much would his word count for?'

'Quite a lot I think. Why not ask him?'

'I'll think about it. Otherwise we'll have to consider other ways of getting at the truth.'

Barry looked puzzled. 'How can you be sure about Nash?'

Lisa explained, 'Because he read something in Alan's file, the one relating to the original conviction for murder. It was in a transcript of Alan's first interview, just after his wife's car had been found. During the course of questioning, Dundas accused Alan of slitting his wife's throat and dumping her body in the North Sea.'

'I don't get the point, why was that significant?'

'Because what Mike spotted, was the date of the interview. When Dundas said that, Anna's body hadn't been found. She was still technically no more than a missing person. So how did Dundas know her throat had been slit? How did he know she'd been dumped in the sea? The bloodstains in her car could just as easily have been there if she'd been shot, her body could have been buried. Mike checked back and found Moran had been interviewed the previous day, during which he used the very same phrase. In other words Moran knew precisely how Anna Marshall had been killed. He directed Dundas to that line of questioning.'

'What alternatives does that leave?'

'I'm not going to discount the police option altogether,' Marshall said. 'I just don't think it's sensible to rely on it exclusively.'

'That doesn't answer Barry's question,' Lisa pointed out.

'About the alternatives? Well, there's the press for one. But they've to be extremely careful about libel. They'd probably need stronger evidence than the police. Launching a full-scale press investigation would take weeks, if not months. We don't have that long.'

'No other way that springs to mind, I suppose?'

Marshall eyed Lisa suspiciously. The question had been posed innocently, a little too innocently perhaps. 'There's always the possibility of resolving matters ourselves.'

'Ah yes,' Lisa said. 'I wondered when we'd get round to that option. But tell me something, with your background in civil engineering, you've been able to work out all this, but what about the third person?'

'What third person?' the others chorused.

'There must be a third person involved. If a substantial number of people are receiving bribes they'd need a paymaster. Someone to act as go-between, to protect Harrison's and Corps's identities.'

'Couldn't they have done it anonymously? Like Brown's payment?' Barry asked.

Lisa shook her head. 'No, there's a world of a difference between the payments to Brown and the way the bribes would be handled. Brown's payments were made to a criminal who'd set up an elaborate network of bank accounts to obscure the money laundering. The people getting the bribes aren't criminals as such. They'll appear to be perfectly respectable. Upright citizens doing normal nine-to-five jobs. The payment to them would have to be untraceable. That means cash, and Corps and Harrison would need someone to dole out the funds.'

'OK, I buy that,' Marshall agreed. 'I see your point, but I was thinking there's someone else, a fourth man.'

'Why?' Barry looked even more confused.

'There's another part of the scheme Corps and Harrison couldn't have carried out for themselves; the industrial sabotage.'

'Why not?' Shirley asked.

'Because they wouldn't want to risk being caught and they don't have the practical knowledge. You've already heard my opinion of Corps. Harrison's an office man, a financial expert, and wouldn't know one end of an excavator from a camel's backside, if it was painted yellow.'

'If there were two others involved, that would leave Corps and Harrison vulnerable to exposure. You know, "when thieves fall out", that sort of thing,' Lisa suggested.

'The difference is, these men wouldn't be outsiders. They have to know both the industry and Broadwood's operations.

Which means Rourke has more than one viper in his nest.'

'If you're right, Corps and Harrison would still be vulnerable.'

'Maybe, maybe not; perhaps they have some hold over these men that will ensure their silence. Exposure would be bad enough for Corps and Harrison, but it could be equally bad for the others. And they had the fall-back situation, where they could threaten a visit from Brown.'

'How do you plan to find these men?' Lisa asked.

'I wouldn't think that's too difficult. Rourke always kept management as streamlined as possible. So there won't be many to choose from. However, that isn't the only unresolved issue.'

'What more can there be?' Barry asked.

'One more death that must be connected, but for the life of me I can't see how. Think about the murders Brown's committed that are linked to all this. The motive's now become clear. All except for one: Gary Watson. What was the motive for his murder?'

'I'm lost,' Barry confessed.

'Gary Watson was the Broadwood employee who fell to his death from the top of a Broadwood building site,' Lisa told him.

'I remember now. You said his death was made to look like an accident,' Shirley recalled.

'Right, but we don't know the motive for Watson's murder.'

'Might they have needed to silence him?' Lisa wondered.

'Highly unlikely, Watson was a site foreman. He wouldn't have been in a position to find out anything damaging. As far as the running of Broadwood was concerned he would have little or no weight.'

'He may have accidentally seen or heard something perhaps?' Barry persisted.

'Very improbable. The likes of Harrison or Corps rarely find themselves in the company of site workers such as Watson. The chances of him stumbling on anything incriminating would be extremely remote. I think we have to look elsewhere for the motive behind Watson's murder. Trouble is, I'm not sure where.'

'I'm beginning to see what you meant when you said you need more evidence,' Lisa agreed.

'It might help if you had a plan,' Barry suggested.

Lisa groaned. 'Don't even think it. Alan's plans frighten me silly.'

Marshall grinned. 'The idea of burgling Corps' or Harrison's house to get the evidence has crossed my mind.' He smiled at Lisa. 'But I don't need to involve you if it frightens you.'

'That's a lousy thing to say,' Lisa told him indignantly. 'I went all the way to Leeds and back, risking arrest for harbouring a fugitive. I aided and abetted you whilst you broke into Hobbs and Hirst's offices, drove the getaway car, and you have the nerve to say: "if it frightens you". Everything you do frightens me. That doesn't mean I'm going to back off helping.'

They were still debating the issue when Lisa's mobile rang.

'Hello, Mike. Yes, but we're a bit tired.' She listened to what Nash had to say. 'OK, I'll ring you back a bit later, we've got the information, and Alan has a germ of an idea.' She closed her phone. 'Nash wanted to know what progress we've made,' she explained.

By late morning their plans were made. 'I vote we grab a couple of hours' sleep,' Marshall suggested.

'Whilst you two have a nap I'll check out the information we need,' Barry told them.

'Are you sure this is the right way to go about it?' Lisa asked. 'After all, it's been a long time?'

'I'm absolutely certain. It's high time I talked to Harry Rourke again.'

Marshall slept on the settee in the Dickinsons' lounge, whilst Lisa retired to the spare room. Lisa was undoubtedly more comfortable, but her companion had deserted her. Nell curled up on the rug alongside her master.

When he woke up Marshall went through to the kitchen. Shirley and Barry were seated at the table. Their expressions were serious. 'There's been an item on the news,' Barry told him. 'We heard it on the local radio. Officers from the Serious Fraud Office raided Broadwood Construction this morning. Apparently they're still there, examining documents.'

'I'd better wake Lisa, get her to phone Nash,' Marshall said immediately. 'This could scupper our plans unless we nip it in the bud.'

'I'll go,' Barry said, but subsided in his chair as Shirley kicked his ankle.

'What was that for?' he asked when Marshall had left the room.

'Sometimes, Barry, you fail to see what's under your nose. How you manage as a keeper, I'll never know.'

'You mean, Alan and Lisa. . . ?'

'Of course. Why do you think she's gone to all this trouble for him, risking her career and everything?'

'Oh,' Barry said. There didn't seem to be anything else to say.

Marshall looked down at Lisa. He'd knocked on the door but failed to rouse her. Seeing her asleep, he was reluctant to wake her, but knew it was necessary. For the first time he realized what an attractive woman she was. Not only that, but she'd risked so much for him. He reached forward and shook her shoulder gently. 'Lisa, it's Alan. Wake up. We've things to do.'

She opened her eyes and smiled. 'Gosh, I was well away.' She sat up, the duvet slipping enough to expose her breasts. Marshall turned away, the glimpse of her semi-nakedness, despite the bra, acutely embarrassing. He could feel the blood pounding in his ears.

'What's the problem?' she asked as she pulled hastily at the duvet.

Marshall explained.

'Right, let's see what we can do. Do you mind?' She thrust back the duvet and slid her legs over the side of the bed. As she dressed, Marshall turned his back, suddenly aware of a hunger he'd thought long dead.

chapter twenty-three

Lisa Andrews' car stopped at the end of the lane. The watching officers had plenty of time to take in the registration number from the safety of their car. The leader had chance to focus his binoculars on the driver and establish that Lisa was alone in the vehicle. 'OK, this is it.' They followed her to Netherdale, maintaining a discreet distance. They followed her car into the Netherdale railway station car park. They followed Lisa after she left the vehicle and headed into the concourse. They followed her to the ticket office, heard her purchase a return ticket to Leeds and bought two for themselves. They followed her on to the train and took seats in the carriage behind hers. At the next station they watched Lisa leave the train and followed her on to the platform. When they left the station they saw her climb into the Dickinsons' Land Rover. They looked round in desperation for a taxi, but the rank was empty. When they caught sight of the man driving the Land Rover, they reached for their mobile phones. It was undoubtedly Alan Marshall. He'd made no attempt to disguise himself. Sadly, hoodwinked once again by the fugitive's duplicity, they were unable to follow him.

Urgent messages were passed to all units in the area. Half an hour later the Land Rover was stopped, much to the surprise of its occupants: Barry and Shirley Dickinson.

Confident of the way the deception had been carried out, the police broadcast an alert for Shirley Dickinson's car. Later that evening they discovered it, in the car park of the next railway station down the line.

Mike Nash was driving. 'That was a brilliant piece of deception, which one of you thought it up?'

'I seem to get the blame for everything, according to Lisa,' Marshall replied, 'so I'd better own up to that as well.'

As they neared their destination Lisa sensed a change in Marshall's mood. He seemed tense. 'You're not nervous are you?'

'Not really,' Marshall replied. 'I used to like Harry, until he turned on me. That hurt at the time because it was so out of character. If it had been anyone else I mightn't have cared, but I was vulnerable; Harry deserting me was the last straw. I'm not saying I lost the will to fight but it all seemed hopeless.'

When they reached the outskirts of Leeds, Marshall directed Nash to take the ring road towards the western edge of the sprawling city. The evening rush hour had passed, so their progress was relatively quick. They followed a local signpost that pointed the way to a village named Calverley, in the no man's land between Leeds and Bradford. Although it was dark, Lisa could see that the built-up area had given way to fields and small wooded copses. She was surprised how closely the countryside encroached towards the city. They switched to a smaller road, similar to one of the country lanes around Kirk Bolton. After they'd driven for about ten minutes, they pulled to a halt at the end of a long tarmac drive. Large wrought iron gates blocked their way. 'Looks as if we're on foot from here,' Nash commented, pointing to a pedestrian gate alongside the main ones.

A quartet of motion-sensitive security lights sprang to life as they walked towards the front of the house, bathing the whole area in a stark halogen glow. Behind these Lisa could see a large, stone-built farmhouse, its exterior soot-blackened to match the walls alongside the drive. They walked unchallenged across the tarmac to the front door. Marshall pressed the bell and they heard the chimes resounding within the building.

Dinner had been eaten in silence. In Tara's case it was diplomatic. In Harry's case sullen. During the first few minutes Tara tried one or two conversational openings but without response. Eventually she demanded, 'What's gone wrong now?'

'I've had the quarterly figures from the accountant,' he told her bitterly. 'I've only looked at the bottom line so far and that's bad enough. On top of that, there's this bloody investigation by the Serious Fraud Office.'

'What happened there?'

'It was totally weird. They arrived mob-handed, started going through all our files, pulling out contract after contract, examining them. Then, all of a sudden, the bloke in charge got a phone call, following which they upped sticks and departed. Without a word of explanation, just warned us they'd be back, and took all the stuff they'd been looking at with them.'

When the meal was over he stood up. 'I'm going into my study to look through this report properly. Then I've got to decide what I'm going to do. I don't want to be disturbed by anything or anybody. Got it?'

'Yes, Harry. If I come in, you'll know the house is burning down.'

That had been an hour ago. Now Tara hurried to answer the door before the caller had chance to press the bell again. Harry's temper and patience were almost exhausted.

She opened the door and stared at the trio standing there. She thought momentarily of Jehovah's Witnesses; then discounted the idea. Admittedly one of the men was carrying a folder, but they didn't seem the type. If anything, they seemed threatening. One of the men was dressed in black, which contributed to the image. The presence of the woman was comforting, if only slightly.

'Yes?' Tara asked nervously.

'Is Harry about?' the man standing directly in front asked. Tara looked at the speaker properly. There was something vaguely familiar about him.

'He left instructions he wasn't to be disturbed,' Tara told them. God, she thought. I sound like a bloody butler.

'I think he'll want to see us,' the man insisted.

'I've told you. He can't be disturbed,' Tara answered coldly. She made to close the door.

The move was blocked by the second of the men, the silent one. He braced the door with one arm.

Tara pushed but to no avail.

'Harry will want to be interrupted, once he knows who we

are and why we're here,' the speaker insisted.

'I've told you twice. Harry said no calls, no visitors. Please leave.' Tara pushed against the door again, but with no success.

'I'm sorry,' the second man said, as he leaned on the door. Tara found it opening despite her resistance. Then the trio was inside the hall. Tara was on the verge of panic. The woman spoke for the first time.

'Don't worry. This is for his benefit. We'll tell him you did your best to stop us.'

'Where's Harry lurking?' the first man asked.

'I'll tell him you're here.' The last semblance of Tara's resistance crumbled. 'Who shall I say wants to see him?'

'No. We'll announce ourselves. Just tell us where to find him.'

'Don't be scared. We're not here to harm him,' the woman added.

Tara was scared, not only that they would hurt Harry but her as well. She pointed to a door leading off from the hall.

Rourke was staring intently at the computer screen. He didn't look up when the study door opened. 'I told you I wasn't to be disturbed.'

'That's not a nice greeting for an old friend, Harry.'

Rourke looked up at the strange voice. His study seemed crowded. He briefly noticed Tara, hovering nervously in the doorway, uncertain whether to venture in or stay outside. Her indecision might have been influenced by the man standing directly behind her. Harry transferred his gaze to the man and woman directly in front of him. He didn't know the woman, but when he focused on the man, recognition came immediately. 'Alan Marshall! What the hell are you doing here?'

'That's a damned good question, Harry. I reckon you're the only one who can answer it.'

The cryptic remark was lost on Rourke. 'I thought you were wanted by the police? I can't believe you've suddenly appeared. You've picked the worst possible time for a social visit. Who are these people with you?'

'I'm sorry, this is Lisa Andrews. She has a vested interest in what happens to me. Lisa, this is Harry Rourke. Rourke owns

Broadwood Construction. He used to employ me. Rourke was the man who sacked me after I was charged with Anna's murder. A very caring soul, is Harry.'

Marshall turned to face Tara. 'I'm sorry if we scared you, but we need to talk to Harry and I wanted to surprise him. It's been nearly ten years since he fired me. He might have forgotten me.' He held out his hand to her. 'I'm Alan Marshall and this is Lisa.'

'I'm Tara,' she replied cautiously, shaking hands.

'What did you say about sacking you?' Rourke stood up and came round the side of the desk.

When Marshall replied the bitterness in his voice was apparent. 'So you can't remember? I suppose I was just some worker who'd proved unreliable by getting arrested. OK, so just sit in your fancy office and have him sacked. Don't give him the satisfaction of a personal letter. That might make him feel as if somebody cared. Instead, have the company secretary send him a little note telling him he was in breach of contract and that his contract had been terminated. Send it care of his prison cell.'

'Harry, you didn't do that. Tell me you didn't,' Tara sounded disgusted.

'No, I bloody well didn't.' It was Rourke's turn to be angry. 'I'm not sure if it's your memory or your brain that's failing, but you've got the facts all wrong. I didn't sack you, you resigned. I was all set to visit you. I'd requested permission for a prison visit; then you resigned. That seemed as if you were admitting you were guilty. I lost interest in you then.'

'No, Harry, it's you who've got it wrong,' Marshall told him quietly. 'But I can understand why. Tell me, how did you know I'd resigned?'

'You sent a letter.'

'Did you see it?'

'I didn't see it myself. I was told about it.'

'If I were to tell you the statement about that letter of resignation was a lie, designed to prevent you contacting me, what would your reaction be?'

'I'd say, prove it.'

There was a long silence as Marshall looked at his former

employer. Then he reached inside the folder he was carrying. 'I'm not one for keeping souvenirs, but for some masochistic reason I kept this.'

He produced a single sheet of paper and passed it to Rourke. Rourke stared at the tersely worded note. 'Like I said, Harry, you were deceived, just as I was. We were taken in by a very cunning, devious and ruthless man who'll go to any lengths to get what he wants. I think it would be best if you were to sit down. I've a few more shocks for you.'

Tara suggested they move into the lounge, where Lisa looked round appreciatively. The leather suite, comprising a couple of three-seater settees and four armchairs, didn't overcrowd the large room. Expensive-looking occasional tables adorned with lamps were distributed randomly around. The curtains were luxurious, as was the carpet.

'Why are you here?' Rourke asked wearily. 'Apart from finding out whether or not I fired you? This is a really bad time for me, and I can do without the police thinking I'm involved in helping you escape.'

'I understand how bad a time this is for you. But I shouldn't worry about the police.' Marshall glanced sideways, a smile fleetingly appearing on his face. 'This isn't a social visit, Harry, far from it. This is business, pure and simple. Except that it isn't pure and it's far from simple.'

'I don't understand.'

'You've been having a rough time recently, haven't you? Things have been going wrong, and it's getting worse. You've been losing contracts you should have won. Big contracts too, and that's worrying you. Then all this vandalism on top: sabotage, which was aimed at uninsured risks. I bet the bill for that runs into millions? And now the SFO is investigating you. Things must have got pretty bad. Almost enough for you to consider a takeover bid. Or you would do, if the offer price wasn't so ludicrously low.'

Rourke's head jerked up at the last sentence. 'How the hell did you know that?'

'I not only know about it. I know who the bidder is and the

price they're offering. I even have a copy of the offer document.'

'How did you get that? Don't tell me you're mixed up in this? Is this some perverted sort of revenge?'

'That's a fairly low opinion you've got of me, Harry. I'm not mixed up in it. At least not in the way you mean. Didn't you ever think that all these events were linked?'

Rourke was past words. He merely shook his head.

'Well they are, and I can prove it. And if you think that's bad, there's worse to come.'

'How could it possibly get worse?' Tara interrupted.

'Believe me, it does. And it would have succeeded, but for a little bit of luck. Imagine a scenario where you've received a bid for the company, but the offer is too low, even as things are. I guess you'd stick out for a better offer, but the bidders don't want to pay more than they need. They may even retract and get Broadwood for less. How do you think they'd go about that?'

Rourke shook his head, bewildered.

'Simple; they arrange the one event that would guarantee the collapse of Broadwood Construction: the removal of Harry Rourke. They could have you killed, but they had a better idea. What would happen to Broadwood if you weren't there to run it, Harry? If, for example; you were serving a life sentence for murder?'

Rourke's expression changed as Marshall explained. From disbelief to incredulity; from incredulity to acceptance; from acceptance to anger. It took three repetitions of the plot before Rourke grasped it fully. That was when the anger kicked in. 'Tell me who's behind this. Tell me and I'll kill the fucking bastards with my bare hands.'

'Join the queue!' Marshall told him. 'Some of us have prior claims.'

Rourke looked at him in astonishment. 'You mean Anna's death was connected to this? All that time ago? It's been going on that long?'

Marshall nodded. 'Anna discovered the plot and had to be silenced. I had to be framed for her murder to prevent me snooping around. Before I go any further, I've a question for you. There's one aspect of the whole business that still puzzles me.'

'Fire away.'

'Don't use the word "fire", it makes me twitch. I want to know everything you can tell me about Gary Watson.'

Rourke stared at Marshall open-mouthed. 'Gary Watson?' he echoed, 'You mean the foreman on the Wharfside development, the one who fell from the building?'

Marshall shook his head. 'Not fell. Gary Watson was murdered. Thrown off that building, his death arranged to look like an accident. The killer's confessed to Watson's murder along with all the others.'

'I don't get it,' Rourke said. 'You're talking about a plot to undermine Broadwood and ruin me. What could Watson's death achieve?'

'Precisely; so why was he murdered? Tell me everything you can about him.'

Rourke told them all he knew. His last sentence gave Marshall the motive.

'Now we know the worst. What the hell am I going to do?' Rourke asked.

'I've been thinking about that. I've come up with a plan.'

'If you want my advice, Tara,' Lisa told her, 'you'll emigrate immediately. Alan's plan will probably have you robbing a bank or kidnapping someone. He's got some very immoral ideas since he was in Durham Prison.'

Marshall ignored her and began to outline his idea. When Marshall finished Rourke looked at him in awe. 'You really think this will work?'

'Why not?' Marshall countered. 'It depends on you. Do you think you can do it?'

'How long will it take?' Rourke asked.

'I reckon it should be wrapped up by Friday. Probably Thursday will be the critical day.'

'It would be ideal if you could keep out of the way during tomorrow, Wednesday and Thursday,' Lisa suggested. 'But I don't suppose that's practical.'

'Actually it is. I've been planning to visit all our sites since the vandalism. I go round the bigger ones regularly, but it would do no harm to visit the others as well. I can do that over the next few days without raising suspicion. If I didn't appear in the office between now and the weekend they wouldn't think it out of the ordinary.'

'The way your temper's been recently they'll probably think their prayers have been answered,' Tara commented.

Rourke smiled ruefully, but Lisa picked up on Tara's implication. 'That's a good point. You can't afford to seem suddenly cheerful, in case word gets back.'

'You don't need to worry about that,' Rourke assured them. 'All I'll have to do is think about how much this has cost me.'

'That's fine, but you must give the impression you're going to reject the bid. I'm not sure how, because nobody else is supposed to know there is one. It must be something big enough to get everyone gossiping. Hopefully that'll catch them off balance. Then we can hit them.'

Rourke was beginning to enter the spirit of the game. 'I've got some quotes on my desk for replacement excavators. I haven't done anything with them yet, but I could get them faxed through to home and ask the office to ring the salesmen and make appointments for next week. It'll give the salesmen a stiffy, but commit me to nothing specific. The last thing anyone considering accepting a bid would do is order expensive plant and machinery. More important, the news will go round the office like wildfire.'

'That sounds perfect.'

'So what do I do after that?'

'Sit back and wait for things to happen. They'll move pretty fast but you can't do anything more. I'll keep in touch and tell you when it's safe to break cover.'

'Suppose nothing happens?'

'It will,' Marshall reassured him. 'And when it does the tremors will be felt far and wide.'

Tara broke in. 'What intrigues me is how you found all this out?'

Marshall glanced at Nash for approval. 'Go on,' Nash told him, with a smile. His only reaction so far.

Marshall told the whole story. As he spoke, Lisa watched the expressions of his audience. Rourke shook his head when Marshall had finished. 'It's as well you did. I'm not sure I'd have believed you if you'd come to me without evidence.'

'If I hadn't turned into a criminal, we wouldn't have discovered the plot until it was too late, if at all.'

As their visitors were preparing to leave, Harry and Tara escorted them into the hall. 'You know, Alan, I still find it incredible that you've managed this, especially with the police chasing you. Are you still wanted for murder?'

'I don't think so.' Marshall looked at his companions.

'Tell him.' Nash nodded.

'I'm afraid I didn't complete the introductions. This is Detective Inspector Nash from Helmsdale CID. Lisa's, or should I say DC Andrews', boss. I couldn't introduce him until we were absolutely sure about you, Harry. As to the rest, well, I had an incentive, didn't I?'

Rourke nodded soberly. 'I did wonder. We forget with all this talk of business and plots that behind it are people's lives. So you're doing it for revenge?'

'Partly, I had to clear myself too.'

'If you hadn't, I'd have spent the rest of my life in prison. Whatever the reason I'm bloody glad you did. I owe you; big time.'

'You can repay me later.'

'That's a promise,' Rourke told him.

'It's time we were off, Alan,' Nash reminded him. 'Mr Rourke, for the time being all communication should be through me, or from mobile to mobile.' He gave Rourke his card. 'And, one more thing. I want you to take extra care until this is all wrapped up.' He looked across at Tara. 'That applies to both of you. Make sure no harm comes to you and that nobody can get at you via Tara. Remember, these are desperate men playing for very high stakes. They'll stop at nothing. We're only talking a matter of days, but you now know what they're capable of. Be on your guard.'

'Are you sure it's necessary? You're not overdramatizing?'

'You haven't seen the files on the murders Brown's committed, and the "accidents" he's arranged. If they've one person like Brown, they may have others. Don't forget we haven't identified everyone yet. Until then, trust nobody. Keep clear of tall buildings and out of the way of excavator blades and deep trenches whose sides could cave in. When this is over I'll need a statement from you.'

On the return journey they discussed the meeting. 'What still surprises me is how easy it was,' Marshall said. 'I admit I wasn't thinking straight at the time, and later I didn't want to dwell on the past, but I never doubted that letter originated from Harry.'

'And he simply took Harrison's word for it,' Nash replied. 'He believed you'd resigned without asking to see your letter. I bet Harrison had one ready in case Rourke asked for it. As you say, it was dead easy.'

'That's because Harrison was in a position of trust,' Marshall said quietly. 'What possible motive could he have for lying about something that was apparently no concern of his?'

'Even tonight, I don't think Rourke would have believed you, had you not taken the evidence along,' Lisa added. 'Unless we'd introduced Mike earlier.'

'Harrison's worked for him over twenty-five years. It must have come as a hell of a shock.'

'What do you remember about Harrison?' Nash asked.

'Not much really. Not in a business sense anyway. He was the perfect second in command, quietly efficient. A good manager and administrator. Apart from work I can only recall a couple of things.' Marshall thought for a moment, 'No, three actually.'

'What were they?'

'He'd a passion for gardening; roses and orchids in particular. He used to win lots of prizes at local shows with his blooms. Gardening and girls were his two main hobbies. He was forever chasing women, without much success. Freddie had a sort of smarmy charm. Some girls fell for it; others found it a turn-off.'

'And your other memory?'

'Nothing important; just one of those small things that mark people out. He'd spent time abroad with the RAF. That might have been where he met Corps. Whilst he was out there, Harrison developed a craving for curry. We used to go out for a drink when a contract was completed and we'd almost always finish up at an Indian restaurant. Freddie used to order a curry so hot nobody else could go near it. He must have a stomach of steel.'

'I have to say, none of it makes him sound like the monster who'd calmly order all these murders, just like ordering a curry,' Lisa commented.

'That's what people always say after a murderer's identity is revealed,' Nash told them. 'You must have heard it dozens of times: "He was such a polite, quiet man. Helped old ladies across the road, carried their shopping", that sort of remark. I know, because I've met a lot of them. And the very worst ones seemed perfectly normal, average blokes you wouldn't give a second glance to. Until you found out what they'd done.'

'Is everything going to plan, Harry?'

'More or less. Rourke's been like a bear with a sore head recently and we know why. He asked me to work out the cost of the vandalism.'

'I bet that came to a pretty penny, didn't it?'

'It did by the time I'd finished manipulating the figures – and the projections. It was under £1 million but I made it up to almost £3 million by adding in everything I could. Including a few things that definitely won't happen.'

'I should imagine he was a little upset?'

'Not half as angry as he was after he received the offer Darren Cowan sent him. That nearly provoked a heart attack. Whilst he was still seething about the bid, I rang the auditors and told them Rourke wanted the latest quarterly results as soon as possible. I asked them to add in a notional cost for the vandalism of £2.75 million. What with that and the £400,000 I'd paid Brown via Valley Services, I knew the results would make bad reading.'

'How did he react to them?'

'At one stage I thought half the office staff would walk out. Except

the SFO had arrived by then and the mayhem got worse. I thought we'd succeeded in every respect, but for some reason they stopped their investigation and left. Maybe something more urgent has come up.'

'What about the next phase of the operation?'

'I can't do much until I contact Brown. I tried all last week without success. I'll try again later this week and then let you know.'

'OK, but don't ring on Thursday evening. I have a by-election meeting that night.'

'How's that going?'

'Couldn't be better. We're streets ahead in the polls. My agent's ecstatic. He reckons if it's decent weather on polling day we might even top the general election majority. The party hierarchy are making some very encouraging remarks as well. On Thursday I've got the deputy leader speaking on my behalf. He's actually staying at my house overnight on Thursday. The leader in the upper house will be on the platform as well.'

'That's excellent, Julian. It seems as if everything is about to fall into place quite nicely. As soon as I contact Brown we can start implicating Rourke.'

'Have you worked out how?'

'I'll give the police an anonymous tip-off that should lead to Brown's arrest. Then I'll point them towards Valley Services. The police will follow the money trail back from Brown via Valley Services to Broadwood Construction. With that and Brown's confession they'll arrest Rourke, and Broadwood will collapse. We step in. Buy Broadwood and the future's plain sailing.'

'You don't foresee any last minute hitches?'

'Relax, Julian, every detail has been taken care of and there's nothing to connect us with any of it. Nothing, I repeat, nothing can possibly go wrong.'

chapter twenty-four

Their subterfuge to deceive those watching the Dickinsons' cottage the following morning involved nothing more complicated than Marshall and Lisa hiding under a blanket in the back of the Dickinsons' Land Rover. Seeing the keeper pull up near a pheasant release pen and take a sack of feed out, the officers lost interest and returned to their post. Once the coast was clear, Barry let them out and told Lisa, 'Your car is parked at the other end of this ride where I moved it to last night.'

Once again they headed for Leeds. To ensure complete success for the scheme concocted by Marshall and Rourke, they had one more visit to make.

Linda finished loading the washing machine and glanced at the clock, 11.15. She was making coffee when the doorbell rang. A man and woman stood by the front door. Their car was parked across the drive. 'Can I help you?'

'Good morning. My name's Alan and this is Lisa. It's Linda, isn't it?'

Linda looked at the couple questioningly. As she was still puzzling over their identity, Marshall began to tell her the reason for their visit. As he spoke, her mouth widened. As fact followed fact, surprise turned to shock, shock to astonishment and astonishment to horrified acceptance. She invited them in. They sat and talked for hours. By the time they finished they'd convinced her. Once she was persuaded, Linda was eager to help. Her keenness should have raised suspicions. When Marshall put forward his plan, Linda suggested a couple of modifications before they agreed the final details.

After they left, Linda walked over to the picture window

in the lounge. She stared out for a long time, at the immaculate lawn, the neatly stocked flower beds and the shrubs and numerous rose bushes that marked the border of the property. She pondered all that her visitors had told her; then turned and began to make preparations. She'd a busy couple of days ahead.

'Superintendent Dundas, DI Nash here. Sorry I couldn't get back to you before. Things have been pretty hectic here, makes things worse when we're so short staffed. Still, I've got some good news for you.'

'Really?' There was a wealth of sarcasm in the single word. 'That's not what I've been hearing. I understood one of your officers has been suspended for consorting with Marshall. More than just consorting by all accounts. Do members of your force often sleep with convicted murderers who are on the run?'

'Ah, you mean DC Andrews. Actually, that's part of the reason I rang you. Yes, the girl's been stupid, criminally so, as it turns out. But we've been able to turn it to our advantage. We've been leading her to think we believe the story she and Marshall have cooked up between them. That way, she now thinks he's about to be cleared of all charges. Utter nonsense of course, but she's swallowed it, and more important, so has Marshall. I've actually had a phone call from him. I'm not sure where they've been hiding but I managed to convince him it was safe to come out. I'm supposed to meet him sometime tomorrow night. He's going to phone me with the details. When we do so, I think it would be a good idea if you and some of your officers were present when I make the arrest. It'll likely be on your turf. What do you think?'

'That sounds perfect. Well done, Nash, a splendid piece of police work. So good I reckon it would be an ideal opportunity to have the press and media there. It'd make a pleasant change for them to see us succeed in such a high profile case.'

'Great idea. Of course, we can't tell them much until I know the venue.'

'Leave it to me. I'll clue them in to begin with. Then I'll have my men ready to tip them off as to the time and the place when you give me the word.'

Nash put the phone down and looked across the room at Ruth and Clara. 'Hook, line and sinker,' he told them.

Freddie Harrison felt completely relaxed. He wandered through to his lounge after dinner and flopped down in his armchair to watch TV. He'd intended popping out to the greenhouse to check some seedlings he'd planted a couple of weeks ago. They were a new strain and he wanted to ensure their progress, but it was a cold, frosty night and they could wait another day. He really couldn't be bothered.

He belched slightly. A reminder of the curry he'd just eaten; hot and spicy. Freddie burped gently again, then settled back to watch *Coronation Street*.

At some stage during the programme Freddie remembered he still hadn't contacted Brown. That would also have to wait until the following day. Freddie wouldn't risk phoning from his own number. As always he would ring from the office.

At the end of the programme Freddie flicked the TV remote and was transported in an instant from Manchester to Albert Square, London. He had just started to watch *Eastenders* when the doorbell rang. He heard voices. Obviously visitors were being greeted. A few minutes later Freddie heard the lounge door open. 'Who was it?' he asked without turning his head.

'Hello, Freddie, you murdering bastard.'

Harrison looked round. Shock and fear combined, the room swam before his eyes. 'Marshall,' he whispered.

But it wasn't only Marshall. Beside him was a strikingly handsome girl Freddie didn't recognize; and behind her was another man. Harrison tried to speak but fear clogged his throat.

'Cat got your tongue, Freddie?' Marshall moved forward two paces. 'Surprised to see me, are you? Of course you are. It means everything's gone pear-shaped, doesn't it?'

Harrison's head jerked slightly. Little more than a twitch but it was a tangible sign he understood. He stared back in shock as Marshall continued, 'What's going wrong with the world, Freddie? You can't rely on tradesmen any more, can you?

Sending Brown to slit my throat and frame me for murder. And here I am, large as life, and twice as ugly. Oh, but pardon me. I'm forgetting my manners, I haven't introduced you, have I? This is Lisa Andrews.' Marshall's tone was light, almost conversational. Then suddenly the voice changed, took on a harsher note. 'Lisa, this is the man who paid Brown for killing Anna, just as he paid him to kill Moran. Tell me, Freddie,' Marshall leaned forward again as if seeking a confidence, 'did Brown ask for extra for killing Lesley Robertson, or did you get a two for one discount?' He turned and began pacing the room.

'He told Brown to make mine look like suicide, but Brown messed up, didn't reckon on "man's best friend". I bet Freddie would have been wild about that, but fortunately it wasn't his money.'

'Brown's confessed, Freddie. But first, he told me lots of interesting things. Now he's visiting with the police and telling them lots and lots of interesting things. Things like the death of the former chairman of the planning committee and the way he pushed Gary Watson off a building. Oh yes, Freddie, we know it all.'

Harrison was stunned at the scope of their knowledge. He wished he could act but he felt rooted to the chair.

Marshall spoke again. Again his tone was severe, like that of a judge or an executioner. Harrison was beginning to loathe the sound of his voice.

'All those killings because you hatched up a plot to rob Harry Rourke. Rob him of his contracts, his company, and finally, to rob him of his liberty as well. Such a neat scheme, but one that was bound to have teething troubles.

'When Anna found out, you knew if she told me you'd finish up inside. So you had her killed and framed me. It worked so well you decided to repeat it by framing Rourke.'

Harrison spoke for the first time, his voice a barely audible whisper. 'You can't prove a word of this.' There was no denial.

'Oh but I can, Freddie.' Marshall held up the documents from Hobbs & Hirst. 'These are copies of course. The police seized the originals this evening, shortly before they arrested Corps.

We arranged that little event to take place at his election rally. I thought you might appreciate that dramatic touch.'

On and on Marshall continued, taunting Harrison all the while. Harrison realized he should resist but couldn't. He wanted to rise, to leave his chair. To leave this room, leave his house. To be anywhere, except here within the range of Marshall's voice, Marshall's rage, Marshall's knowledge, Marshall's judgment, and Marshall's hatred. He thought it must be shock; he felt strangely weary. He realized denial was useless. Marshall knew everything. Marshall hadn't come seeking information. Marshall had come seeking revenge.

Freddie found his voice. 'I hope you don't expect me to confess or beg for forgiveness. Is that what you want?'

'No, my original plan was to kill you. After all, I served time for a murder I didn't commit. Perhaps I could trade that one against one I did commit. What do you think, is that fair?' Marshall spread his arms wide like a prosecuting counsel appealing to a jury. 'You robbed me of my wife. You framed me for her murder and you robbed me of my love for her.' Marshall leaned forward and his cold, pitiless eyes drilled into Harrison's. 'You robbed me of that love when you got Moran to lie.' Marshall's eyes were no longer cold, they were as hot as molten lava. 'You robbed me of that love,' Marshall's voice was quiet now, quiet but deadly, 'when it was all that I had left of her. You killed Anna twice. You slaughtered her body then you besmirched her memory. Can you think of a good reason why I shouldn't kill you, Freddie? Can anyone here think of a good reason why I shouldn't kill Freddie?'

For the first time Harrison knew he wasn't going to escape. It was all over. He knew it and was powerless to prevent it.

Into the silence after Marshall's final question a voice answered quietly, 'Yes, I can. I can think of one very good reason.'

Everyone turned towards the speaker. The woman standing in the lounge doorway held a small but extremely efficient-looking automatic pistol in her hand. 'Would the three of you go across to that settee and sit down.' She waved the pistol to emphasize the point as Freddie stared at her, his expression vague.

She turned to him. 'Do you recognize this gun? I took it out of your safe yesterday morning when I was showing them all those interesting documents and that very nasty video you have of Chris Davidson with those poor little boys.

'I loved Gary,' Linda Watson continued. 'It wasn't a perfect marriage but it was a good marriage. I remember the day he died; the day they came and told me he'd fallen from that building. All these years I've believed it. Believed it was an accident. I was hurt and upset when he died, grieving and in need of consolation. And there you were: kind, considerate Freddie. A shoulder to cry on. A helping hand for a widow alone. You timed it perfectly, didn't you? Made your move on me when I was at my most vulnerable: lonely and in need of companionship. So I became your mistress. Not for love; affection was the best I could feel for you. It wasn't the same as what I'd lost, but it was something.

'That was until yesterday morning, when these two arrived with their incredible tale of murder and plots, of fraud, and lies, and deception. I found it hard to credit what they were telling me. Until they played the tape, and I heard the man you paid confessing. Telling how he pushed Gary from that building. You had him murdered, just so you could get me. Do you have any idea how that makes me feel, Freddie? I'll tell you, shall I? I feel dirty; cheap and dirty. I don't know if I'll ever feel clean again. When I found out, every warm feeling I had for you was washed away in an instant. And what replaced it? I'll tell you, hatred. You should never underestimate the power of a woman's love, Freddie, or her capacity to hate. But then it's a little late for you.'

Linda turned towards Marshall. 'You asked a question. You asked if anyone knew a good enough reason for you not to kill him.' Marshall nodded. 'Well you can't,' Linda told him. 'Because I have already claimed that pleasure.'

'Go on, then.' Harrison spoke to her for the first time. 'Shoot me and have done with it.'

'You'll die when I'm good and ready, and not a minute

before,' Linda snapped. Then she smiled. 'But at least I gave you a good send-off. After all I'd heard, Freddie, I still made you your favourite meal, a parting gesture. A really hot, really spicy curry to send you on your way to Hell. Don't you think that was nice of me, Freddie?'

Harrison attempted to rise from his chair, trying to fight this strange feeling of inertia. 'For God's sake, get it over with,' he snarled. 'Shoot me, damn you.'

'No, Freddie. I'm not going to shoot you. I've something far better in mind. We're all going to sit here quietly and watch you start to die.'

Harrison stared at her, uncomprehendingly.

'I made the curry extra hot and extra spicy, to conceal the taste of the additional seasoning. Of course, it does say it's odourless and tasteless on the packet, but you can't always trust what the packet tells you. Can you? I checked it on your computer. It told me what the effects were. The nervous system gets attacked first, but the effects can still be reversed at this stage. You'll be immobile soon, Freddie. That's because the motor nerves have been attacked. But that's not fatal. It isn't until the convulsions start that the irreversible stage has been reached. Then you'll know. You'll know that death is inevitable. But what you don't know, Freddie, the best part of the joke is that it won't kill you tonight, or tomorrow, or the next day. This poison is so good it'll keep you alive for years to come. Just think of it, you'll have all that time to think about what you've done. That's all you will be able to do of course, because if I got the dose right you'll be totally paralysed. I do hope so,' Linda added thoughtfully. 'I measured it ever so carefully.'

'Where did you get the poison?' Lisa asked in revulsion.

Linda turned and smiled. There was a sort of sick horror in the sweetness of that smile. 'That's the best bit. I think it's so appropriate. I got it from Freddie's own greenhouse. It's his favourite weedkiller, and look, it's killing this weed.' She pointed at Harrison and began to laugh.

It was then that the first tremors began. It was then he finally realized that it was all over.

Linda had walked to the lounge door and was through it before Nash reached her. He heard the click of the lock being turned from the outside. 'Damn,' he glanced at his watch. 'Twenty minutes before the rest of the team get here.' He reached for his mobile and dialled the control room.

Nash and Marshall tried the windows; the double-glazed units were locked, the keys removed. Linda Watson left the house carrying a small briefcase containing all Freddie Harrison's disposable assets. Her planning had been meticulous. She waved cheerfully to them as she began reversing her car down the drive. There was nothing they could do to prevent her departure. They stood at the window, watching. None of them gave a thought to Harrison, still sitting helpless in his armchair.

When Mironova arrived she unlocked the lounge in time for the paramedics to remove Harrison to hospital. With them, they took an empty box of weedkiller Nash had salvaged from the kitchen waste bin.

At the prearranged time, when the rest of the police and their media entourage were in place, Marshall emerged from the house flanked by Nash and Lisa, who had taken hold of his arm with one hand, and his jacket collar with the other, as though she were detaining him. They were surrounded by uniformed officers, many of them armed. Cameras flashed as the press, TV and radio reporters crowded closer. The officers formed a circle around the trio. In the centre of this group were Superintendent Dundas and DS Smailes. Nash turned towards Marshall, reached out and began to shake his hand. Dundas stood, open-mouthed. 'Nash, what the hell are you doing?' he blustered. 'Arrest him!'

Nash glanced at Dundas, then held up a hand to quiet the babbling questions from the media. 'You were told there would be some meaningful arrests made this evening. This man'– he indicated Marshall – 'is Alan Charles Marshall, who has been accused of murdering three people. And this' – he indicated Lisa – 'is DC Lisa Andrews, who has for the last week been working undercover, to bring the persons responsible to justice. I imagine what has happened tonight will give them both great pleasure.'

Nash nodded slightly to Clara, who signalled to the edge of the crowd. The Chief Constable of Yorkshire Central Task Force, accompanied by Gloria O'Donnell stepped forward. The senior officer began his statement. 'Officers from a combined task force have this evening arrested Julian Corps. He will be charged, along with Frederick Harrison, with conspiracy to murder and a host of other offences. The murders include those of Anna Marshall, Councillor Jeffries, Stuart Moran and Lesley Robertson. All charges against Alan Marshall have been dropped. The arrests are the culmination of a brilliant operation led by Detective Inspector Nash of Helmsdale CID. He and his small team, although under-staffed, have uncovered a conspiracy to rob and defraud involving millions of pounds over the years. Other arrests will follow.'

Then the media went wild. The mêlée to get from the senior officers to Nash, from Nash to Marshall, Marshall to Lisa Andrews was so bad that at one point Nash thought riot police would have to be brought in.

Eventually Nash and Marshall escaped to the police car. 'We'll need a statement from you, of course, but I hope this is the end of a nightmare,' Nash told him.

'I hope so too,' Marshall agreed. His eyes slipped to Lisa, who was busy fielding questions. 'Let's call it a chance to look forward instead of dwelling in the past.'

The following day's *Netherdale Gazette* carried only one story, headlined: POLICE BLOW THE WHISTLE ON BIG BUSINESS, a story that had been carried across the national press that morning. It showed photographs taken the previous evening and statements issued by both chief constables. Under a separate banner headline, PARLIAMENTARY CANDIDATE ARRESTED, the article described the detention of Julian Corps in lurid detail. There were photos of Corps being led away from the rally in handcuffs alongside election posters of him. Another shot had Nash chuckling. The photo showed the deputy leader of Corps's party peering furtively from behind the curtain of the theatre hosting the rally, as police swooped to make the arrest. The caption read: SHADOWY CABINET MINISTER. Further down the page Nash read another piece with equal interest. 'In an operation linked to this investigation police raided the offices of Leeds solicitors, Hobbs & Hirst, and removed a quantity of documents. The *Netherdale Gazette* has also learned that another man involved in what is being described as a massive conspiracy was found unconscious at his home in suspicious circumstances. He is being treated under guard at hospital. Police are anxious to interview a woman, Mrs Linda Watson, who they believe may be able to help them with their enquiries'.

Nash closed the paper and handed it across his desk to Ruth Edwards. 'Thank goodness that's over. All we need to sort out now is the possible involvement of Smailes. But that's not down to me; that's your department. Then, perhaps we can return to some semblance of normality. Who knows, I may get a day off.'

Ruth smiled. 'And I can return to my proper job. Not for the first time, you've used some fairly unorthodox methods, Mike. I realize they've been necessary, but I'd hate to go away thinking that's how you normally go about policing this area.'

Nash shook his head. 'We've been through some fairly trying times over the last few weeks,' he pointed out. 'But I wouldn't change anything.'

'I'd better get off then. I've still got my packing to do.' She smiled again as she stood up and turned to leave, but paused and looked back at Nash. 'No regrets, then?'

'That you're leaving? Of course, but I'll always have the memory of us working together. And who knows, one day we might do so again.'

He reached to answer the phone. 'Hello, boss, it's Viv. I'm fit enough to come back to work. Thought you might be a bit pressed without me?' Pearce stared at the phone in confusion, listening to the laughter and wondering what Mike Nash found so funny.

After Ruth left his office, Nash thought about all that had happened. It had been the second time he and Ruth had worked together. On this occasion she'd even stayed at his flat.

Normally, the presence of such an attractive woman in such close proximity would have set his pulses racing, but that hadn't happened. Was it simply because she was a fellow officer? Or could it be that he was getting old? Nash smiled wryly, a smile that was interrupted when he sneezed violently, once, twice, three times.